C000055750

HAUNTED FALLS

Cover Art by: Steve Daniels
Back Cover by: Warren Martin

THE AUTHORS

KEN FARMER – After proudly serving his country as a US Marine (call sign 'Tarzan'), Ken attended Stephen F. Austin State University on a full football scholarship, receiving his Bachelors Degree in Business and Speech & Drama. Ken discovered his love for acting when he starred as a cowboy in a Dairy Queen commercial. Ken has over 39 years as a professional actor, with memorable roles *Silverado, Friday Night Lights* and *The Newton Boys*. He was the OC and VO spokesman for Wolf Brand Chili for eight years. Ken now lives near Gainesville, TX, where he continues to write and direct quality award winning films like *Rockabilly Baby* and write novels like *The Nations* sequel, *Haunted Falls*.

BUCK STIENKE – Captain – Fighter Pilot - United States Air Force, has an extensive background in military aviation and weaponry. A graduate of the Air Force Academy, Buck (call sign 'Shoehorn') was a member of the undefeated Rugby team and was on the Dean's List. After leaving the Air Force, Buck was a pilot for Delta Airlines for over twenty-five years. He has vast knowledge of weapons, tactics and survival techniques. Buck is the owner of Lone Star Shooting Supply, Gainesville, TX. As a successful actor, writer and businessman, Buck lives in Gainesville with his wife, Carolyn. Buck was Executive Producer for the award winning film, *Rockabilly Baby*.

Buck and Ken have completed six novels to date. The first was *BLACK EAGLE FORCE: Eye of the Storm, BLACK EAGLE FORCE: Sacred Mountain* is the second *Return of the Starfighter*, the third. A historical fiction western, *The Nations*, the fourth. The fifth novel, this time back to the Black Eagle Force series: *Black Eagle Force: Blood Ivory* and *Haunted Falls* makes our sixth.

HAUNTED FALLS

BY

KEN FARMER
&
BUCK STIENKE

Copyright 2013 by Ken Farmer and Buck Stienke. All rights reserved.

This book, or parts thereof, may not be reproduced in any form with out prior written permission from the authors.

ISBN-13: 978-0-9891220-3-0 Paper
ISBN-13: 978-0-9891220-4-7 E

Timber Creek Press
Imprint of Timber Creek Productions, LLC
312 N. Commerce St.
Gainesville, Texas

DEDICATION

HAUNTED FALLS is dedicated to the American Indian, most particularly the five civilized tribes of the Indian Territory. The Cherokee, Choctaw, Creek, Seminole and the Chickasaw. These tribes or Nations were forcibly moved to what is now Oklahoma by the Indian Removal Act of 1830 over what the Cherokee called *Nunna daul Tsuny* or *The Trail Where They Cried*. Known today as The Trail of Tears. The eastern portion of the Territory was known as the Nations.

This novel is a work of fiction. Names, characters, places and incidents are either the products of the author's imaginations or are used fictitiously. Any resemblance to actual persons, living or dead, business establishments, events or locales is entirely coincidental.

ACKNOWLEDGMENT

The authors gratefully acknowledge the help from Alex Cord, Loree Lough, Kathrine Boyer, T.C. Miller and Doran Ingrham for their invaluable help in proofing and editing this novel.

This book is licensed for your personal enjoyment only. If you're reading this book and did not purchase it, or did not win it in an author/publisher contest, then please purchase your own copy. Thank you for respecting the hard work of these authors.

Contact Us:
Published by: Timber Creek Press
timbercreekpresss@yahoo.com
www.timbercreekpress.net
Twitter: @pagact
Facebook Book Fan Page:
http://www.facebook.com/TheNationsSeries
214-533-4964

First printing -6/18/2013

ENDORSEMENTS

Haunted Falls opens with a Michener-esque description of the Chickasaw Nation's Arbuckle Mountains, and by Page 2, a high-action gunfight will make them want to run for cover! Daring characters, gritty dialog, a hair-raising mystery, and the most exciting history lesson of their lives guarantees that Farmer-Stienke fans will add *Haunted Falls* to their "keepers" shelf. (Loree Lough, bestselling author of 100 award-winning novels, including The Lone Star Legends series and 5-star A Man of Honor.)

Buck Stienke and Ken Farmer started the story of U.S. Deputy Marshal Bass Reeves in their first book, entitled *The Nations*. *Haunted Falls* continues the story of Bass Reeves as he joins other U.S. Deputy Marshals in pursuit of the infamous Dalton gang. It is full of adventure, romance, some history, excitement and a unique paranormal twist. There is something to entice all readers. You will not want to miss this sequel. - Katherine Boyer - Midwest Book Reviewer

If you've read Ken Farmer and Buck Stienke before, you already know how good they are. If you haven't you're in for a big treat. I am in awe of their intellect, knowledge and craftsmanship. Enviably prolific, in the time it takes me to write a comment or review of their work, they turn out an entire novel that engages and compels. With *HAUNTED FALLS*, they've done it again. It continues where *THE NATIONS* left off. Masters at creating mood, they lull you into the pleasures of a tranquil, pastoral scene and then hit you with an explosive, heart-pounding, breath-holding, violent action leaving you shocked.

Everything is bathed in an ambiance of mystery, an elusive, foreboding threat. What's better than a bank robbery by the Daltons, the Youngers, or the James gang? Yes, it's been done before but not like this and not by Farmer and Stienke. Better than ever. Their dialogue takes you right to another era and culture. The wonderful Bass Reeves is back as the 'colorful', first black U.S. Marshal. When two villains attempt to take their horses, Bass and Jed out-fox them, out-shoot them and do it all with great humor. I am not going to tell the story. Farmer and Stienke do it so well and do it with a twist of the supernatural.

HAUNTED FALLS is a treasure of fully realized characters, authentic language, great detail, an involving story, and all composed with seductive skill. It is a true western. You **WILL** enjoy this book. And that's an order! -

Alex Cord, Star of Stage, Screen and Television and now author of *A Feather in the Rain* and the just released, *Days of the Harbinger*.

HAUNTED FALLS

NASHOBA TOHBI - Sacred Wolf

Timber Creek Press

WWW.TIMBERCREEKPRESS.NET

OTHER NOVELS BY
TIMBER CREEK PRESS

MILITARY ACTION/TECHNO

BLACK EAGLE FORCE: Eye of the Storm (Book #1)
by Buck Stienke and Ken Farmer
BLACK EAGLE FORCE: Sacred Mountain (Book #2)
by Buck Stienke and Ken Farmer
RETURN of the STARFIGHTER (Book #3)
by Buck Stienke and Ken Farmer
BLACK EAGLE FORCE: BLOOD IVORY (Book #4)
by Buck Stienke and Ken Farmer with Doran Ingrham

HISTORICAL FICTION WESTERN

THE NATIONS by Ken Farmer and Buck Stienke
HAUNTED FALLS by Ken Farmer and Buck Stienke

MYSTERY/SCIFY

DAYS of the HARBINGER by Alex Cord

Coming This Fall

LEGEND of AURORA by Ken Farmer and Buck Stienke

TIMBER CREEK PRESS

CHAPTER ONE

INDIAN TERRITORY
CHICKASAW NATION
1894

"Honey angry today," said Montford Anoatubbi of the Chickasaw Nation.

The white man behind him spit a long stream of amber tobacco juice at the off-white limestone outcrop to their right. "Yep...five inches of rain'll do 'er every time."

Just past daybreak, the brilliant azure blue sky, absolutely free of clouds, allowed the morning sun to shine upon the backs of the two men on horseback as they followed a large snow-white wolf-dog along a switchback. The huge animal led the way down a well-worn game trail toward a fast moving, churning mountain creek at the bottom of the ridge. They had started out that morning after taking shelter during an all-night rain storm in a cave high on a tree-covered granite ridge of the Arbuckle Mountains in the western portion of the Chickasaw Nation.

The underlying granite of the Arbuckles dated back some 1.4 billion years. Thrust-faulted igneous rock had been overlain by thick limestone sediments during the Paleozoic Era—when the entire central portion of North America was under a shallow sea—and folded numerous times in its early geologically active period, often giving the appearance of Christmas ribbon candy. The ancient range had eroded down to a height of only 1,412 feet above current sea level and numerous thrust outcrops stuck up through the loamy soil in evenly spaced rows like the rib cage of some gigantic prehistoric monster.

Much of the area was covered by a wide range of oaks, pecan, hickory, cottonwood, walnut, sycamore and cedar trees interspersed with meadows of grama, buffalo and blue stem grasses. The spring-time sweet scent of dogwood blossoms filled the dewy early morning air.

One rider was white, the other Indian—each wearing basically the same type of clothing—worn Levis, cotton shirts and work boots. They had tied their black broadcloth jackets behind the cantles on top of their soogans as the day had already begun to turn warm. The white man sported a full dark mustache and wore a faded blue cavalry-style bib-front shirt with a center-creased gray Stetson—he also wore a leather shoulder holster in addition to a belt gun. The Chickasaw's shirt was a newer store-bought calico and his hat was a black beaver felt, tall-crowned, uncreased and with a Red-Tailed Hawk feather stuck in the porcupine quill and bead hat band—the traditional type preferred by the Chickasaw.

Abruptly the wolf stopped; the hair along his back and shoulders rose up as he looked across the creek and growled. The white rider reacted. "What is it, Boy? Smell someth..."

His words were cut off by a storm of gunfire from the brush on the other side of the raging creek. Montford, leading a pack donkey loaded with panning and camp gear, went down first as his horse was hit twice in the chest—trapping his right leg underneath. The startled donkey broke free, brayed and scrambled back up the incline. Montford struggled to extract his rifle from his saddle boot and took a round to his head, spraying the rocks and grass behind him with a red and gray mist—killing him instantly.

The other man dove from the back of his horse to the left just as his blood bay mount was hit by a fusillade of bullets. His hat flew off as he hit the ground, rolled and scrambled on all fours down toward the creek bank. He drew the Smith and Wesson .44 Russian revolver on his right hip as he reached cover behind one of the numerous rocks and boulders that lined the creek.

Rocks that were near or in the water in this part of the Arbuckle Mountains were known as *slick rock* because of a coating of many layers of calcium carbonate—called travertine—they received from the water of the area. Both man and horse had to be extremely careful when crossing any running water—a misstep could instantly plunge them into the normally swift current.

He crawled through a shallow eddy behind a rock that was little bigger than a number two washtub as shots peppered the water and rocks nearby. There was blood oozing from his side, both front and back, just above his hip. *Damn, went clean through. Guess I'm lucky,* he thought as he looked down...*Naw...if I was lucky, wouldn't have got hit atall.*

The exit wound was bleeding the most—he pulled up his shirt and ripped bigger holes in his blood-soaked union suit. He took the chaw of tobacco from his mouth, split it in two and stuffed the biggest chunk into the larger hole, the smaller in the front, and then tried to tuck his shirt back in his trousers to help hold everything in place.

Another shot ricocheted from an adjacent rock, showering his face with glass-like rock splinters. The dog crawled up next to his leg as he wiped the blood dripping down into his right eye from a cut just above his eyebrow. "Dang, wish I coulda got to my Marlin. Could git their attention with a few of those 45-70 rounds..." He glanced back up the embankment. "Looks like Montford's had it and we're up the hill and over the mountain, Boy."

The wolf-dog cocked his head.

The only thing he could see across the creek was a cloud of gray gunsmoke from the rounds being fired at his location. He rose up and snapped off three quick shots from the double-action Russian, spreading them one foot apart. He heard a cry from across the eighty-foot wide rapids.

"Lucky again...Looks to be at least three, meby four more over there. We need to get us some better cover...What do you think?" he said to his companion as he broke over the Russian, removed the spent cartridges that automatically stuck up, thumbed in replacements and snapped the pistol closed.

Nearly ten feet away was a larger boulder with the remnants of a tree trunk wedged against it from previous high water.

"You know, if we can make it to that big rock over there with that tree, we'll have cover from two directions...Come on, son!" he shouted to the dog above the roar of the whitewater as he triggered off two more rounds across the creek and jumped up.

On the third step, his leather-soled boot slid off the top of a melon-sized rock at the water's edge at the same time three more shots were fired in his direction from across the creek. A fine spray of red blossomed briefly as he grunted, dropped his pistol and splashed headlong into the raging torrent. More shots were fired at the large animal as he sprinted behind a deadfall up on the bank.

"Fools! Cain't even hit a dog?" one of the men on the other side of the creek said to his comrades.

"What'n hell, Cougar, you think that hound is gonna tell somebody?" asked Ox, a huge square block of a man.

"We taken care of them two. The Lighthorse'll raise hob if'n they try to pin this on us," said Bobo as he rose up from his hiding place in the bushes.

"All right, grab Fleming's body, we'll bury him in the tailin's back at the dig," said Cougar "...we got another stop to make on the way."

The swollen rapids of Honey Creek tumbled the man's body downstream at between eight and to twelve miles per hour. The body briefly hung on the roots of a tree wedged between two boulders and then was ripped loose as much of his shirt tore away. He was then forced through a sieve between two rocks into a hole where he was rolled down to the bottom of the creek, back up to the surface and back down to the bottom again in a deadly cycle.

Suddenly his eyes snapped open underwater and looked up at the light above. He instinctively curled into a ball and as he hit the graveled bottom again, he pushed with all his might and shot to the surface. Grabbing a quick gulp of air above the churning water, he ducked back down, lunged to the right, cleared the hole and was back out into the main stream again.

On the bank, the wolf-dog, running along a game trail through the thick woods that paralleled the creek, easily kept pace with the surging water. His eyes never left the tumbling, bobbing and rolling figure that was his master.

The man tried to grab a boulder off to the side of the main channel, but it was too slick and he was washed on downstream. As he bobbed to the surface once again, he looked down the creek and his heart froze.

Honey Creek disappeared—it cascaded over the seventy-seven feet of Turner Falls. *Oh Jesus, my only chance is to ride the flow to the bottom an' take my chances on that thirty-foot deep pool...Hope to hell I don't hit that big rock in the middle...Ain't like I got a choice.* He flattened out his body—his feet pointing in the direction of the falls—hands at his sides before he hit the slick coating. Over thousands of years, Honey Creek had deposited layer after layer of the fine-grained, multicolored travertine. The coating had thickened to the point that the falls did not drop straight down the block fault, but rather had smoothed to a near forty-five degree gradient—it was like hitting black ice.

He shot out into the middle of the pool at the base at almost thirty-five miles per hour just narrowly missing the large boulder in front of the falls. The impact with the water took his breath away as he plunged almost two-thirds of the way to the bottom. Once the water slowed his momentum, he started to kick his legs to bring himself back to the top. His lungs were near bursting and blackness was closing in as his face broke the surface. He took in several great draughts of air, shook his head—causing him to see stars—painfully struggled his way back to the falls, grabbed another breath of air and dove under the cascading water. He surfaced on the other side and pulled himself onto a two-foot ledge that extended in front of a prehistoric cave that penetrated deep back into the mountain.

Somehow he managed to drag himself up eight feet to the level floor of the cave where he curled into a fetal position on the damp rock. His hand went to the side of his head as he felt of the deep gouge that was still oozing blood—the semi-darkness of the cavern began to swirl around him with multicolored lights and then mercifully went totally black.

The wolf-dog ran to the side of the falls, worked his way along the skinny rock ledge and passed behind the thundering water. Unerringly, he headed into the cave's interior to the unconscious body, nuzzled him with his nose and then lay down beside him, placing his head on the figure's shoulder. The warmth of the big creature's body would save the man's life. The dog didn't know that, of course, he just wanted to be as close as possible to the only master he had ever known...

LOG CABIN
HONEY CREEK DOWNSTREAM

A very handsome woman in her mid-thirties opened the back door of the cabin and threw a dishpan of soapy water out into the yard. She was wearing man's clothing—work boots, brass-riveted canvas denim pants and a plaid flannel store-bought shirt. Her long copper-colored hair was pulled back in a low-tied ponytail at the base of her neck.

She shook the last of the soapy water from the pan, pushed a loose strand of hair from an attractive face accented by a spray of freckles across a small straight nose. She stepped back inside as the spring pulled the screen door closed with a bang. Angie O'Reilly walked back to the counter, took the white porcelain bucket from its hook and poured fresh water into the pan.

She turned at a noise that appeared to come from the porch. Angie walked to the front door of the large one room cabin, picked up the doubled-barreled shotgun propped against the wall next to the door.

"Who is it?" There was no answer. "Faith an' you don't want me to ask again."

"Just want to talk to you, ma'am," came a voice from other side.

She reached out with the muzzle of the shotgun, lifted the metal latch from the wooden hook and stepped back as the door swung open reveling two coarse-looking men. "I'd be moving back down the steps if you don't want me to separate you from your pockets."

"No cause to be hostile, lady…"

"Do it…Do it now!"

"Better do as she says, Cougar. That scatter gun will take us both out," said Bobo, standing behind and slightly to the side.

Cougar was a big, rough, round-shouldered man and a face with a nose that had lost more than one disagreement. Bobo was a skinny, pock-marked faced half-breed in his late twenties with dark beady eyes.

The two men slowly backed to the steps and down to the ground in front of the hand-hewn plank porch. Ox sat his horse just outside the slat fence, holding the reins to three horses. One had a body draped over the saddle.

"Now, what it is that you'd be wanting? I told you brigands to leave me be," she said as her green eyes flashed and she brought the shotgun to her shoulder.

"Mr. Baldwin just wants to give you another opportunity to take his generous offer for your claim, ma'am," said Cougar as he held up both hands.

"You can tell that high-binder, Jason Baldwin, the answer is the same. Me family have all died, and me husband is buried here. I'll not be going anywhere...Now get off me property," she said as she cocked both hammers with audible clicks.

"You may wind up being buried here too, with that attitude...Let's go boys," Cougar said as he and Bobo backed all the way out the open gate to their horses.

"That may be, but I'll not be goin' alone."

"We'll be back," said Cougar over his shoulder

"That'll be your last mistake," she said as she watched them ride off back toward a rock causeway that crossed Honey Creek.

Angie went back inside, uncocked the shotgun, propped it against the wall in its usual place, walked back over to a ladder-back chair at the table and sat down. She leaned forward, cradled her head on her arms and her body racked with sobs.

FALLS CAVE

The man's body shook with the cold as he instinctively reached out and pulled the big animal closer to him. Abruptly, the dog's head came up and looked toward the curtain of water that cascaded past the opening. From the side where the narrow ledge protruded, a barefoot girl, seven to eight years old—with corn-silk hair and wearing a faded calico print dress that had been sewn from a flour sack—walked between the wall of water and the lip of the cave. She went straight toward the man and dog lying in the semi-darkness, squatted down beside the dog and began to pet him. "He's hurt," she said.

The dog whined and licked her hand. She reached over and placed her hand on his forehead. "He's got the fever too."

The man responded to her touch and his eyes fluttered open. His hand again went to the swollen and inflamed gash along the side of his head. "Ow," he said as he moved his hand away. "Who are you?" he asked as his eyes slowly tried to focus on the little girl.

"I'm Anna. What's your name?"

"I...I..." He drifted back into unconsciousness before he could finish.

"Come on puppy, you come with me. We have to get help," she said as she got up and walked back toward the ledge. The dog obediently followed her.

LOG CABIN
HONEY CREEK DOWNSTREAM

Anna walked with a purpose through the thick woods along one of the numerous game trails that ran by the creek, the big white animal at her heels. Downstream from the falls, they came to a small clearing with a one-room log cabin, barn, corral, privy and smokehouse. Light gray smoke drifted up from the chimney built of native rock.

"Go there," she said as she pointed to the cabin.

The animal whined, took a step, looked back at her and whined again.

"Go!"

He turned and trotted up to the slat fence, lightly jumped over it and padded up to the covered porch that extended across the face of the cabin. He sat down in front of the thick wooden door and scratched once.

From inside came Angie's voice—"I told you not to come back!"—as she jerked open the door pointing the shotgun out to the porch.

The wolf-dog lay down and covered his nose with his paws, whined and looked up with his big golden eyes. She quickly looked down at the movement. "Well, who are you?" she asked as she looked all around outside and then lifted the barrel of her gun.

He rose up on his haunches and lifted one front paw. She stepped back inside and asked, "Ohh…Are you hungry?"

The wolf-dog got up, trotted down the steps, turned, looked back at her and whined.

"Not hungry…You're somebody's aren't you?"

He woofed, turned a circle, walked toward the gate and looked back again.

"You can almost talk…You want me to follow you, is that it?"

He woofed and spun around in a circle again, turned and jumped back over the gate and looked at her.

"Can't get any more obvious than that…All right, just a moment and I'll get me shawl." She grabbed her green woolen shawl from the peg just inside the door and stepped back out on the porch, closing and latching it behind her. "'Lay on, McDuff, and be damned he who first cries, 'Hold, enough!' as Mr. Shakespeare wrote in Macbeth."

He cocked his head first to one side, then to the other and then turned and took off back the way he had come.

"Don't know Shakespeare, huh?" Angie said as she cradled the shotgun in the crook of her left arm, opened the gate and followed the big dog down to the trail along the Honey.

"Hey, big dog, would you be wanting to slow down a mite?" she shouted at him as he disappeared around a turn. Seconds later, his broad head appeared around a tree up the trail. He gave her a short whine and sat down until she walked up. "I only have two legs…You got to go easy, would that be suiting you?"

The dog spun around three times and started back down the trail—slower, this time. He looked off to his right where another white female wolf padded through the trees, keeping pace with him.

The big animal led Angie to the edge of the falls and right up to the narrow ledge behind the roaring water. He turned and looked back at her.

"In the old cave? I wish you'd of said something. Could'a brought a coal oil lamp."

The dog cocked his head at her.

"I suppose that you'd not be needing a light in there, do you now?"

He gave her a short bark.

"Didn't think so. Didn't know Shakespeare either…Well, let's be going," she said as she pointed behind the falls.

He turned and padded along the narrow ledge and disappeared inside. The other wolf sat down at the edge of the woods and watched as Angie held her shotgun to her chest, turned sideways and inched her way along the ledge behind the falls to the darkness of the cave. Once inside, she waited a moment until her eyes adjusted to the diffused light coming through the wall of water. She looked around until she saw the white animal lying next to a dark form, and then walked over with no little trepidation.

"Saints preserve us! It's a man!" she exclaimed as she lay her shotgun on the floor of the cave and knelt down. She felt of his head. "Still alive...but feverish...Oh, Lord, help me, he's been shot...twice," she said to herself as she saw the wounds in his side and his head. Angie removed her shawl and draped it over his shivering body. "No way I can get you out of here, you're a bit too big for the likes of me to carry...Have to try to treat you here. Gotta go get some stuff. I know you can't hear me, but..."

Then his eyes fluttered open and he looked up her through squinted lids and said hoarsely, "You've growed a mite..."

"What?" she asked, but he had passed out again. "Delirious...you stay here, dog. Keep him warm. I have to go get blankets and medicine...Understand?"

The dog lay down beside his master again, put his head back on his shoulder and looked up at her as if to say, "I know."

"You sure you don't know Shakespeare?"

FALLS CAVE

Boy looked up from beside the man's side as Anna walked back into the cave. She was carrying his hat, Marlin lever action .45-70 rifle and the pistol he had dropped at the edge of the creek. She laid the hat and guns over to the side and caressed the side of his face gently.

His eyes slowly opened and he looked up at her. "Wish you'd make up yer mind…'Er you…you gonna be big or little and why are there two of ya?" he managed to get out as he squinted at her.

"I'm neither. I'm Anna and I'm only one…I brought your hat and your guns…Your friend didn't make it…But he said not to worry."

"Do what?…Ahhhh!" He put his hand to his head.

"Your head is hurt, but it will be all right. You just have to rest. Your puppy is with you and there is help coming." She glanced at the falls. "I have to go now." Anna got up disappeared around the edge of the falls.

"Wait," he tried to shout, but it hurt too much. His eyes closed…

LOG CABIN
HONEY CREEK DOWNSTREAM

Angie had a large wicker basket sitting on her table next to a coal oil lamp. She had already placed several blankets, a quilt, a Mason jar of warm beef broth, some bandages, and a clean man's union suit and shirt inside. She was blending some warmed hog tallow with turpentine into a paste in a small porcelain bowl.

On her stove, she had stripped the bark and new spring buds off some white willow branches that grew along the creek and was boiling it in a pot along with some stinging nettle. She didn't know what it was, but one of her Chickasaw neighbors had told her that the boiled mixture would reduce pain, cut fever and speed healing.

Angie O'Reilly was unaware that just three years later in 1897, chemists working at Bayer AG, in Germany, would produce a synthetically altered version of salicylic acid—the primary ingredient in white willow bark and leaves that alleviated pain and fevers. It would be called 'Aspirin'.

She took the boiled mixture, poured it through a strainer into another Mason jar, wrapped it in a dish towel made from a feed sack and put it into the basket with the other items. Finally, she went outside to the smoke house and sliced several chunks of cured ham. Back inside, she grabbed a couple of cold biscuits, wrapped them with the ham in a cloth and added it to her stash. Finished, she put on a warm woolen jacket, stuffed a pair of scissors and some phosphorus matches in her pocket and headed out the door—basket in one hand, shotgun and lantern in the other and a blanket-covered canteen over her shoulder. As an afterthought, she walked back over to a sideboard and took a Smith and Wesson .32 caliber, five shot rimfire pistol from a drawer and slipped it into her coat pocket. *Don't know if he's an brigand or what...no need on taking chances,* she mused.

It was getting late in the afternoon and she had to get back to the cave, build a fire and minister to his wounds before dark. *He'll never survive the night in that cold, damp cave.* She stepped out onto the porch to be greeted by Boy, sitting facing the door.

"How would you be knowing I was ready to head back to the cave?...Oh, never you mind. It was bit of a silly question, I suppose."

He turned and raced ahead of her back to the falls.

Fifteen minutes later, the sun approached the western horizon and was casting long blue shadows as it disappeared behind the tallest ridges and switchbacks of the Arbuckles. Angie worked her way along the narrow ledge and back into the cave. She stopped just inside, set her basket and shotgun down, pulled a match from her pocket and lit the lantern. Its first feeble glow only penetrated partially into the dank interior. She turned up the wick to nearly full height, illuminating the entire front room of the cave. Already lying next to the man's inert form, the big dog's eyes glowed red in the lamp light, making Angie start and gasp, "Oh! May the saints preserve me," she said as she crossed herself and moved over closer to the pair.

She sat down her basket, shotgun and the lamp and then reached out to touch his forehead. He groaned and stirred.

"Still a bit feverish...better tend to these woun..." Angie stopped as she noticed the hat, rifle and pistol lying on the other side of the figure. "Faith and what in the world? Where did those come from?" she muttered and then noticed the pistol was a match to the one still strapped in his shoulder holster.

The man's eyes opened and he squinted up at her for a moment. "Wish you'd make up your mind," he finally whispered hoarsely.

"What is it you mean?"

17

"Well, 'er you gonna be big 'er…little?"

"I'm not understanding what you're asking…and where did those guns and hat come from?"

"You brought 'em when…" He started to say more, but drifted off again.

"Daft he is…out of his head." She removed her sewing scissors from her pocket and started to unbuckle his shoulder holster so she could cut what was left of his shirt and long handles off. She stopped and looked around the prehistoric cave and could just make out the ancient petroglyphs on the near wall. Strange creatures and what the Indians called images of the sky gods that were carved into the stone long before the Chickasaw of the Muskogean branch of indigenous people arrived there in 1832. Angie knew that her husband's people held this cave to be sacred, very spiritual and some even thought it to be haunted. She couldn't help but wonder as she crossed herself again, *Where did that hat and other guns come from? I know they weren't here before…and who or what is he…*

***

CHAPTER TWO

UPSHUR COUNTY
TEXAS

Six men rode two abreast down the rutted red dirt road through the thick piney-woods of east Texas. Gilmer Road ran from the town of Gilmer in Upshur County to Longview in Gregg County. A small portion of the farming and lumber supported community extended into the western part of neighboring Harrison County.

All the men were dressed in three-piece black or gray broadcloth suits and an assortment of hats from a couple of derbies, a bowler and to fedoras. They were not 'cowboys' as depicted in the popular dime novels, but looked more like business men or law officers—but, law officers they were not.

The group included Mason Frakes Dalton, known to family and friends as "Bill"—a surviving member of the Dalton gang.

Bill came by the outlaw trade honestly, if that can be said as an oxymoron. His mother, Adeline Younger Dalton, was aunt to the Younger brothers, Cole, Jim, John and Bob, as well as cousin to the James boys, Jessie and Frank. The Daltons, Youngers and the James' all rode the outlaw trail together at one time or another in years past.

Bill's brothers, Bob and Grat had been killed in an attempted dual bank robbery in the Dalton's home town of Coffeyville, Kansas—October 5, 1892. His younger brother, Emmett, had been wounded and was serving a term in the Kansas State Penitentiary, later renamed the Lansing Correctional Facility. Some would say it wasn't overly bright to try to rob two banks in your own hometown on the same day—perhaps that's why Bill didn't participate in the disaster.

He did, however, put the gang back together with Jim Wallace, Big Asa Knight, Jim Knight, Three-fingered Dynamite Dick Clifton and George Bennett—all former members of the Dalton gang.

"What time you 'spect we'll get into Longview, Bill?" asked Big Asa.

He pulled his silver plated pocket watch from his vest and glanced at it. "'Bout 2:30 or so, if'n one of these ponies don't throw a shoe."

"We're twix and 'tween with our back-up horses back yonder in Gilmer," said Wallace.

"We'll need those replacements if we have to make a run fer it," offered Bill.

"Reckon I'll have to blow the safe?" asked Dick.

"Hope not...but that's why you're along, Three-fingers. Bank should be still open if'n we get there 'fore three."

"Well, we need to stop for just a bit. Gotta drain my lizard," said Bennett.

"All right. Let's pull up there by that loblolly...Anybody else need to take care of his business, better git 'er done, 'cause we ain't stoppin' on the return trip. You gotta pee...you'll do it in yer brogans," said Dalton.

The six men walked their horses east on Fredonia Avenue toward the downtown business district of Longview—it was 2:50PM. The thriving timber and farming community had recently paved its main streets with bricks from their own local plant. The heavy red clay required for brick-making was very abundant in Gregg County like many other counties in the heavily forested area of Texas east of the Trinity River. In addition to the streets, many of the newer structures going up were also of brick, including the First National Bank of Longview.

"Looks like they got themselves a new building," said Jim Wallace as the bank came into view some one hundred and fifty yards down the street. "Still had the wooden one, last time I was here."

"That was three years ago, Jim...lumber, brick business and that new plow factory puttin' this town on the map...that's why we came," said Dalton as he tipped his hat to a group of ladies crossing the street.

"I'm gonna ride on in. You boys follow one at the time…and spread out…We'll all tie up at the bank.

Bill rode past the City Marshal's office just as a short, stocky constable, Rosco Chattaway, stepped out of the door. The twenty-three year old law officer was wearing a dark blue wool uniform with brass buttons completely down the middle of his thigh-length coat. Across the front of his flat-topped, short-billed cap, was the word *CONSTABLE* in polished brass letters. He watched as the rest of the gang slowly rode separately to the bank down on the corner, dismount and tie up.

Chattaway studied them for a moment longer and then turned to reenter the office. "Marshal, they's some men just rode into town sorta one at the time and they all tied up in front of the bank…Never seen 'em afore."

"And?" City Marshal Matt Muckleroy asked, not looking up from his paperwork.

"Well, I could see they was wearing side arms under their coats and appeared to be a mite…fidgety."

He looked up. "How do you mean…'fidgety', Rosco?"

"They was lookin' around, ya know, sorta nervous-like. Then all but one went into the bank…I think they're ne'er-do-wells up to no good…sir."

The rotund marshal removed his wire-rimmed reading glasses laid them on his desk, got to his feet and adjusted his gunbelt. "You know what I tol' you about thinkin' Rosco…but you make a good point. Head down to Sheriff Brownlow's office. I'll go the other direction and start roundin' up a posse…just in case. Tell J. D. to put his deputies on the roofs on the other side of the street and catty-corner from the bank, I'll put mine behind the water troughs and inside the saloon directly across from the bank…Be sure he reminds his men to take a caution…ya hear?"

"Yessir." The constable stood there for a moment and then glanced around the marshal's office with a blank look on his face.

"Today, Chattaway…Today!"

"Yessir…uh, I was jest wonderin' if'n I should get my gun…sir?"

"Rosco, if brains were dynamite, you couldn't blow yer nose…Of course get yer gun!"

"Right, sir," he said as he went to the gun rack on the back wall of the office, removed a Remington single barrel shotgun and headed to the door.

"And rounds, Rosco, rounds. Not much good without ammunition, now is it?"

"Oh…yes, sir. I mean no, sir…sir," he said as he wheeled around to the cabinet next to the gun rack and grabbed a box of shells. "Got 'em, sir," he said as he held up the box.

"Go, dammit! Just go!" the marshal screamed as Chattaway hustled toward the door. "Boy's gonna make an old man of me…if I survive atall….Dumber'n bucket of rocks," he mumbled and jumped as the door slammed. Muckleroy shook his head as he grabbed his dark blue frock coat and headed out to round up his posse.

"Wallace, stay out here and mind the horses…'n keep yer eyes open…The rest of ya'll with me," Dalton said as he, Big Asa, Jim Knight, Three-fingered Dynamite Dick and George Bennett entered the lobby of the bank through the double nine foot tall glass-inset doors.

Bill glanced at Big Asa and Knight. They nodded back, walked up to President Joseph Clemmons desk at the side of the lobby and Big Asa handed him a note that read: *This will introduce you to Charles Spreckelmeyer, who wants some money and he is going to have it. Bill and Friends.*

Clemmons looked up from reading the note only to see the bore of a Winchester pointed at his face just six inches away. Jim Knight had carried the .44-40 caliber rifle inside the bank under his long morning coat. The banker swallowed hard as he noticed Dalton and the others had spread out and also drawn their weapons. *Oh, my heavenly days, that letter I got last week announcing that Bill Dalton was gonna rob my bank wasn't a hoax.* An elderly woman customer screamed and fainted.

"Everyone!…Hands in the air!" said Bill. "You do not want me to say it twice…Banker, I suggest you move yer lard ass," he added, cocking his pistol and waving it in Clemmons direction. "Just put everythang from the teller's drawers in one of yer canvas bank bags."

The president grabbed a bag from under the counter and moved from teller to teller collecting ten dollar bills, some twenty dollar bank notes and stuffing them in the bag.

At this point in the history of the US, there was no Federal Reserve System. Banks issued their own private currency in paper, as well as the national currency—what was referred to in the post civil war south as *Yankee dollars*—along with gold and silver coins. The president and the treasurer or another officer usually signed the bank notes by hand with pen and ink. Bank notes issued by a national or state bank were honored throughout the nation and the territories.

"Come on, old man. That's good enough...hand me the bag...Dick, see anythin' outside?"

"Looks quiet, Bill...meby too quiet...Uh...Jim jest signaled...it's clear," said Three Fingers from his station by a window.

"You citizens git down on the floor...All right, boys, let's get the hell outta here," Dalton ordered as he moved toward the front of the lobby.

George opened the left door, looked around and stepped out onto the boardwalk followed by Bill, Big Asa, Jim and then Dick. As soon as they were all outside, a nervous Rosco hiding behind a water trough on the other side of the street, touched off a round from his ten gauge shotgun that took Wallace's hat off.

That shot started a fusillade of fire pouring down on the bandits from the top of the buildings and across the street. Wallace, hit several more times, fell from his saddle to the brick street and lay still. Bill and the others all fired quickly at the puffs of gray gunsmoke, and then ducked back inside the bank building.

In the Pine Tree Saloon directly across from the bank, a traveling drummer, Archibald Maywether, dressed in a plaid suit and a green bowler, was just raising his glass to take a sip when the first round from Bill Dalton's revolver came through the plank walls. The bullet took his little finger off and shattered the whiskey glass—Archibald had not even ordered another shot. He and the other patrons quickly dove to the floor, covering their heads with their hands or trying to find shelter as more bullets came through the saloon walls and windows whizzing like angry bees.

"Rosco, you idiot! You were told not to fire unless I gave the order...Me! We coulda had the whole damn bunch when they was gittin' on their horses...Did yore mama have any children that lived?" Marshal Muckelroy shouted and then sat down heavily behind the water trough.

"Marshal, you all right?" asked Rosco.

"Unnn...took a shot to my chest..."

Rosco looked at the hole in the marshal's vest. "Don't see no blood, Marshal...meby it went clean through and didn't touch nothin'."

Matt glanced at his less-than-bright constable, and then pulled a leather coin purse out of his upper vest pocket. A flattened .45 caliber slug fell out along with several dented silver dollars. "Damnation! Hit my money pouch...Think I got a couple of busted ribs."

"Well...beats the other choice...sir," offered Chattaway.

City Marshal Muckelroy turned another steely gaze at Rosco and started to say something when the outlaws opened fire from the bank. The sheriff and city marshal's posses all ducked for cover and started shooting back at the bank building.

After thirty or forty seconds of furiously exchanged gunshots, the bank doors opened and Clemmons, four tellers and three customers were pushed outside in a group followed immediately by Dalton and his gang.

The panicked deputies and possemen continued shooting in the confusion as Bill and the others mounted their excited horses and raced west down Fredonia Street firing their pistols back at the townspeople as sparks flew from the horses' pounding hooves.

When the gunsmoke had cleared, it was discovered that in addition to the outlaw, Jim Wallace, Longview residents George Buckingham and Charles Learned were also killed in the battle. It was never determined whose bullets killed the two men. Wounded in the fight included City Marshal Matt Muckleroy with a heavy contusion and broken ribs and citizens Walter McQueen and T.J. Summers. Over two hundred rounds were known to have been fired in the gunfight.

Rosco Chattaway walked across the street to where the dead outlaw Wallace lay, picked up the man's fedora and studied the several buckshot holes through it. He turned the hat over and printed on the sweatband inside was the name of the store that sold it—W.O. Dustin, Ardmore, I.T....

OSAGE COUNTY, IT
CHEROKEE NATION

It was just dark-thirty with a thin horned moon rising above the trees. The myriad stars, unpolluted by moonlight, were winking into view like thousands of tiny campfires across the heavens.

In the distance, a pack of coyotes began tuning up with their mournful chorus, shortly to be answered by the woman-like scream of a catamount.

"Peers as though we just as well make camp by that branch over there, Bass. Looks as though we won't be the first...they's already a fire pit been built 'n I kin see a stack of deadfall close by some other traveler left," said black US Deputy Marshal Jed Neal as he pointed to an open area with a small circle of fire blackened rocks next to a wet-weather stream.

"Spect so, Jed. Be after midnight before we could git to Sand Springs anyhoo...Not inclined to wake Marshal Patrick's household...John L. can be a mite testy when he's woke up in the middle of the night."

"Not to say nothin' of the kids...What's he and Nellie Ruth got now...three?"

"And one in the oven...Gonna ketch up to you and me if'n he don't watch it."

"Reckon they figured out what's causin' it?"

"Oh, I mind they did." Bass chuckled as he dropped the reins to his buckskin stallion under a large sweet gum near the tiny meadow and removed the dally to the pack mule from his saddle horn. "I'll unsaddle, give the boys a rubdown 'n a bait of grain if'n you'll start a fire."

"Works for me...Could use a hot cup of Arbuckle."

"That and my stomach thinks my throat's been cut."

"I'll slice us up a couple rashers of fat-back to mix in with the beans and I spy some saxifrage lettuce an' some yeller hop clover over by the branch. We'll have us some greens too. Pitch me one of those airtights from the pannier…Hellova thing, puttin' beans in cans. Makes trailin' a mite easier."

"It does, it does."

Nineteen year veteran US Deputy Marshal Bass Reeves, the first black marshal west of the Mississippi and his black partner, nine year veteran Jed Neal, leaned back against a log back a few feet from the camp fire. Each was nursing on a graniteware cup of post-supper coffee.

"You know, I'm gittin' a bit concerned 'bout Jack. He was supposed to check in yesterd'y," offered Jed as he blew on his coffee. "Hot."

"Yeah…well, could be he jest cain't git to a telegraph…Could be he's jest bein' ornery…been known to be that way on occasion…and could be he's playin' it close to the vest…bein' undercover and all…Could be he's sick…'er meby stove up…Or could be…he's found his ownself a honey…"

Bass and Jed looked at each other for a second.

"Nah," they said at the same time and then both jumped as a high-pitched piercing trill seemed to come from a big red oak at the edge of the clearing.

"Sonofabitch! Screech owls scare the pee outta me…like they sneak up and do it apurpose…Made me spill my coffee," he said as he licked the back of his hand.

The horses and pack mule seemed to agree with Jed as they snorted and stomped their feet in agitation.

"Meby that one did, Jedadiah. Meby it seen you was 'bout to take a sip of yer coffee 'n was just needin' a laugh."

"Yeah, well I 'spect he got one...Anyways...think John L. will be able to go with us down to the Chickasaw Nation?"

"I 'magine...Tobe can take over while we're gone. He'd want to go his ownself, but the lumbago's got a purty good holt on him, 'n Boot too...The ridin' don't bother him much, but the gittin' on 'n gittin' off is a bit tetchy."

"Ain't it the truth...our time's acomin', I reckon..." He reached in the pocket of his dark gray broadcloth coat, pulled out a small brown paper sack and extended it toward Bass. "Lemon drop?"

"Pass. Think I'll load up my pipe...Hmm, got com'ny...white men." Bass looked off into the darkness and tapped the side of his nose.

"Damn...You and that Injun nose. How d'you tell they be white?"

"All peoples have different smells, white, black, Injun, Chinee, Mescan...Lived with the Creeks for mor'n two years after I run off from massa Reeves durin' the war..."

"Hellooo the camp," came a call from the darkness back toward the trail.

Bass switched his cup to his left hand and palmed his .41 cal Colt from his shoulder holster with his right. He hid his hand and pistol behind his hip and draped the flap of his coat over them. Jed glanced over and held up two fingers with a question on his face. Bass nodded.

"Come on ahead, but we'd take it as bein' real polite if you keep yer hands on the reins...the both of you."

"We're peaceable...jest seen yer fire 'n smelt yer coffee," replied the voice.

"Tie yer mounts to our picket line over by the trees. If'n you got cups, we'll share our coffee," said Bass.

Jed got to his feet as two men walked from the darkness of the trees into the flickering light cast from the camp fire. The first was a smallish, pinch-faced, gaunt man with a full mustache, wearing a brocade vest under a dark green morning coat and a John Bull hat. The other was a big man, on the heavyset side, with a three-day stubble of a beard and wearing a tan canvas jacket over a gray linsey-woolsey vest—a battered fedora sat askance on his head. Both wore side arms around their hips, under their coats—each carried a tin cup.

"We're much obliged for the coff..." he stopped. "Damn, Newt, we stumbled on a camp of manumitted darkies."

"Yeah, Bailey, couldn't tell from back yonder. They kinda blend in with the night, don't they?" Newt chuckled.

"You boys want coffee or not?" Jed said with a touch of steel in his voice.

"Why shore. We was jest funnin' with ya. Ain't that right, Bailey?"

"'Course...Say, you fellas got some fine lookin' horse flesh back there."

"They'll do to ride the river with...Have a sit," offered Bass as he pointed to a couple of large rocks on the other side of the fire with his cup.

"Oh, think not. We'll pass on the coffee...but take yer horses instead," Bailey said as he threw his cup at Jed and simultaneously reached for the Remington on his hip.

Bass' Colt roared. Bailey screamed, spun to his right and then to the ground as the .41 caliber ball struck him just under his holster, tearing it from the belt, and then bouncing off his hip bone.

Jed drew and fired at Newt just as he was clearing leather. His round struck the big man square in the center of his chest. Newt grunted and sat straight down on his butt. He looked down in disbelief at the red spot that was growing on his once white boiled shirt just above the V of his vest.

"Damnation, nigger...You done kilt me," he said and then fell to his back as the cloud of gray gunsmoke began to drift away with the soft evening breeze.

Bass got to his feet, holstered his Thunderer, walked to the little man and rolled him over with his foot. Bailey looked up at him in no small measure of pain.

"You God damned smoke bastard. You was waitin' fer me to make a move."

"I was," Bass said as he bent down and unbuckled Bailey's damaged gun belt, slung it toward Jed and kicked the pistol—still in its holster—out of reach. "Recognized you right off, Bailey Biden, soon as you got inside the fire light. Got warrants on you and yer runnin' mate, Newt Fletcher, jest last week...Aggravated Larceny, Attempted Murder, Murder, Larceny of Horses, Griftin' and several other minor warrants.

Been lookin' fer you and here you are, walkin' right into my parlor."

"Just who the hell are you?"

"Well, some call me one thing…some another. You can call me United States Deputy Marshal Bass Reeves."

Biden rolled back over. "Oh, my holy God in heaven…we had to pick Bass Reeves to rob…Son of a bitch, son of a green bitch…jest my luck."

"Shackle this miscreant, Jed, and see to his wound. Intended to jest hit his shooter, but he moved a mite…'Spect it's only a flesh wound though…I'll roll big-un there in his soogan 'nd we'll load 'em on his own horse in the mornin'…Ol Doc Thacker will want to deal with the body fer the death certificate."

"Hope John L. has got a vacancy in his jail…fer this nabob," said Jed as he snapped the heavy shackles on Biden's wrists. "If not, reckon we can chain him in the outhouse out back."

"Aw, now marshal, ya'll wouldn't do that…would ya?"

"Don't see why not…you'd be in good comp'ny," Jed said as he poured a little coal oil mixed with wood ash on Bailey's flesh wound.

"Ow, ow, ow! God dammit to hell! That burns, nigger!"

Jed poured a little more on and rubbed it in with his finger. "There, how's that?…Better?"

FALLS CAVE

Angie squeezed the water out of the cloth and wiped the last of the fever sweat from his face. The bandage she had wrapped around his head to keep the turpentine and tallow poultice on the nasty wound just above his ear. She had stitched it together with linen thread and it would need to be changed soon. The man groaned and pushed the blankets down and away from his bare shoulders. She pulled them back up and tucked them under his chin. The big white wolf-dog, lying on the opposite side of the man, cocked his head and licked his hand that was outside the covers.

"Hot...hot," he mumbled and then opened his eyes and looked up at her trying to focus. "Am I dead?"

"Not yet, laddie. Ye came fair close to seeing the good Saint Peter though...Thirsty?"

"Yes, ma'am, I surely am."

She helped him sit up a little and lifted the canteen to his parched lips. He moaned in pain. "Feels like I been kicked in the side."

"Ye were shot there as well as alongside your head. I could poke me finger all the way through...your side, not your head...Begorrah, but it missed your vitals." He took a deep swallow and she pulled the canteen away. "Uh, uh...Slowly. Drink slowly...in sips."

"Yes, ma'am." He took several small sips and looked up at her. The morning daylight refracting through the falls glinted from her green eyes and seemed to give her a glow around her loose copper colored hair hanging down past her breasts. "You sure I ain't dead?"

"The saints be praised, I can assure you that you're quite alive...although I'm not sure ye should be...Why do ye keep asking?"

"'Cause you look for all the world like an angel...or at least what I picture one to look like."

"Go on with your blarney. It's guaranteeing ye that I'm no angel...and judging from all the bullet and knife scars all over your body...neither are you...Would ye be having a name? And how did ye come by all those scars?...Is it an outlaw you'd be?"

"That's a whole passel of questions...which one you want me to answer first?" He raised up the blankets and looked underneath at his body and the bandage wrapped around his middle. "...and why am I nekked as a jaybird?" He nervously put the blanket back under his chin.

"I had to remove your clothes...what was left of them, to doctor your wounds...Besides they were wet. You'd have caught the pneumonia...Now, how about let's start with your name."

"You go first."

"All right. I'm Angie, Angie O'Reilly."

"Well, Angie, Angie O'Reilly, I'm mighty pleased to meet you. My name is...is..." He paused and rubbed his fingers across his forehead and glanced back up at Angie. "My name is...Well kiss a fat baby...I don't know what my name is...Ahhhh!" He put his hand to the side of his head and touched the bandage. "Ahhh, got me one whale of a headache. If'n I was a drinkin' man, I'd say I had a hangover, but I don't drink."

"If you don't can't remember your name, how do you know you don't drink?"

"Cain't answer that neither…jest know I don't like the taste of the stuff."

Angie held the Mason jar with the willow bark elixir up to his lips. "Here, drink yourself some of this. The Chickasaw say it will make the pain more tolerable."

He took a shallow sip. "Ack, that stuff is bitter…Tastes like seed ticks smell."

"Drink some more."

"Cure me or kill me, right?" he said as he took another draught.

"One or the other," she said as she took the jar and put the lid back on.

"I thought whiskey tasted bad…got nothin' on that stuff."

"Let's try something else…What's the beastie's name?"

He looked over at the dog, scratched his ears and was rewarded by another kiss. "Boy…I just call him Boy…" The big white animal cocked his head again at the mention of his name. "…Now ain't that funny, know his name, but not my own…'nd he ain't mine…Think I b'long to him. He jest showed up one day, not too long ago when I first hit the Arbuckles."

"Well, he saved your life by fetchin' me here. He's pretty smart…even if he doesn't know the Shakespeare."

36

"Come again?...Oh! I understand. No, ma'am, he's partial to Keats."

Angie looked at him for a moment then said, "Ye must be feeling better, ye'd be funning me."

"I am startin' to feel a mite better. Must be that Kickapoo joy juice you made me drink, but, no ma'am, ain't funnin' you. Got a book of Mr. Keats poems in my parfleche...Is it about? I read to him on occasion."

"No, there wasn't anything except what ye were wearing or was strapped to you...except those extra guns and your hat that somehow showed up when I left to go get me medicine and truck."

"The little girl brung 'em...Is she here?" He looked around the dimly lit cave.

"Little girl?"

"Yeah, seven, eight years old. Corn-silk hair, sky blue eyes...said her name was Anna...'Er was I dreamin'?"

Angie gasped and brought her hands to her mouth. Her eyes began to fill with tears...

***

CHAPTER THREE

SAND SPRINGS
CHEROKEE NATION

Bass and Jed rode down the red dirt Main Street, the early morning sun at their backs—with their pack mule and the two outlaws in tow. Bailey Biden—hands shackled to his saddle horn along with the lead rope to Fletcher's bay mare carrying his blanket-wrapped body—grimaced in pain at every step his horse took.

"Damnation, marshal, any chance of seein' a doctor 'bout this hole you put in my hip?"

"Wish to hell you'd quit that whinin', Biden. You'd think you was agonna die...Hell, had a worst place on my lip and never quit whistlin'," quipped Jed.

"If'n you hadn't a tried to rob us poor unsuspectin' travelers, you might not have got yerself shot...You ain't the sharpest knife in the drawer, ya know. Just be glad I wus feelin' benevolent," said Bass over his shoulder.

"Poor unsuspectin' travelers, my ass," Biden grumbled.

Bass pulled rein in front of a set of hitching rails along one side of a six foot long water trough. The sign that hung from the porch over the boardwalk was painted with: CITY MARSHAL.

The door to the office opened and a straw-haired, freckled-faced young man in his early twenties wearing a store-bought collarless shirt under a gray wool vest with a deputy marshal's shield affixed to the front, stepped out.

"Marshals Reeves and Neal! Dang, I was goin' to ask what ya'll were adoin' over in our neck of the woods, but it looks like you got some riff-raff for us...Well, at least one, that is."

"Yep, they was two, Homer. Tried to get a bit fractious and Jed punched that one's ticket draped over his horse there. He went by Newt Fletcher. This'un here is Bailey Biden...needs some patchin'. They's dodgers on the both of 'em...Got room in yer steel hotel, there?"

"Yessir, got a vacancy...Specially fer Biden there. Marshal Patrick's been on the lookout for him since he heard he wuz on the scout up this way. Figured he and Fletcher wuz over to Catoosa the hell-hole, though...It's gittin' to be known as the Hole-in-the-Wall of the Nations and all."

"Where's John L., by the way? He sleepin' in?"

"No, sir. He's over to Lucinda's havin' breakfast with Tobe and Molly...Ya'll head on over there, ifn you like. I'll see to yer stock and take these two over to Doc Thacker's."

"Oooh-lále, but a stack of Lucy's buttermilk flapjacks, covered in butter 'n sorghum and a half-inch thick slab of ham already makin' my mouth water," said Jed.

"Mine too," said Bass as he dismounted and pitched the key to Biden's handcuffs to Homer. "We'll do the paperwork after breakfast...you don't mind."

"'Spect that'll do, marshal," Homer replied.

He nodded at the young deputy, turned and headed down the street toward Lucinda's Cafe with Jed alongside. They walked almost a block when a big, red-headed, bearded man astride a black Tennessee mule headed in the opposite direction in the street, pulled rein.

"Hey! Ain't you that man-killin' nigger marshal Bass Reeves," he asked and spit a stream of tobacco juice in the red dirt street.

Bass just slightly turned his head and looked out at the shaggy giant of a man dressed in faded bib overalls, sack-cloth black jacket and a battered slouch hat. "Must be yer day, mister. Right on all three counts...since two are obvious and I have killed a few men in the line of duty."

The man stepped off his mule, whipped the reins around the nearest hitching rail and stepped toward Bass and Jed. "Been lookin' fer you...You kilt my brother over to Salisaw last year."

"Looks like yer right again. Did kill a Parkin "Jawbone" Bannack in Salisaw in the process of servin' a warrant fer assaultin' a woman...one Josephine Taylor...Pert near beat her to death...That be him?"

"You had no call killin' him...She wuz just a harlot."

"Well, one, no matter what her occupation was, she was a human bein' and two, he drawed down on me with his scatter gun...Needed killin'...Don't cotton to child 'er woman beatin'."

"Don't give a damn what the reason...I ain't carrin' no gun, but I aim to stomp a mudhole in yer black ass deep enough to bury a wagon in...Knuckles 'n skulls...jest me and you, nigger. Knuckles 'n skulls," he said as he pulled off his coat and hat and draped them on the hitching rail.

"Well, don't see no keep-off signs tacked on me." Bass turned to his partner. "You, Jedadiah?"

"Not today...Mistakes must run in yer family, mister...Ya'll must be some special kinda stupid...Want me to hold yer coat 'n truck, Bass?"

"Appreciate it," he said as he removed his coat. He then unbuckled his twin reverse holstered gun belt with matched .38-40 Colts, his shoulder holster and finally, his hat. "Don't lose 'em."

"Not likely." Jed grinned.

Bass rolled the sleeves of his off-white boiled shirt up to his elbows and stepped into the street. For one of the rare times in his adult life, he had to look up at another man as he towered at least six inches over his own six feet and three.

"You got a name, big 'un? Figger yer back name is the same as yer brother...Bannack?"

"Folks jest call me Bear Man."

"Who'd a guess..."

Bass's head was rocked from a smashing right cross that staggered him and left him seeing stars. He quickly backed up and moved to his right. "Damn, big man, you ain't got fists...you got hams with fingers."

Bear Man swung another round house right that Bass partially ducked as it glanced off the back of his head.

"Watch 'em, Bass...he could fell an ox with them hands."

"Tell me somethin' I don't already know," he said as he feinted left and then stepped right and buried his fist up to the wrist in Bear Man's stomach just below his sternum.

The big man let out a whoosh of fetid air followed by a sharp breath and dropped his hands to his belly. "Shit!...Swallered my bacca," he wheezed.

Bass took the opportunity to throw an overhand hammer fist to the top of his head. The man's knees buckled for a moment. But as the marshal stepped back to let him catch his breath—Bear Man swung a wild haymaker, catching Bass on the right shoulder almost knocking him off his feet. Reeves cautiously circled, trying to shake the feeling back into his numbed, tingling arm and countered with two trip-hammer hard left jabs, one to Bannack's already misshapened nose and the second to his mouth.

The giant spit out a front tooth, shook his head like a angry bull—slinging blood to both sides—then charged Bass, grabbing him in a bear hug, lifting him up and squeezing—bending him over backwards. "How you like that, nigger? Now you know why I'm called Bear Man...I'm afixin' to break yer back."

"Don't…think…so," Bass managed to wheeze out as he put his hands up under the blood covered bearded chin and tried to push his head back—but to no avail. Then he spread his arms wide and slapped both hands hard as he could against each side of the man's head directly over his ears—simultaneously rupturing both ear-drums.

Bannack dropped Bass and grabbed his ears. "Ahhh! Son of a bitch!"

This time, the marshal didn't give him a chance to recover as he drop-kicked him as hard as he could in the crotch. Bear Man jerked his hands from his ears to his mangled privates, back to his ears and then back to his crotch. His eyes crossed and he dropped to his knees and whimpered—"Eeiiiii"—as he toppled over on his side like a felled tree, hands still between his legs. Dust billowed up around him as he lay mewling like a newborn kitten. He curled up in a fetal position and then lay still.

"Well, reckon it's true what they say, Bass…Intense pain will make a man pass out…Want me to shackle 'em?" asked Jed as he walked up and returned the jacket, hat and fire arms.

"Guess not…Think he's paid enough fer his lesson…He won't be ridin' anywhere fer a spell…don't 'spect."

"Probably not, at that…" Jed chuckled. "Good thing you done some prize fightin' at county fairs in yer younger days…"

Bass splashed water in his face from the horse trough, took a faded red wild rag from his coat pocket and dried off. "Shore glad *he* hadn't…We'd be agoin' at it yet."

"Well, don't know 'bout you, but I'm still hungry."

They walked through the eight foot tall single glass paned door to Lucinda's Cafe ringing the three inch brass bell hung from the header. The two men paused briefly, hung their hats on a hat-tree by the door before they spotted Tobe, Molly and Marshal Patrick at a nearby eight foot long table. A gray-muzzled red and white border collie lay underneath, his head resting on his paws. The dog jumped up when he saw who had entered and ran over, wagging his tail and wiggling all over.

Bass knelt down and the dog licked his face as he scruffed both of his ears. "Boot! How you been, boy?"

"Hey, 'member me?" Jed chimed in.

Boot—both front feet dancing up and down—gave Jed kisses too and then pressed his head against the marshal's leg to enjoy the petting.

A tall trim man, in his sixties with an unruly shock of salt and pepper hair, a white handlebar mustache and matching eyebrows got to his feet and stuck out his hand. "Plague take it! Bass Reeves and Jed Neal…As the day is long, it's good to see you…Say, where'd you get that mouse under yer eye? Looks fresh," said retired marshal Bassett.

"Good to see you too, Tobe…"

Jed interrupted Bass, "The other feller looks a sight worse, believe me…he's still nappin' in the street down in front of the mercantile."

"I need to run him to the hoosegow, Marshal?" asked City Marshal Patrick as he got to his feet.

"Naw, leave him be, John L. He'll be all right in a day 'er two, 'cept fer singin' soprano a while...nice to see you," Bass said as he gave the strapping young law officer a back-slapping hug. "How's the family 'n that purty wife?"

"They're fine, little James has been on the colicky side this past week 'n Nellie Ruth's 'bout to pop any day now."

An attractive blonde woman in her fifties confined to a tall wicker-backed wheelchair on the opposite side of the table spoke up, "I've got her and the kids out at the ranch ''til the baby comes...Those children will be the death of me, yet."

"You wouldn't have it any other way, woman. You know how much you love those grand babies," said Tobe.

Molly Allgood Bassett batted her golden brown eyes at him. "I was talkin' about you and John L. You're worse than a pair of four year olds..."

"Well, see thangs ain't changed much 'round here...Yer still a purty as ever, Molly."

"Go to hell for lyin', same as stealin', Marshal Ree..."

"Ya'll gonna keep jawin' in the middle of the aisle, blockin' my way?" A matronly woman in her early fifties, her gray-streaked hair up neatly in a bun, interrupted Molly. "Or would you like to take a seat so I can serve you? Marshal Neal looks like he's about to pass out from hunger."

"Miss Lucy, you hit the nail on the head. Smelt yer cookin' two blocks down the street."

"Aw, shush, go on with you. Sit and I'll bring your usual...still buttermilk pancakes and ham for you and eggs over medium, sausage, biscuits and gravy, Marshal Reeves? With coffee and a cold pitcher of sweet-milk?"

Bass nodded. "Yessum, thank you."

"You know what I like, Miss Lucy…jest keep bringin' those flapjacks "'til I hollar calf-rope…'n bring me a big glass of clabber, too…if you please," Jed added.

"Don't let your eyes get bigger than your stomach, Marshal," she said with a twinkle as she walked away.

Later after Lucy had cleared away the dishes, everyone was having coffee in her heavy white porcelain mugs. Jed had undone the bottom three buttons of his vest and was leaning back in his chair.

"…and well, that's purty much the story…We wuz hopin' John L. might be able to come with us…but what with Nellie Ruth afixin' to deliver…" Bass looked around the almost empty restaurant.

"Man's place is to be near his wife during birthing…Even though he's mostly in the way," Molly said as she glanced at John L. "'Sides, I think this one is going to be a girl…your first."

"You haven't said that before," John L. retorted. "How do you know?'

"She's carrying the baby high. The other three, all boys, she carried low…you'll see."

"Ding dang! A girl! What do you know 'bout that?" He turned to Bass. "Marshal, meby I can catch up to ya'll after the baby comes and…"

46

"I'll go," Tobe interrupted.

"You'll do no such of a thing, Tobias Reese Bassett. You know that..."

Tobe interrupted his wife of ten years. "Mollydarlin', Jack is my friend. If it wadn't for him...Well...'nuff said. I'm goin'. We'll be takin' the train most of the way, anyhoo...End of discussion."

"It'll most likely taken us a week, what with changin' trains in Tulsa 'n takin' the Iron Mountain to Wagonner." Bass paused to take a sip of his coffee. "Then catchin' the MKT down cross the Red to Denison, Texas, 'n the Southern Pacific west to Gainesville..."

"Made that trip back in '85 when I delivered that diamond ring to Lorena Matthews keepin' my promise to that dying cowboy...'Spect Gainesville's growed a mite...Big cotton, cattle 'n railroad center on account the Chisholm Trail ran a tad to the west 'n it was a Butterfield stage stop. Hear tell they's now a jerk-water run up north through Ardmore, IT, all the way to Oklahoma City...Don't run everday, though," Jed added.

"See?" Tobe said to Molly. "Beats hell out of sittin' a saddle 'n sleeping on the ground fer purtnear a month."

"Hard-headed old...What about Boot? You know he'll grieve..."

"Oh, I think he's got another adventure in him...Don't you, son?"

Boot's head jerked up at the mention of his name and he gave a short 'woof' and then licked Tobe's hand.

47

Bass glanced at Jed and then nodded a reluctant acceptance. He hoped he wasn't making a mistake…

ARDMORE, I.T.

The gilded hand-painted letters on the ornately carved dark mahogany door read: JASON ALEXANDER BALDWIN - BARRISTER. Bart "Couger" Hess knocked on the brass plate set on the side with no small amount of trepidation.

"Come in," came the answer from inside.

Couger turned the glass knob, eased the door open and jerked the slouch hat from his head as he stepped inside the newly appointed plush office.

Almost all the buildings in down town Ardmore were either brand new or in the process of being rebuilt from the fire that had gutted the town just a few months earlier. Ardmore—Gaelic signifying high grounds or hills—was just nine miles south of the Arbuckle Mountain range and an equal ninety miles distance between Oklahoma City on the north and Dallas, Texas on the south.

"Mr. Baldwin in, Miz Kerry?" Cougar asked of the dowdy, somewhat overweight matron sitting behind a cherry secretarial desk.

Her expression was as if she had been sucking on a lemon as she looked up over her pince nez glasses perched on the end of her nose. The once dirty blonde hair, now streaked with gray and wrapped in a tight bun on the back of her head did nothing to alleviate the severity of her demeanor. "I'll see if he's available," she said as she got up and entered a mahogany door behind her station. In a moment, she returned to the reception area. "Mr. Baldwin will see you now," she said brusquely as she looked him up and down with undisguised disfavor.

"Thank you, ma'am," he said as he entered the still open door, closed it behind him and moved toward one of the new burgundy leather wing chairs in front of Baldwin's seven foot wide black walnut Chippendale desk.

"I didn't say you could sit, fool...Next time you come into my office, wear clean clothes...and leave those filthy boots outside in the hallway...My God, man, do you ever bathe?"

"Yessir, oncet a week, whether I need to 'er not."

Baldwin rolled his eyes. "Now, what do you want? I trust you have good news."

Jason Baldwin was an arrogant, portly man in his fifties with mutton-chop whiskers and a full head of dark brown hair graying at the temples—with a penchant for expensive European suits and Cuban cigars. He looked up with disdain at the unkempt man.

"Uh...yessir and, uh...no sir."

"What the hell does that mean? My God in heaven, I'm surrounded by imbeciles."

"We, uh, taken care of those two placer prospectors that wuz bringin' that gear they bought at yer store to their claim on the Honey...Fleming got hisself kilt in the process..."

Baldwin removed a cigar from a side pocket of his satin brocade vest and snipped off the end with a pen knife. "No big loss...he was dumber than you...if that's possible." He warmed the cigar with a match then stuck it in the side of his mouth and lit the end. "The advantage of having the only hardware and mining supply store in the area keeps us apprised of who's finding color...continue."

"Sent Bobo back to gather what gear he could...saddles an' such and he tracked down their pack donkey. The equipment they had bought is already back in yer store. The donkey is at our claim camp..."

Baldwin jerked the cigar from his mouth and blew a huge cloud of blue smoke. "Fool! Take that donkey off somewhere and shoot it. What if someone recognizes it as belonging to those two prospectors?...Then what?"

"Well, sir, we, uh, then went by the widder O'Reilly's place like you said to..."

"And?"

"...and well, she run us off with that big double-barreled Greener of hers. She weren't foolin' neither. Said to tell you her answer is the same."

"I've had it with that red-headed wench...I want her gone... gone! Do you understand me?" Baldwin slammed his pudgy fist down on the top of his desk.

The big man jumped. "Want us to burn her out?"

"God dammit man, are you deaf? I said gone...Don't give a damn how. When I hire someone I don't tell him how to do his job...Her allotment is the biggest claim on the Honey and I have a client that wants it! There's a new strike over at Ravia...Same white quartz outcropping. I want to wrap all those claims along the Honey up...Just get it done or I'll find someone who can..." He paused, swiveled his chair around, stared out the window for a moment, and then turned back. "On second thought...I know the Sartain brothers down in Fort Worth...handy with guns and do what they're told without scruples. Twins, Rafe and Raff...heard tell Rafe braced John Wesley Hardin out in El Paso once. Got seven, eight men in their outfit...need more men anyway...Marshal Lindsey's getting a bit too nosey...Now get the hell out of my office and go do your job."

"Yessir." The chastised man quickly turned, opened the door and headed toward the outer entrance.

"Hillary! Bring your note pad and get in here."

"Right away, Mr. Baldwin," she replied as she entered his inner sanctum and closed the door behind her.

FALLS CAVE

"...we were picnicking on the west side of our property on the ridge at the top of the falls and she was over near the creek picking Indian paint brushes and wild jonquils...Oh, how she loved those flowers...Anyway, I saw her lean down to pick up something at the edge of the water...she slipped on a rock, fell into the Honey and it swept her down the falls to the pool..." Angie paused, choked back her tears, took a deep breath and continued, "...we never found me daughter's body..."

"Just don't understand it, I know I seen her...well, seen somebody. How else could I know what she looked like?...Or her name?...Even talked to her...Jest cain't believe it was the fever."

"Lord works in mysterious ways...sometimes." She helped him sit up and handed him the Mason jar of broth. "Drink this...That's been over two years now...and then one day I went down to the Honey to draw wash water. Saw something glint in the sunlight from a gravel bar beside an eddy...It was a cluster of small gold nuggets. Well, needless to say, it didn't take long for the word to get out when I had them assayed in Ardmore...Just a few months later, me husband was murdered, bushwhacked on the way back from Ardmore...Shot in the back he was."

"Right sorry to hear 'bout yer husband, ma'am."

"The wagon and mules showed up at the barn...there was blood on the seat...I knew then..." Angie handed the big dog still laying beside his master a cold biscuit. He gently took it from her fingers, looked up at her as if to ask, "May I eat it now?" She nodded. "Go ahead, it's all right." He flipped it up into the air a short distance, caught it and wolfed it down in just seconds.

"We got our one hundred and forty acre allotment from the tribal council almost ten years ago...me husband, God rest his dear soul, was half Chickasaw...It gave us a little over a half-mile of frontage along the creek...There have been numerous nefarious attempts to get our...me land. From phony suitors to out and out grifters...But the worst has been a barrister in Ardmore...Jason A. Baldwin, is the moniker he goes by. He not only is a lawyer of some ill repute, but he also owns the assay office, the hardware store and the mercantile..."

"What's ill repute?"

"Crooked as a dog's hind leg."

Boy lifted his head up and looked at her.

"No personal reference intended," Angie said to him.

"Oh, right. You said lawyer."

"Anyway, he started out by making me a legitimate, but less than generous offer for me property...Now that has degraded to outright threats and he's shut me off from buying supplies and even me food at his stores. I have some Chickasaw neighbors...kin to me late husband...that manage to slip myself some necessaries and every three months or so, I take the wagon down to Gainesville...It's a two day trip, each way...I have notified the resident US Deputy Marshal about what's been going on. He said he'd look into it...That's been over three weeks and he's been quiet as a wee church mouse."

"This Baldwin don't sound like particular nice feller," he said as he reached over and put his hand on one of his pistols.

"You hold it right there, laddie!" Angie whipped out the .32 from her coat pocket and cocked it.

"Whoa, ma'am...Easy now. I was just gonna wipe 'em down...Start rustin' mighty fast in this here damp cave."

"I still don't know who you are...What with all those knife and bullet scars you carry around...For all I know you're a highwayman or worse still...work for that divil his own self, Baldwin."

"Well, you got nuthin' on me...Don't know who I am neither...Seems like I know a lotta things 'ceptin' that...Guess I cain't blame you for bein' tetchy. 'Spect I'd be on tenderhooks too...wuz I in yer shoes." He moved his hand away from his guns and clasped his fingers together over his stomach. "Would appreciate it though, you'd point that shooter somewheres else…Don't think I could handle anymore holes in me…fer right now." He paused. "It's plain and simple, sure 'nuf, that somebody wanted me dead. I kin see one bullet bein' a huntin' accident…but not two."

"It is sorry I am," she said as she put her Smith and Wesson back in her pocket. "You're right, I am a bit on the edge. Some of Baldwin's hired guns paid me a visit just before your animal showed up and led me here…

"Do you think you can walk? Me cabin isn't too far and it's a lot more comfortable than this dank cave…You've been unconscious, off and on, for almost five days…It's a wonder you haven't caught a case of the croup."

"Reckon I could give it a try. 'Spect that's enough sleep fer anybody. Legs ain't hurt much 'cept for some skint places 'n bruises. They's a little swellin' in my right knee, but it's been steady goin' down…Head feels like somebody's inside beatin' on a big bass drum, an' I'm still a seein' two of you on occasion, though."

"Here, drink the last of this." She handed him the jar of willow tea. "I'll make a trip to the cabin with all this stuff…and your guns. Then I'll come back and help you. Your boots and pants are dry. They're on the other side of the fire…Do you think you can get them on while I'm gone?"

"Give it a shot, ma'am," he said before taking several big swallows and draining the jar. He made a wry face and his body shook at the taste of the bitter medicine. "Don't cotton much to walkin' anywheres barefoot and nekked...Pardon my language."

She turned her face, smiled and pulled the clean union suit and a folded flannel shirt from the basket. "Here, put these on...belonged to me husband. He was about your size...I'll be back in a bit."

"Yessum...Boy, you go with her...He'll look out for you, ma'am."

"Of that I have no doubt. None whatsoever...You sure he doesn't like Shakespeare?" she said over her shoulder as she picked up his weapons along with her basket and they headed toward the ledge beside the falls.

"Well, not from me, anyhows," Jack added with a forced smile.

ARDMORE, I.T.
MARSHAL'S OFFICE

Deputy US Marshal Selden Trullery Lindsey opened the telegram from Sheriff Brownlow in Gregg County Texas. He scanned the yellow flimsy for a moment. "I'll be damned." Selden turned to another deputy, Loss Hart, working on a cup of coffee at a desk across the room—his feet propped up on top. "Loss, been a bank robbery down in Longview, Texas...Git this. They're purty sure it was Bill Dalton."

"No shit? Hell, thought he was still in Californee."

"Meby, meby not...One of the outlaws was killed...had a hat made at Dustin's. Why don't you take this description over to the hat shop and see if Waymon made a hat for somebody

55

matchin' it...I'll bet a five dollar gold piece, that if'n it was Dalton, they headed north toward the Kiamichi's to throw any posse off their trail...We'll catch the train over to Antlers...Good chance we can cut 'em off, if'n they're headed this way."

"Makes sense to me. I'll see to our horses after I check this out at Dustin's. He remembers everybody he ever made a hat for," Loss said as he took the telegram from Selden, grabbed his hat off the hook and headed out the door.

Marshal Lindsey was a big, broad-shouldered man nearing six feet and two inches and weighing over two hundred pounds. He was square-jawed and sported a big black full mustache. Selden and Loss had served out of the Paris, Texas, US Marshal's office since 1890 and he knew in his gut that Dalton and his gang would eventually head toward the Arbuckles.

There were rewards totaling about $35,000 offered by various organizations for the apprehension of Bill Dalton—dead or alive. This was a huge sum of money in 1895. In today's money, it would be the equivalent of over $930,000. Every lawman and bounty hunter in the territory would be on the lookout for the last of the Dalton Gang...

"Jim Wallace," said Loss as he came through the door an hour later. "Waymon said no question 'bout it...Got a brother, Houston with a place up near Elk...I done dropped the horses off at the train yard with the hostler...Train fer Gainesville will be through in little over two hours."

56

"Yep, know of the Wallace boys. Couple of ne'er-do-wells if they ever was...I've suspected their place was a line house for outlaws for some time, now...Always has a plow sweep hung in a tree nearby the log cabin. They bang on it to let anyone they might be shelterin' that they's laws in the area...Good work, Loss...Just time enough to load up some trail supplies...Who knows...might git lucky."

FALLS CAVE

He was stamping his foot into his calf-high cavalry boot as Anna slipped into the cave.

"Dang, girl, coulda knocked. Mighta caught me a dressin'."

"I'm sorry, kinda hard to knock on water."

"Got a point there." He squatted down, making his brown eyes level with her blue ones. "Tell me, Anna, where do you go?"

She pointed toward the water cascading past the cave entrance. "There...Are you feelin' better?"

"Yes, I am, missy...Now what do you mean, 'There'?"

"Just, there..."

"Where do you stay?"

Pointing again. "There."

"Is Angie O'Reilly yer momma?"

She hesitated and glanced toward the rushing water. "I'm not allowed to say."

"What do you mean...yer not allowed to say?"

"I'm just not supposed to...I'm only allowed to help..."

"Who? Who is sayin' yer only allowed to..."

She quickly glanced at the white sheet of thundering water. "I've already stayed too long...I have to go now...I'm glad you are feeling better...I like your puppy."

She turned, ran to the ledge and disappeared from his sight around the corner.

"Well, slap a'nt Gussie in the face...if that don't beat all."

Angie and Boy entered the cave from the same ledge Anna had just left seconds earlier. The dog stopped and glanced around the cave then to the wall of water and whined. He lay down, facing the falls.

"Oh, I'm glad you were able to get dressed...Are you feeling a bit better now?"

"Did you see her?"

"See who?"

"Anna...She left just a hair before you came in...You didn't see her?"

Angie caught her breath. "N...No. No one came out while I was walking up...Praise be to the saints...you see her again?"

"I did...talked to her too...and this time there weren't no question 'bout it...She was a real as you er me..."

***

CHAPTER FOUR

KATY TRAIN STATION
DENISON, TEXAS

The big black 6-2-2 coal-fired steam locomotive, number 101, pulled in to the red brick Katy depot. Her last stop had been Gainesville, thirty-five miles to the west—the next, after Denison, would be Paris. On the other side of the long two-story depot, a 4-4-2 black and silver MKT locomotive from Dallas, bled off her boiler over-pressure with a huge cloud of steam.

Marshals Lindsey and Hart stepped down from the first passenger car behind the tender on the 101. They briefly looked about and then headed back down the train to the livestock car to see about the transfer of their horses to the MKT northbound.

"Think we got time to get the plate lunch at the Harvey House before the train leaves, Sel?"

"Don't see why not, got better'n a hour 'fore she pulls out fer Antlers. Looks like the yardmaster and the hostler already 'er movin' our horses," Selden said as he pointed down to the livestock car just past the mail car. "Ol' Black stands out in a crowd, don't he?"

"Yep, hellova horse. Seventeen hands, too big fer me...have to get a box jest to git on 'em."

"Hell, you need a box to git on yer own 'n he's not quite fourteen hands."

"Aw, hush...That ain't so," said the 5'8" Hart.

Lindsey and Loss Hart entered the crowded Harvey House restaurant inside the KATY depot. They looked around trying to find a couple of empty seats.

"Selden!"

Lindsey turned to his right to see Bass standing and waving near the side of the room.

"Well looky yonder, Loss, it's Bass, Jed...'n another feller. Wonder what the hell they're doin' here?" Selden said as he waved back.

"Not gonna find out standin' around...Looks like he's got a couple extry places on their bench at the table...Musta knowed we wuz comin'. Come on, I could eat the side boards out of a gut wagon."

Hart and Lindsey made their way across the busy Harvey House restaurant toward Bass's long table.

"Bass! What er you and Jed doin' in these parts?" Selden said as he held out his hand. "An' who's this feller?"

"Selden, good to see you…Loss. Want you to meet Marshal Tobe Bassett from up Sand Springs way."

"Tobe, heard tell 'bout you. It's a real pleasure. Always glad to meet a good lawman."

"Marshal Lindsey, heard a lot 'bout you too. Pleasure is all mine," Tobe said as he shook Selden's and then Hart's hand.

"I'm Loss Hart…worked with Lindsey here fer the past four years…Pleased to meet cha…Who's this here under the table?"

"That's my best friend, Boot…Well don't jest sit there, son, shake hands with the man."

Boot raised his right paw, Loss took it and gave it a shake. "Pleased to meet you too, Boot."

"Ya'll grab a seat. One of the Harvey Girls will be back in a minute 'er two…Name's Annabel, a real sweetie," said Bass.

As if on cue, just as the marshals all took a seat at the boarding house style table, a wasp-waisted young lady, no more than nineteen, approached. Her flaxen hair was done in a tight bun on top of her head; she wore a white long-sleeved shirtwaist blouse, buttoned all the way to her shapely neck, a light gray lindsey floor length skirt and a white ruffled apron. Her pert button nose had a small splash of freckles across the top that seemed to fit perfectly with her deep blue eyes and alabaster skin.

Harvey Girls—as they were called—were all between the ages of seventeen and nineteen; weren't allowed to wear any type of make-up and had to sign a three year contract with the railroad. All the girls were required to live above the restaurant in a private dormitory—with a live-in house mother. Living and working in a Harvey House was tantamount to a young ladies finishing school. They weren't allowed to accept courting gentlemen during their contract period, but it was extremely rare for a Harvey Girl to remain unmarried for very long after they left employment in the famous chain of restaurants. It was considered a great honor to be chosen as a Harvey Girl on the Santa Fe line.

Former railroad man Fred Harvey is credited with creating the first restaurant chain in the United States—the original Harvey House was opened in Florence, Kansas in 1878. The chain would eventually grow to eighty-four restaurants along the AT&SF tracks. The last Harvey House would be built in the Gainesville, Texas Depot in 1901. The popularity of the Harvey Girls remained strong even well into the twentieth century with the release of the movie, *The Harvey Girls* starring Judy Garland in 1946.

"Gentlemen, welcome to the Harvey House. My name is Annabel, I will have the pleasure of serving ya'll today," she said with a melodious Alabama lilt to her voice. "Our special today is fried chicken, yeast rolls, mashed potatoes, cream gravy, speckled butter beans and steamed cabbage…With peach cobbler for desert." Her smile seemed to light up the room and her even white teeth set off her naturally red full lips. She was indeed a beautiful young woman.

"Sounds good, Annabel. Could we git some coffee while we wait?" Bass asked as he glanced at the other marshals and got confirming nods.

"Yes sir, Marshal...bless your hearts. I'll be right back with a pot and cups...Don't ya'll go way now...ya hear?" She smiled an infectious grin at the men, turned gracefully and headed toward the kitchen.

"My goodness, never thought I'd see a girl as purty as my Nellie Ruth, but dang, that Annabel comes close," Tobe offered.

"She does, she does," confirmed Jed.

"Now, you were gonna tell me what ya'll were doing down thisaway before we were so pleasantly interrupted," said Selden.

Bass glanced around to make sure there were no eavesdroppers. "Well, purtnear six weeks ago, you sent a telegram to the Judge 'bout a claim jumpin' complaint an' harassment on that gold strike over in the Arbuckles. Judge Parker turned the affair over to me and I sent Marshal Jack McGann down there with a Chickasaw Lighthorse undercover as placer miners...Sorry I couldn't let you know, Sel, the Judge thought we best keep it close to the vest...Never know who might git holt of a telegram...Jack's failed to check in...been nigh on to ten days now...Ain't like him. Ain't like him atall...We were headed yer way."

Well, Bass, as you'll recall, met Jack, the last time I's in Ft. Smith an' ain't seen hide-ner-hair of him in our country. But then again, heard he's purty good at undercover work...Who's the Lighthorse workin' with him?"

"Montford Anoatubbi."

"Good man, know him too...Don't know as I'd worry too much. If anythin' had happened, 'spect we'd a heard somethin'...Don't you think, Loss?"

"Yep, an' we been doin' some investigatin' our ownselves. Got a jakeleg lawyer in Ardmore...the one we sent the complaint 'bout harassment to the Judge about...that seems to be acquirin' a lot of claims. Folks just up and sellin' out on the cheap...Startin' to smell like uncle Chester's stink bait...Jest ain't got nothin' we kin sink our teeth into as yet..."

"But we do have a situation we could use some help on," Selden interrupted.

"That would be?" asked Bass.

"We're on the trail of one Mason Frakes Dalton, better known as Bill...He an' his gang robbed a bank down to Longview...two citizens and one outlaw were kilt an' a bunch others wounded. We think the gang's headed toward the Arbuckles an' we kin head 'em off at Antlers...Like I said, could use a little help."

Bass glanced over at Jed and Tobe.

"If we got a chance to git the last of the Dalton's...I'd say it needs to be done," offered Tobe.

CHOCTAW NATION

Bass, Jed, Tobe, Selden and Loss pulled rein at a small general store on the northwest outskirts of Antlers. The wide sign above the covered porch read: DAWSON'S GENERAL STORE.

"Could use a cool root beer," said Jed as he dismounted.

"I'm near outta Brown's Mule, too," added Loss.

The five marshals tied their horses to the hitching rails in front of the small store and stepped inside the front door.

"Afternoon, marshals, what kin I do ya fer?" the grizzled storekeep asked as the screen door slammed shut behind them. He turned and spit a stream of tobacco juice at an old brass spittoon badly in need of a cleaning near the end of a counter and eyed the others as they helped themselves to the wire-capped bottled root beers in a wash tub of cool water.

"Mostly information, old timer," Lindsey said as he fished an eight-inch length of licorice candy from a jar next to the cash register. "Seen any strangers about in the last day er two?"

"Well, now that you mention it, seen some fellers...believe they wuz five of 'em...crossed the road yonder a piece." He pointed north. "Headed west, they wuz...One of 'em, big man, come in an' bought some salt pork, coffee 'n canned peaches, he did...Thought it was kindly funny at the time they cut through the woods 'stead of stayin' to the road...bein' in suits an' all."

"Much obliged," Lindsey said as he pitched a silver dollar on the counter. "That settle us up for the root beers, candy and tobaccer we got?"

"Close enough...Them fellers, they looked kindly in a hurry too...if'n ya ask me."

Marshal Lindsey nodded as they headed out the front door.

Eight miles north and west of Antlers, the marshals negotiated their mounts through the heavy timber toward a logging trail. They were near the base of White Rock Mountain and had just forded Wild Horse Creek. The best tracker, Reeves, had been able to follow the sign left by Dalton's gang he'd picked up near Dawson's store.

"Still five of 'em, Bass?" asked Selden.

"Yep, horses are purty flagged an' I'd say one is lame er wounded...but they be pushin' 'em hard. 'Spect they think a posse is still on their tail."

Boot gave a short bark.

"Somebody up ahead...steppin' out in the trail there," said Tobe.

"Choctaw...huntin'," offered Bass softly. "Shee-ah," he said to the Indian as they got closer.

"Shee-ah, Marshals...I am Manfred Moore," said the middle-aged fairly short Choctaw.

He was carrying a single shot 410 and had six squirrels hung from his belt—five good-sized red fox and one gray.

"Moore? You kin to Tecumseh?" asked Jed.

"Cousins."

"How's he gittin' along?" asked Tobe.

"He's home over to Tushkahomma...makin' babies an' raisin' watermelons...Has seat in Choctaw Nation Tribal Council legislature...He big man now." Manfred laughed.

"Tell him Bass, Jed and Tobe said howdy next time you see him."

"Happy to, marshals. Tecumseh speak of ya'll much...It is honor to meet you."

"Pleasure to meet you too...We're on the trail of..."

66

He interrupted Bass, "Manfred know...Five men pass early this mornin'. They not see Manfred. Left worn out 'n wind broke horses 'bout a mile up ahead...One shot. They are shanks mare...For now."

"Much obliged, Manfred," Bass said as he touched the brim of his hat.

"Take caution, Marshals...they are bad men."

"We know, Manfred, we know...Good huntin'."

"As you, Marshals, as you...Shee-ah, I go," he said as he turned and disappeared back into the deep woods.

"Better unshuck yer long guns, boys an' spread out. I'll take point, Sel, you 'n Jed the flanks. Loss an' Tobe...got our backs...Looks like we may have 'em treed."

"Treed coons kin be powerful dangerous, Bass," said Selden.

"Yep, know that too."

THE FALLS

Angie, the wounded man and his white dog walked around the far edge of the two hundred foot wide pool with the large boulder in the center near the falls. He was walking somewhat stiffly with the help of a black walking stick and looked back at the wolf-dog lying down, staring at the falls. "Boy! Come on son."

The big white animal looked over his shoulder at the couple as they neared the trail that led to her cabin, then he turned back to continue staring at the falls.

"What's with you? Come on."

He finally got up and padded after them, occasionally glancing back at the water.

"You know, the Chickasaw believe that all white animals are sacred and endowed with the ability to communicate with restless spirits," Angie commented.

"Yeah, well what about me?...I seen her too."

"I don't know..." She paused a moment. "They also believe the spirits only let those they want see or talk to them...I suppose that makes you one of the chosen."

"Well, jest don't know that I believe in spirits...er at least never did before." He glanced down at the walking stick. "What'd you call this thing again?"

"It's called a *shillelagh* in the old country. Belonged to me grandfather. They were not only used as a walking stick, but as a weapon of war, too. Originally it was for settling disputes in a gentlemanly manner...like pistols in your colonial days or swords in the days of yore. That knob you have under your hand, laddie, was hollowed out and filled with near two pounds of lead."

He hefted the black shiny stick and lightly swung it back and forth. "An' how'd it git so black 'n shiny?...Never seen wood like it b'fore."

"They were usually made from the blackthorn, rubbed down with butter or lard and placed up in the chimney to cure for six to eight weeks. That gave it the traditional black shiny color and made them very, very hard...It will certainly dent whatever you might choose to hit with it...including a man's head."

"Kin believe that. I'd dang sure hate to git hit with it..."

Boy let out a low whine and looked back at the distant falls again.

"Still wonder how he knew to find you."

"I think I know...I'll get word to me late husband's uncle, Anompoli Lawa."

"A-nom-poli La-wa? What's that mean?"

"*He talks to many*, but his civilized name is Winchester Ashalatubbi...he's a shaman in the Chickasaw tribe...Methinks he will be able to help us understand."

"Works for me."

FT. WORTH, TEXAS
WHITE ELEPHANT SALOON

The White Elephant saloon sat in almost the middle of Ft. Worth's dangerous *Hell's Half Acre* on Main Street. Most widely known for the gunfight between former Ft. Worth sheriff, Longhair Jim Courtright and gunfighter-gambler Luke Short in 1887, the saloon was a popular gambling and drinking site. The survivor of the shoot out, Short, maintained the gambling concession until his death from dropsy in 1893.

The bottom floor of the massive near 4,500 square foot facility was dominated by a stage, a forty foot ornately carved bar—shipped in special order from San Francisco—and numerous tables for eating and the occasional card game. Most of the gambling—poker, faro, roulette and the telegraph hookup that brought in the latest reports of horse races, prizefights and baseball games from all over the country—was located upstairs.

Two exceptionally handsome men stood at the bar directly in front of a famous eight foot oil painting of a nude *Fatima* reclining on a day bed. She was partially draped in a light red gossamer cover. The men sipped on snifters of Courvoisier Cognac XO—they were identical twins. Each was dressed almost the same in tailored black frock coats, gray striped trousers, ruffled-front shirts with silk cravats and flat crowned, three-inch pencil-roll brimmed Stetsons—the only difference was the color of their silk shirts and cravats. Rafe wore a light blue shirt and a dark blue cravat while Raff's shirt was a pale green with a dark green coordinating cravat—their dark hair and icy black eyes typified their Gypsy heritage. They appeared to be what was commonly termed 'dandies'—but dandies they were not. Each wore large rowl silver jingle-bob spurs as was the style in their home state of California.

They were the Sartain brothers—shootists extraordinaire. In the dying days of the old west, shootists or gunslingers were a disappearing breed, but the hubristic Sartain brothers still held sway as deadly guns for hire in the southwest.

A short chunky man in a white jacket and black pants approached the brothers with an envelope. "Mr. Sartain, I have a message for you," said the concierge.

Both men turned and simultaneously said, "I'll take it."

They glanced at one another and grinned.

"You take it brother," Rafe said.

"No, you're the oldest, you take it," responded Raff.

"Only by fifteen minutes…All right, this time." He took the envelope as Rafe handed him a short ivory-handled dagger from his belt sheath. Slipping the razor-sharp blade in the corner, he gave the knife a quick flick to slice the envelope open. He fished the telegram from inside and handed it to Rafe. "I opened it, you read."

Rafe unfolded the yellow sheet of paper. "Well, well, looks like our vacation is over...Baldwin has a little job for us up north. Says to bring six or seven of our men."

"Regular fee?"

"Regular fee...The first half will be transferred to our bank tomorrow upon our acceptance." He turned to the concierge who was still standing next to them waiting for a reply. "You may send one word, my good man...*Agreed*." He handed him a silver dollar.

The man bowed slightly. "As you wish, sir. Thank you," he said and then walked back toward his office.

"Always thought Baldwin was a pompous little man with a belly full of self-importance," said Raff.

"But his money has always been good."

"Ah, therein lies the rub as Hamlet said...I expect we should notify Carson and the boys to meet us at the station in the morning for the train to Gainesville," offered Raff.

"They'll be ready...been getting a bit restless."

"As have we, brother, as have we."

LOG CABIN

"Mighty comfortable cabin you got here, Miss Angie," he said as he reached down from the slat-back rocking chair to scratch Boy's ears. Both he and the big white wolf-dog were as close to

71

the roaring fire as the heat allowed trying to lose the chill of nearly five days in the cave. He took a sip of hot coffee from a white porcelain mug. "An' fine coffee too...Feller could git used to this."

"Don't bother yourself, laddie. The likes of you will not be here any longer than it takes to mend you up...and I need to be callin' you something besides 'laddie'...Methinks I shall call you 'Hank'. You look like you could be a 'Hank'."

He gave a start, sloshing coffee on his hand.

"What is it? Did you have a pain?"

"No, ma'am. It's just when you said that name, 'Hank', it was like a rabbit ran across my grave...like it was familiar, somehow...It has passed...Hank it is. Sounds good as any...and better'n most."

"We'll have a pot of good n' hearty Irish stew in a bit. I'm putting some bread in the oven to go with it. Yourself needs something more than broth to stick to your ribs, don't you know."

"Yessum, just smellin' that stew is makin' my mouth water." The dog gave a woof. "Think Boy's in total agreement too."

"Well, it'll be near to an hour before the bread's done...I just put it in the oven. Got some fresh sorghum and butter to go with it."

"Oh my, that sounds like jest what the doctor ordered...Noticed yer Murphy wagon over to the barn. Looks like a good'un...could use a dose of paint. Not as big as a Conestoga, but a whole lot stouter."

"It serves the purpose. Like I mentioned, I drive it to Gainesville when I'm in need of supplies."

"Horses 'er mules?"

"What? Oh...mules. Two up."

"In the barn?"

"Yes, I stalled them when I made the last trip from the falls. I usually leave them in the paddock, but I didn't know how long getting you here would take."

"What say I go out and give 'em a bait of grain?...Could use the exercise 'fore supper. That walk from the falls done me some good, I'm a thinkin'. Loosened my knee up a right smart."

"Are you sure you'd be up to it?...I don't want you to pull those stitches in your side. You'd be awake this time if I had to sew you back up."

"I'll take yer grampaw's walkin' stick," he said grabbing the shillelagh from the floor beside the rocking chair and heading for the door. "Come on, Boy, lets git us some fresh air."

The big dog rose, stretched and padded toward the door after him.

Hank carefully navigated the four steps from the porch to the ground, testing his knee a bit more on each one.

"Well, that wasn't bad, was it son?"

Boy spun around three times and stretched his legs out in front, chest on the ground, tail wagging in the air.

"No, not good enough to play, jest yet...don't rush me."

The big dog turned and trotted to the gate, jumped over and waited on the other side, his head cocked.

Hank opened the gate and headed toward the barn. "We're goin' to feed the mules...if you must know."

Boy spun around three times again and led the way to the barn.

Inside, Hank limped over to the grain bin, opened the lid, filled the pewter scoop with oats and headed over to the two stalls on the right side of the log barn. "Well, don't know you boys names, but 'spect you don't care much since I'm bringin' supper." He dumped half of the scoop in each of the big red mule's feed buckets. "Looks like ya'll need some hay too."

Boy sniffed behind the grain bin as Hank looked around and spotted the big stack of cut grass from the previous summer over in a corner—a three-tined spring-steel pitchfork stuck upright in the middle. Propping the walking stick against a support pole, he pushed the fork in, got a load of hay and flipped it into the nearest stall. He repeated the action on the second one. "That oughta hold ya'll ''til mornin'."

Grabbing his cane, he turned to head back toward the way they had come in when Boy stopped and rumbled a low warning growl.

"Somebody out there, son?" he whispered. The dog looked up at him then at the left side wall, turned and headed to the opposite end. "All right I'll follow you, then."

They went out the other end of the barn. Boy turned to the left—which was on the opposite side from the house—and crawled on his belly toward the side. Hank crept up behind him and eased a glance around the corner. He saw a big square block of a man creeping alongside of the barn toward the front—he was holding a burning torch by a two foot handle.

Hank pointed back the way they had come and whispered, "Go." Boy turned, headed back through the doorway and disappeared. He slipped back up to the corner, looked around just in time to see the big white animal come around the far end of the barn in front of the man with the torch. They both stopped.

Boy's lips curled back in a silent snarl and he began to advance slowly, like stalking—step by step. The man started backing up when Hank stepped up behind him and swung the shillelagh like a baseball bat. There was a sickening crunch when the knob end made contact, sending his hat flying, and the big man planted his face in the dirt—unconscious.

Hank quickly rolled the still burning torch in the damp ground, snuffing it out. He lifted the prone man's head up by his blood coated hair and checked his eyes. "Dang, she was right. Sure put a dent in this old boy's noggin'...Mighta hit him a tad too hard, not sure he's a gonna wake up...leastwise not anytime soon...Good job, son...We better head back to the house. Not a chance in hell he's here alone." Hank turned him over and unbuckled the man's gunbelt. "Might need this worse 'n you, mister."

Hank opened the front door and hobbled, in followed by Boy. He quickly closed and latched it. "Got comp'ny. Where's my iron?"

"What? Who?"

"Big box of a man with a lit torch, looked like he was fixin' to fire the house…Yer right about this stick, put him out like a light."

"That would be the one they call Ox."

"That fits…I 'spect there's more. We best git ready."

Angie walked over to front of her chifforobe, opened the twin doors and retrieved his Marlin 45-70 and the two Russian six-shooters.

"The only ammunition I saw is in your gunbelt and what would be in the rifle, I'm assuming."

"Have to do," he said as he checked that there was a shell in the chamber of the lever action rifle. "This'un only holds five rounds, but it's like a cannon…drop an elephant if'n there wuz one a chargin'. Got five more rounds in my belt…yer shotgun loaded?"

"Aye, with double-ought buck, it is."

CHOCTAW NATION

The sunlight filtered down only sporadically in the dense woods, illuminating the thick brown coating of fallen slash and loblolly pine needles as well as parts of the trail. Bass led the way as he trailed the Dalton gang's five weary horses—Selden rode to his left and slightly behind with Jed on his right. Loss and Tobe spread out, covering their backs. Hundreds of pine cones in various states of decay littered the forest floor and were the primary reason the wood teemed with squirrels.

So little daylight ever reached the ground that almost no grass or forbs would grow there. Bass detected a slight change in the constant chattering of the squadron of squirrels that jumped from limb to limb in the treetops above them. He pulled rein on his horse and held up a gloved hand. The other marshals stopped and stared into the darkened woods for any sign of movement.

A large slash pine cone dropped from some fifty feet above and bounced a few yards to Tobe's left. He jumped, snapped his Winchester to his shoulder, and then nervously looked around for any more motion. He strained his ears for additional sounds. The old lawman tried to swallow, but found his mouth to be bone dry.

Bass glanced back, pointed to Tobe and silently motioned for him to move left. Without turning around, he held up three fingers and motioned for the others to spread out further right. Something told him, call it intuition, experience or perhaps a sixth sense, that there was danger close by. He couldn't see anything out of the ordinary, but the hairs stood up on the back of his neck, and he wished more than he wanted to admit that the wind was not behind him. He glanced down at Boot, who was sniffing around the base of a three foot thick pine. "Come on old timer, gotta earn yer pay sometime."

Boot trotted on down the trail ahead of Bass. They had only moved forward another eighty yards when Boot's ears alerted and Bass reined to a stop. He noted his buckskin stallion was looking hard in the same direction the dog was staring—but it was too late.

The crack of a .44-40 split the relative silence of the dark woods. Bass heard the sickening thwack of the bullet as it struck home, followed by the anguished scream of a wounded horse. Four other shots rang out almost simultaneously. One cut Bass' reins in two only an inch from his hand.

Black, Selden's prized mount, crumpled to the forest floor, his right shoulder shattered by the first shot fired by Bill Dalton. An unseen pine twig between Dalton and the marshal had deflected the shot low, saving the lawman's life. Selden was momentarily pinned beneath the thrashing stallion as several other rounds whistled overhead in the dim light.

Bass bailed off his mount and sprinted for the cover of nearby tree trunk. He caught sight of a muzzle flash some sixty yards away through the trees over a deadfall. Trying as best he could, he placed the Winchester's front sight on where he thought the shot had come from and squeezed off a round, then followed it up with two more.

"I'm hit," Three-fingered Dynamite Dick yelled as Bass's second shot tore into his left collarbone and exited out his back just above the shoulder blade. He rolled back behind the log, his arm useless.

"Keep shootin'! We got 'em pinned down!" Bill called back as he fired another round at Selden's last position.

Jed moved to his right and used his trusty old Henry to lay down a string of near misses on the outlaws who were trying to maintain a cross fire on the marshals. It was obvious that the gang had set a trap, trying to catch all five of them inside their semicircle. But Bass had spread the group out just in time, making the five against five shoot out in the dark timber more of an even contest than Dalton had bargained for.

Tobe fired five times at the man to his left, sending splinters into the outlaw's neck from a grazing shot that lifted off a three inch wide piece of bark. The aging lawman rolled behind the closest tree trunk as one bandit fired at his previous location. The man with the splinters, George Bennett, took the opportunity to melt back onto the darkness and ran over the hilltop out of range.

Selden crawled away from the panicked horse. He rose to a knee behind some deadfall and fired at Bill's position until his Winchester ran dry, then switched to his six shooter. He fired four more shots with his Colt, but suddenly realized that no shots were being returned. He slipped five of the long .38-56 rounds past the rifle's loading gate and levered one into the chamber. He caught his breath and looked around for his partner. Loss took a couple of shots at a retreating target that Selden himself could not see.

Bass saw a muzzle flash from atop a distant log and took a fine bead at it. A bullet whizzed past his head and buried itself into a pine trunk as he pulled the trigger. His shot caught Dynamite Dick just above the right eye. The sound of his head exploding was like a ripe watermelon falling off a picnic table.

The forest fell silent as a tomb. Even the squirrels had nothing to say about the mayhem that had occurred in a couple minutes of gunfire. Gray gunsmoke floated between the trees, obscuring the view even more.

"You all right, Bass?" Selden called out.

"No holes that I know of," he replied as he looked over to see Tobe holding up a thumb. "We're good on the left. Jed, you and Loss hit?"

"Not me," Jed called back.

"Me neither," Loss reported. "Bastards cain't shoot for nuthin'."

When it became obvious the Dalton gang had disengaged, Bass moved over to Selden's position. The Texan was examining the severely wounded animal and trying to calm it as best he could.

"Shoulder's broke...Cain't be saved."

Bass shook his head and began to draw his Colt. "Cryin' shame to lose such a fine animal."

Selden held his hand up in a signal to Bass and then cradled the magnificent animal's head in his lap for what seemed like an eternity. He then stood up and spoke in a low voice, "He's my horse...My responsibility to...do what has to be...done." His voice cracked slightly as he gently stroked the horse's neck, "I'm sorry son, so, so sorry...God knows I am...please forgive me...I love you, boy," he whispered softly before he placed the muzzle behind the stallion's ear.

Bass turned away as he anticipated the inevitable shot. Still, his body jerked involuntarily and was followed by a chill when it finally came. He turned to see the big man brush his hand over Black's face to close his lids and stood up with tears in his eyes.

Selden holstered his gun and looked out in the direction that Dalton had run off and then directly at Bass. "When we catch up with that worthless son-of-a-bitch...he's *mine*."

Bass nodded. "Purty sure I dropped one of 'em. What you want to do now?...They ain't got no horses, and we be short one."

"We'll check on the one you shot, but there's no good reason to go and track four of 'em in these woods. I already know where they're a headed...We get to Antlers, catch the train back to Gainesville and connect on to Ardmore tomorrow. I'll remount there."

When they got to the body, Boot was sniffing the gray brain matter splattered around.

"Git away from there, Boot, you know better'n that," Tobe admonished his dog.

"Good God-a-mighty, most of his head's gone. No way to tell who 'er what in hell it is," said Jed.

"Look at his hand. That's Three-fingered Dynamite Dick Clifton...got paper on him. You'll git a nice re-ward, Bass," offered Selden.

"We all will, Selden, we all will."

Bass helped Lindsey remove his tack from Black. Jed cut a couple of pine saplings from off the trail a short distance away and they built a travois for Three-finger's body with Seleden's rain poncho. Verification of the deceased by a local judge was required to collect any reward.

Since Loss was the smallest, Selden rode double with him. The group rode for a mile, then walked for a mile until they covered the ten miles back to Antlers. There was fire in all of their eyes...

***

CHAPTER FIVE

LOG CABIN

"Wonder what-in-hell's tak'n Ox so long? Shoulda pitched that torch on the roof an' been back by now," Cougar said as he and Bobo waited with the horses down by the creek.

"Yer brother ain't the brightest er most agile human I ever knowed…Hell, he mighta missed the whole damn house."

"Best go check it out. Hand me my Winchester…an' those two sticks of that dynamite from my saddle bags."

Bobo pitched the rifle to Cougar and then gingerly handed him the sticks from the cotton filled satchel. "Be particular with that stuff now, looks like they be startin' to sweat a bit."

"Intend to," he said as he stuck them in his vest pocket.

They tied the three mounts to some brush and started moving toward the tiny clearing from their hiding place just around a bend in the Honey downstream from the cabin.

"Let's split up. You head toward the front and I'll take the barn side where Ox wuz supposed to go…cain't git to the back, cabin bein' up ag'n the cliff thataway…If'n we cain't burn the bitch out, we'll jest blow her 'n that house to hell and gone."

"Go ahead and open all them swing-in windows, no need in them gittin' shot all to pieces…plus it'll give us an openin' to shoot from. They cain't shoot through these cured log walls…Gotta keep 'em outta throwin' distance…You 'ny good with that ten guage?" asked Hank.

"Passable."

"Hope so. Man's generally more scare't of a scatter gun th'n a rifle er hand gun…Got 'ny more shells?"

"Full box."

Hank nodded then checked the loads in his Russians and the Remington .44-40 he took off Ox, picked up his Marlin and limped to the front window on the left side of the door. "Angie, you keep a watch out yer kitchen window. They's less area to cover back there…Watch they don't come through the barn…That Greener kin reach the barn easy."

Boy growled low in his throat as the hair along his back began to raise up.

"Keep a sharp eye, they're out th…"

He jumped as he was interrupted by a rifle bullet impacting the log wall next to the window. Hank glanced outside and saw a cloud of gray gunsmoke in front of a small copse of cedar trees nearly thirty yards in front of the cabin. He quickly snapped off two rounds from Ox's Remington through the open

84

window and then ducked back down behind the thick wall. Three more shots were fired from outside, one thudded into the log wall, another splintered the edge of the window frame and the third came through the window and knocked a chunk of rock from the fireplace across the room.

"Keep down, Angie!" he said as he saw her standing beside the kitchen window.

She dropped to her knees and peered over the sill. "Don't see anyone...yet."

"You kin bet they're comin' from both directions!" He switched to his rifle and stole a glance out the window to see Bobo sprinting toward a two foot thick oak tree twenty feet closer. He cranked out a round from the .45-70. The little man's feet came completely off the ground from the dead center chest shot as a cloud of red mist momentarily hung in the air. His momentum caused his body to tumble and roll to a stop against the base of the tree where he lay like a rag doll.

"One down."

Cougar flattened his body against the backside of the barn when he heard the boom of the big rifle. "What'n hell? That weren't no shotgun." He crept around to the far side and saw Ox's body lying face up just a few feet in front of him. "Ox! Ox!" He ran up to his brother's body and knew instantly he was dead when he saw his wide open glazed-over eyes. "You God damned whore!" he cried out through his yellow tobacco stained teeth. He moved up to the corner, fished a match and one of the sticks of dynamite out of his vest pocket. Striking the Lucifer on the side of the barn, he held it to the end of the fourteen inch fuse protruding from the stick. It sputtered, hissed and then caught. He took three running steps toward the cabin and launched the explosive the final sixty feet. "Take that, you murderin' bitch!"

"Hank!" Angie screamed as she snapped the shotgun to her shoulder and pulled the rear trigger. The double-ought shot caught the stick flipping end-over-end at its apogee. The dynamite exploded with a tremendous clap of fire and thunder.

Cougar was knocked backward by the concussion—the second stick of dynamite falling out of his vest pocket as he hit the ground. He rolled to his knees, scrambled to his feet and sprinted back toward the edge of the barn. Angie squeezed the front trigger, catching him in the side with a partial load as he rounded the corner. She could hear his yelps of pain as he disappeared into the brush on the far side of the barn.

"Damn, girl, where'd you learn to shoot like that?" Hank asked incredulously from his station at the front window.

"I grew up hunting birds with my daddy back in Ireland. That was an easy shot."

He glanced outside. "'Peers as tho it's over…musta just been the three of 'em…'Spect they'll be others. That dynamite tells me its got serious as a train wreck."

"That's what I told ye."

"Need to make a trip upstream."

"Why?"

"See if'n I kin find where I was shot…Somethin' tells me it's the same bunch of curly wolves."

86

"Possible…but you're not going anywhere "til I fix those stitches. The wound on the back side is leaking now," she said as she noticed the circle of red on his shirt.

Hank looked down at his side. "I'll be danged. Didn't feel it."

"Probably happened when ye levered a round in that rifle or maybe when ye laid Ox out…I'll get me needle and thread and some more turpentine an' tallow."

"Cain't wait."

Angie walked over to her sideboard where she kept her sewing basket, picked out her curved leather needle and some black linen thread.

"Pull your shirt up and sit down on the bed. I have to unwrap the bandages and clean the wounds first."

She unpinned and then unwound the long strip of torn cotton bedding, took a vinegar dampened cloth and cleaned away the old salve.

"Aye, it's lucky you'd be. Yourself only pulled one stitch," she said as she cut away the old thread and re-stitched the exit wound.

"Ow, ow…gosh amighty!"

"Don't be such a baby," she admonished while she unscrewed the lid from the jar of turpentine and tallow. After reapplying the healing balm and wrapping a clean bandage around his waist, she pinned it with two safety pins.

"There, that should hold…unless you decide to get rowdy."

"I'll try to be more careful…You might have a bigger needle in that basket."

"I might at that," she said with a smile. "Now don't you think we should do our Christian duty? Evil as they may have been, they still deserve a proper burial."

"Uh, well, not so fast. The laws will be wanting to look into the matter. Don't think we should even touch the bodies."

She gave him a curious look. *How on God's green earth would he be knowing that?* "Why would you be saying that? Would you be having experience in such matters?"

He glanced up at her face. "I wish I knew…Just seems like the right thing…Do think we should go and track that one you got a piece of…he might not have got very far."

She nodded as he stood, tucked his shirt in and slipped his suspenders back up.

"If you would hand me my hat an' walkin' stick, we'll go see if'n we kin find where he went…Come on, Boy, let's go."

The big dog jumped up from his place by the fire and was waiting at the door when Angie remembered the bread.

"Let me be taking the bread out of the oven first and put it in the bread box…"

"My, my, smells wonderful…meby we could…"

"I think not. There might be a wounded man out there…and they can be more dangerous than they might be otherwise."

"Yep, that is true…Sure smells good, though."

They followed the drops of blood with Boy leading the way from the barn through the brush down toward the creek and came on a small opening next to a grove of persimmon trees.

"Hah! Figured we'd find their horses down by the creek. No way those three walked all the way from town," Hank said as he limped down the embankment—holding his rifle in one hand and the shillelagh in the other. "The one that left the blood trail mounted here." He pointed at the boot tracks that disappeared next to a persimmon tree where the mount had been tied.

Angie nodded, then eyed the dead men's horses. "Saints be praised...he does his work in mysterious ways...We needed some way to get you up the creek past the falls. And would you be looking here what he gives us."

"If you say so, missy...But I think this here stick and rifle and yer shotgun had a little say in the matter."

"The Lord in heaven can work wonders, Hank...Don't you forget it. Help me up on the little one, would you?"

"Yessum." Hank set the rifle and shillelagh on the ground and interlocked his fingers, making a cradle for Angie to step into.

With any easy motion, he eased her high enough to swing her right leg over the horse's flank and into the saddle. "Lucky for you, the previous owner was about your height, won't have to shorten the stirrups."

She slid both feet into the stirrups and took hold of the reins when Hank offered them. He retrieved the Marlin and stick and tied the latter to the saddle of the other horse. With no small effort, he climbed into the seat, grimacing as the stitches and bruises reminded him of their presence.

She heard his involuntary groan as the saddle leather creaked. "It's all right you're being? We don't have to do this today already…Tomorrow is another day…"

"Reckon I'll make it, one way or the other. Don't know why, but something tells me I need to see what there is upstream. We know I came from up there someplace…Meby I can find us answers to who er what I am…Anyways, you know this here country like the back of your hand…Lead on, ma'am."

Their horses topped the rise after the steep climb beside the falls. They had to pick their way around the outcrops and exposed rocks that stuck up through the winter grass like big gray warts.

"There'll be being a game trail over to the left closer to the creek in the woods. The riding will be some easier."

"Cain't say as I'm sorry about that. The climb up the mountain to the ridge top here purt near done me in."

"Would you be wanting to stop and rest a bit?"

"Think not, if'n I got off right now, might not could git back up. So let's head on…No tellin' how far I washed down the creek ''til I hit the falls."

Boy led off up the game trail as if he knew where he was going—maybe he did. He didn't stop, smell bushes or even react to the cottontail that jumped across the trail and into the bushes on the other side.

Sometimes they could see the churning, tumbling Honey other times not as the path meandered close to and then away from the creek. But they could always hear it.

"We've traveled more'n a mile I speculate an' Boy hadn't stopped fer wood, water er coal."

"Methinks he knows where to go."

"Time will tell...Time will tell. I've grown to trust the big guy."

"As have I."

"Only time he slowed, was at the falls...just didn't want to leave 'em."

"They have a special...Look!" A pair of brownish-gray coyotes broke and ran for their lives when Boy spotted them tearing at some of the scraps of spoiled meat left on the dead horse's flank. He growled a warning, his teeth bared in a no-nonsense display of canine disdain for his much smaller cousins. Hank noted the reaction and rode around a large cedar tree just in time to see the coyotes run almost fifty yards off up the switch back. They stopped when they thought they were far enough away from the wolf, turned around to watch as Hank and Angie eased their mounts down the incline.

"I'd say you put the fear of God into that pair, Boy. Don't go gittin' any ideas about chasin' 'em all the way to Fort Sill."

"I think I see the remains of a horse or mule down there," Angie said.

"Think you're right...not much left after five days."

The two rode closer as Boy ran up to the carcass and circled it curiously. He sniffed at the skull, almost bereft of tissue save some dark reddish hair and scalp still firmly attached to the forehead. Every form of carnivore and scavenger in the area had taken turns feeding on the once proud and healthy steed.

"Get away from there, Boy," Hank ordered.

The dog reluctantly complied and rambled back to a position between the two riders. Hank pulled rein and studied the scene dispassionately. Angie looked at the jumble of bones, some of which, particularly had been gnawed down almost flush with the spine. She turned her attention to Hank and tried to imagine what a man with amnesia would be thinking at a time like this. His face gave nothing away at all. *Wouldn't want to play poker against this one.*

"Well, sir. Anything look familiar to you?"

"No ma'am...Ain't much left of this poor creature...but I can tell you it died quick-like. That there's two bullet holes in the chest bone," he said as he pointed at the evidence. "And somebody took the saddle and tack. Weren't no possum or coon neither."

"Was that your horse?"

"Cain't say...meby yes, meby no. Likely had me a half dozen horses in my life. Wish to hell I could remember...Sorry for the language."

"I forgive you, Hank," she replied. "It must be terrible not knowing...Hold on, I'm thinking I see something down the hill there."

He turned and saw another bit of light colored material that could have been a stick, but could also be a bone sticking above a ledge only thirty feet away. His hand went instinctively to his six-shooter as he nudged his mount down the trail. On the far side of the ledge, the remains of both a horse and its rider lay exposed to the elements. "Aw, Jesus," Hank muttered at the gruesome sight.

"Lord have mercy on his soul," Angie said as she crossed herself, her face crestfallen at the find.

Hank painfully dismounted on the uphill side, untied the shillelagh, slipped his hand through the leather strap attached just under the knob and tied the horse to a yaupon holly bush. He made his way to the body and gazed at the shredded calico shirt and ripped and stained Levis. Boy ran up to the body and sniffed the shattered skull and the shirt, and then laid down and placed his head on his paws. He let out a whine then looked back at Hank.

"He wuz trapped 'neath his horse...took one to his head." There was a hole just below the hairline and the entire back of the skull was missing. "We knew him, didn't we Boy?"

He barked twice as Hank slowly circled the body and turned to Angie. "They stripped his tack and his shooting irons...bastards even took his boots."

"That they were...not giving a man a decent burial."

"I'll come back when I'm able and give him one."

"And I'll help you say the right things."

"I would appreciate that. Gotta feeling I knew this man...not much to go on, though. He had short dark hair, the cheek bones tell me he was Injun...and I suppose a lot of calico shirts like this here one get sold."

Boy rose to his feet and began to scout around closer to the creek. In a moment, he picked up an object in his mouth and brought it to Hank. He reached down and took the multicolored remnants of a torn porcupine quill and bead hat band. The hawk tail feather tied to it had been gnawed badly by field mice. Hank stared at the band briefly, closed his eyes and concentrated hard.

Angie dismounted and walked closer to Hank and then put her hand on his shoulder. He slowly opened his eyes, the slightest hint of a tear filled the corners.

"Montford."

"What?"

"A name just came to me when I touched this hat band…Montford. That's all, just Montford…but this is the spot, I know it is an' I was aridin' that other horse…"

"Would it be being his first or last name?"

"No more idea than a pig knows what day it is…Anna told me in the cave he didn't make it, but not to worry…" He turned and looked at her. "Wonder what she meant by that?"

"That he was in the hands of our Lord and Savior forever more."

He nodded. Boy brought him another item from down closer to the water—a tattered rawhide leather pouch, the strap chewed off.

"My parfleche." He pulled up what was left of the flap and removed a chunk of flint rock, a flat piece of steel and a small thin book. It was covered in worn, scuffed leather with faded gold lettering, *Fanny Brawne, My Bright Star by John Keats*. "Fanny Brawne was his love," he said just staring at the book. "He died when he was twenty-five of the consumption…Did you know?"

"No, I'd not be knowing that...Tiz a wonder you can remember so many things, but not your name."

He glanced from the book up to her face. "Meby I'm bein' punished fer somethin' an' don't need to know who er...what I was."

ARDMORE, I.T.

Cougar slid from his horses' back to the dirt street like a sack of potatoes. Partially dried blood covered his shirttail and soaked his pants. The saddle seat, fender and stirrup strap were likewise stained a dark crimson, He had managed to rein up in front of Dr. Dwayne Gibson's office just off Main Street.

Unable to rise, he shouted as loud as he could, "Help me, doc, help me!"

Dr. Gibson came out his front door and saw him lying beside his horse—his entire left side soaked with blood. "You there...," he said to some business men walking down the boardwalk. "...help me with this man...And tie his horse up."

Two men ran over and picked Cougar up by his shoulders and feet while a third tied the horse to a hitching rail and loosened its girth.

Dr. Gibson held the door open. "On that table over there...be particular with him now."

"Baldwin...Somebody git Baldwin," Cougar managed to wheeze out.

The men laid him on the cypress topped table and backed away like he had some kind of dread disease.

"One of you go get Jason Baldwin like he asked...You better hurry, too."

He grabbed a pair of scissors and began to cut away the blood-soaked clothing. "Hand me some of those towels stacked on that cabinet over there," he said to the other man that was still there. "Now!" he snapped when the man just stood there staring at the multiple puncture wounds in Cougar's side.

"Yessir...sorry. Just never seen that much blood before," he said as he grabbed a hand full of the white towels.

Gibson folded one of the towels and pressed it against the wounds in an effort to staunch the flow of blood.

"Don't let me die, doc. Please don't let me die!"

"Doing the best I can, son. Just try to relax."

"Cain't...It hurts...Oh God, it hurts."

Jason Baldwin rushed into the doctor's office. He glanced down at his henchman as the doctor lifted the blood-soaked towel and recoiled from sight of the pasty white skin and dark red and purple wounds. "What the hell happened out there, Cougar? God dammit, man...can't you do anything right?"

"She...she went 'n kilt Ox 'n Bobo, Mr. Baldwin...She kilt my brother!"

Baldwin locked eyes with Dr. Gibson. The doctor just shook his head, his mouth a grim frown.

"She killed you too, Cougar...That Irish bitch killed all of you," Baldwin said as the big man took a ragged last breath and exhaled with a weak death rattle. His sightless eyes lost focus as his final pain drifted away along with his condemned soul.

"See to the body, Gibson and send me the bill. I have to go find the sheriff," Baldwin said as he spun on his heel and headed out the still-open door.

The doctor stared blankly as Jason Baldwin left his office—he just shook his head and covered Cougar's body with a sheet.

Sheriff Milo Cobb stood nervously in front of Baldwin's desk. The potbellied, mustachioed man held his somewhat worn brown fedora in his hands, slowly rotating it through his fingers.

"What did you need to see me about, Mr. Baldwin? Got here quick as I could."

"Of course you did...Cobb, need you and a couple of your deputies to get out to the widow O'Reilly's place. I have information that she murdered three of my men. Cougar and Ox Cole and Bobo Green. Cougar made it into town and died about thirty minutes ago over at Doc Gibson's. He was shot all to hell. Amazing that he was able to make it into town."

"Yessir, damn shame, knew those boys."

"I want that murdering bitch arrested and locked up, you hear me?...And you don't have to be none too gentle about it."

"Yessir, I understand...Uh, do you know what they were doin' out there, sir?...Uh, for my records, you know."

"Certainly. I had sent them out to deliver a very handsome offer for her property and she gunned them down like dogs...Why, she had even threatened them the last time they were by to pay their neighborly respects...they go past her place on the way to work my claim on the Honey...She's a menace to the good people of this area...probably somewhat unbalanced since the passing of her daughter and husband. I'll talk to the judge about getting her committed...Now go do your job, Sheriff."

"Yessir, I'll get a couple of men and head out first thang in the mornin'...Never make it out there 'fore dark today."

"Well, whatever, just see to it...You're running for re-election, aren't you Milo?"

LOG CABIN

The sun was high in the sky as Sheriff Cobb and two deputies rode into the clearing in front of the cabin. They pulled rein at the slat fence between the house and the wagon road.

"Blazes! Looky over yonder, Sheriff...That'd be Bobo Green. Knowed him," said one of the deputies, pointing at the body next to a big oak. "Better holler, Sheriff, she might taken us fer more Baldwin men," he added wryly.

"Good idee, Kyle...Miz O'Reilly!" he shouted cupping one hand to the side of his mouth. "Miz O'Reilly...It's Sheriff Cobb...Haloo, the woman of the house. Anybody to home?"

Angie stepped out on the porch. Boy slipped out beside her and sat down. "What is it you'd be wanting, Sheriff?"

"Uh, well, uh, ma'am, got a report they wuz some shootin' goin' on out here an' some folks got kilt. Reckon we need to talk about it. Now, how about we step down an come in the yard?"

"Do whatever would be pleasing you, Sheriff Milo Cobb. There is nothing I'd be trying to hide from the law," she said as she stepped down the four steps from the porch to the ground. Boy followed and moved in front when she got to the bottom. He sat down between Angie and the front gate.

"Deputy Kyle, you and Horace go find all the bodies an' look 'em over good."

"Yessir…come on, let's get er done before them bodies start to stink 'ny worse," Kyle said to the other deputy. They tied their horses to the fence and headed directly toward Bobo.

"The other one's on the far side of the barn," Angie offered.

Hank leaned up against the wall next to the open window peeking outside between the curtain and the sash. He held her Greener ten gauge in his hands.

"There'd only be two bodies here, Sheriff. God rest their souls and may the Saints watch over them," Angie said as the Sheriff stepped into the yard.

"Got yerself a new dog, I see. Best keep him under control so's I don't have to shoot 'im."

"You'd be shooting my dog, Sheriff…yourself will die where you stand…"

"Well, well, looks like Baldwin was right. You threatenin' me, woman?"

"I'd not be having to threaten the likes of you…But I'd be happy to make a promise."

"Not today, woman. Yer under arrest for murder. The third one, Cougar Cole, made it back to town an' died in Doc Gibson's office...Said you'd kilt 'em all."

"They did come on my property with intent to burn me out and when that failed, they fired a number of rounds at me house." She turned and pointed to the bullet holes in the logs and window frame. "Then the hooligans tried to use dynamite to blow up me house...That was their mistake."

"I don't give a damn what you say, I'm arrestin' you fer the murder of Cougar an' Ox Cole and Bobo Green. You'll hang fer what you done." He pulled a set of iron shackles from his left coat pocket and stepped toward her.

Boy rose up, the hair stood along his back and his lips curled in a barely audible snarl. Milo moved to draw the Colt on his hip...

Hank pulled both hammers back into the cocked position and started to step out the door when he heard the sound of pounding hooves enter the clearing. He could hear a voice.

"Best hold it right there, Sheriff."

The sheriff's hand froze where it was and he turned to see an elderly Chickasaw in a black suit and a high-crowned black hat with a Bald Eagle feather in the hat brim, stepping down from his horse. Beside him, a younger, stocky, Chickasaw in gray stripped pants, white boiled shirt and gray wool vest also dismounted—pinned on the vest was the circle and star badge of the Chickasaw Lighthorse. He too wore a tall crowned, uncreased black hat with a Red-Tailed Hawk feather and carried a Winchester rifle in his hand.

"What 'n hell 'er you an' Sixkiller doin' here, Ashalatubbi?" asked the sheriff as they came through the gate.

"We were goin' to ask you the same question, Cobb."

"Well, if'n it's any of yer business, I'm fixin' to arrest this woman fer murder...three counts."

"Not likely," said Ben Sixkiller.

"Angie O'Reilly's husband was half Chickasaw. That makes her Chickasaw. This is Chickasaw Nation and she is under our protection...You are out of your jurisdiction," said the older Indian.

"The hell you say! This woman killed three white men. I'm takin' her in, and that's a fact." He turned back toward Angie and drew his six-gun. Instantly, there was a blur of white as the wolf-dog reacted, followed by a scream of pain as Boy latched on to his wrist. The sound of a sickening crack resonated above the growl coming from deep in the animal's throat. Cobb's Colt dropped to the ground from his useless fingers. "Get 'im off! Fer God's sake, git 'im off!"

"Boy, that would be enough, thank you," Angie said.

The big dog glanced up at her, then back at the sheriff now on his knees in pain, and turned loose of his wrist. He backed up and sat down beside Angie again and looked up at her as if to ask, "Did I do good?"

The sheriff remained on his knees, his left hand wrapped around his wrist with blood oozing out between his fingers. He stared at Ashalatubbi and Sixkiller. "God damn you redhides, this won't stand...guarandamntee you that."

Ben slowly levered a round into the chamber of his new '94 Winchester. "Meby I kill you now for trespass on *redhide* land...Sheriff."

Kyle and Horace walked up.

"What's goin' on, Sheriff...'er you wounded?" asked Kyle.

"Damn dog tried to kill me."

"Looky what we found."

Kyle held up a stick of dynamite and Horace held up the burned out torch.

"Found this dynamite over next to the barn and Horace found that there torch next to Ox's body...Had his head caved in...wadn't shot. Didja know that?...Uh, Ox that is, not Horace...he's right here," reported deputy Kyle.

"Just shut yer pie hole, Kyle...an' keep it shut," the sheriff grumbled.

"I told you they attacked me house. Methinks I acted in self-defense...It's taking care of that wrist, I'd be doing if I were you, Sheriff."

"Do you need help gettin' on your horse, Milo?" Ben Sixkiller asked.

Cobb just glared first at Angie, then at Sixkiller. "I'll manage," he said through gritted teeth as he wrapped a bandana around his broken, bleeding wrist.

"We'll take the dynamite and torch as well as the bodies for evidence at the hearing in front of the Chickasaw council. We will send the bodies in to Ardmore tomorrow," said Ashalatubbi.

Cobb's two deputies helped him into his saddle, and then they mounted their horses and rode out.

As they disappeared down the wagon road back toward Ardmore, Hank stepped out onto the porch…

***

CHAPTER SIX

GAINESVILLE, TEXAS

Five hungry lawmen and Boot walked out of the Turner Hotel, a large two story wooden structure facing California Street a half block from the Santa Fe Railroad depot. Each had taken the opportunity to wash off the trail dust and get a shave downstairs in one of the local tonsorial parlors after returning from the unsuccessful mission to intercept the Dalton gang. Selden raised his hand to flag down the passing horse-drawn trolley that ran down steel tracks centered in the bustling boulevard.

"No sense walkin' when we can ride."

Bass eyed the green coach with yellow trim. "They's got restaurants and saloons in 'bout every block in this town. How far we got to go?"

"Only 'bout eight blocks to The Painted Lady, but my poor old feet are about worn smooth out from the walk to Antlers.

Got me a big blister on my left foot size of a banty hen egg from them boots."

"Noticed you were a mite gimpy, Marshal," Tobe said with a grin. "Anybody got a spare nickel?"

"I'll spring for all of us, and you boys can buy me a beer...er two, in trade," Selden said as he tossed the conductor a shiny two bit piece.

All five took their seats on the red leather-covered benches set in rows. Boot curled up next to Tobe's feet.

Jed looked out the open window at the stores going past as he remembered his first trip to Gainesville. It had been a solemn one to deliver a diamond engagement ring to a young lady named Lorena Matthews. He had found her cowpoke husband-to-be, Blue Davis, shot and left for dead by the sociopathic outlaw, Ben Larson, in the Cherokee Nation and made the man a vow to deliver the memento just before he passed away. *A promise is a promise. Man either does right or he don't.* Bass had been taken with the young black man's sense of honor and got him a job with the US Marshal's Service.

"Marshal Lindsey, if'n you don't mind me askin', what's so special 'bout this Painted Lady place?...Me being a married man with six kids and all. The missus wouldn't go for me messin' with some trollop."

Selden broke into a hearty laugh. "Jed, you can tell your wife you stayed downstairs and kept your britches on...I chose this place 'cause the steaks are the best this side of Fort Worth."

"Takes a load off my mind, it does…How many folks live in Gainesville now? By the looks of all the brick buildings, they must be doing good 'round here."

"'Spect so, cotton is king in Cooke county and with the town being a crossroads of the Butterfield Stage and the Santa Fe. The Chisholm trail passed close by, just to the west, but that's a thing of the past, what with the coming of the railroads and all. The town marshal told me there are over 35,000 folks livin' here now."

"That 'splains why they call this here street California," Bass noted. "Say, Mike Compton still the sheriff here? Worked with Big Mike a time 'er two…Good lawman."

"Nope, retired last year, Taggart Wacker's sheriff now…Most call him Tally…just not to his face," said Selden with a chuckle.

They all guffawed, Jed almost swallowed his chaw.

The trolley passed a buckboard loading up at Osborne's mercantile store. A husky young man tossed another sack of flour in the wagon and paid no attention as the people hauler passed by. The county courthouse loomed into view as the trolley approached the intersection of Dixon Street. Bass glanced over to the corner of the courthouse square where a statue commemorating the local war dead from the War of Northern Aggression back in the 1860s stood, but the former slave was unable to read its inscription. The soldier's distinctive Confederate kepi conveyed meaning of the stone monument to him anyway. He merely shook his head and went back to enjoying the ride.

Selden reached up and grabbed the tasseled cord connected to a spring mounted brass bell. He gave it a tug, signaling to the conductor that one or more of the passengers wanted to disembark. The balding seventy year old man pulled to a stop as the trolley came up to the Commerce Street intersection on the west side of the courthouse. A pair of attorneys, each carrying a similar black leather satchel, crossed behind the trolley and stepped up over the hand-cut limestone curb onto the bricked California Street sidewalk.

"Appreciate the lift, old timer," Selden said to the conductor as he passed by and descended the two metal steps and onto the red brick street.

"You betcha, Marshal," he replied with a gap-tooth grin as the other four lawmen followed suit.

The sight of five lawmen piling off the trolley car caused one of the two lawyers to throw up his hands in jest. "We surrender, Marshals! You boys got us surrounded."

"What's the charge?" Tobe asked. "Impersonating a lawyer, I'd venture."

Both barristers laughed. The one with the sharper wit shot back. "Ya'll caught us red-handed. Guess we'll jest throw ourselves at the mercy of the court…Say, would one of you two marshals be Bass Reeves?" addressing Jed and Bass.

"Guilty as charged," the big man said with a grin.

"Heard a lot about you…all good, I would assure you." The man extended his hand. "Proud to shake your hand, sir."

Bass shook his hand, and grinned. "Nice to make yer acquaintance."

The two defense attorneys watched as the group of lawmen headed north on Commerce Street. One looked at the other and remarked, "I'm kinda glad those guys work out of the Fort Smith office. They could be hard on business around here."

Outside The Painted Lady Saloon, the raucous laughter of a rowdy crowd mixed with the sound of a rinky-tink piano player working on a lively ragtime tune—an early Scott Joplin melody entitled *Maple Leaf Rag*. An ornate sign attached to the wrought iron railing around a fourteen foot high balcony over the sidewalk proclaimed the establishment for all passerby's to see. A smaller sign painted on the glass front just beside the double doors marked the address, 311 North Commerce Street. Directly next door at 313 was another of Gainesville's ninety-five drinking establishments, the Red River Saloon. A reveler didn't have far to go in order to bar hop.

Selden led the way inside, with his partner Loss holding the door open for the other three men. He took a glance up and down the street to insure they had not been followed by any nefarious characters intent on doing them harm. Being a lawman in the 1890s was still a full time job, with plenty of enemies created by the good ones.

Lindsey spotted a corner table large enough for five and as far away from the boisterous thirty-foot San Francisco bar as the layout allowed. Sawdust covered the wood floor and was speckled with spilled beer, whiskey and tobacco juice from those patrons too drunk or too lazy to use the spittoons that were strategically placed on the floor. The long ornate walnut bar dominated the south wall, with a polished brass rail designed for a foot rest running the entire length and with a twelve foot high, three mirror back-bar. The brick building itself was only 25 feet wide, but a full ninety feet deep and featured a fourteen foot high ceiling with embossed and enameled tin panels. The kitchen was located in the rear, and a narrow hallway led out to the private wagon yard and stable behind plus the outdoor conveniences.

The senior lawmen took the back three seats that offered a view of the crowd, leaving Jed and Loss with a scenic view of the wall—rank had its privileges. A slim, but attractive waitress stopped by and handed the men a menu each. She noted the badges on the men and smiled.

"My name is Ruth Ann, now what can I get you gents to drink while you look over the menu?"

Tobe spoke up first, "Rye whiskey for me."

All the others simply replied, "Beer."

Selden set his menu down before she had even traveled ten feet from the table. "I'll tell you what, their Delmonico steaks are sumpthin' else…aged and marinated…What I'm gittin'."

Bass didn't begin the pretext of trying to read the menu. All the other lawmen already knew he couldn't, so he just agreed to Lindsey's suggestion, as did Loss. Tobe held out for the 20 oz T-bone, medium rare and Jed opted for the man-sized chicken fried steak with fried dill pickle slices and sawmill gravy. The cute girl returned with a cork lined round tray laden with their drinks, took the men's orders and departed toward the kitchen.

LOG CABIN

Angie, Hank and Winchester sat at her dinner table, each with an after-supper cup of coffee. Boy was curled up in his place by the fire.

"It's a bit of the shame Ben Sixkiller couldn't be staying for the supper," said Angie.

"It was important that he get the evidence and the bodies to the council while they were still in session. We appreciate the loan of your wagon and mules...I'm confident he will have them back by tomorrow," offered Winchester Ashalatubbi.

"It's sure that will be fine, uncle."

"'Sides, those bodies were already gittin' a touch ripe...pardon the expression...How is it you say your Chickasaw name ag'n?"

"A-nom-poli Lá-wa," he said slowly. "Anompoli Lawa...he who talks to many...Just call me Winchester."

Hank chuckled. "Probably easier at that. Ain't known to have the most agile tongue."

"You know your animal is Nashoba Tohbi or white wolf and is very sacred to the Chickasaw," said Winchester as he glanced at him lying by the fireplace.

Boy raised his head and his golden eyes returned the look at the shaman as if he knew he was being discussed.

"Figured he was mostly wolf...got some dog in 'im too, I wager...Smartest animal I ever seen, an' fer some reason is totally devoted to me. Don't rightly recall exactly how we joined up...but joined together we are."

"Do you have any family that is no longer with us?"

"You could hold a gun to my head, shaman, and I couldn't tell you."

"Could be he's your father or brother from another life...I feel he has known you before and has returned to assist you...There is an aura about him. This is why he can see and communicate with the spirits."

"But what about himself, uncle? He sees and talks to me...me lost daughter, Anna, too."

"I think it's through the spirit wolf, child...Ababinili in his wisdom knows she is not at peace, that she was not properly buried according to our beliefs."

"Aba...Ababin...what? Who is that?"

"The Great Spirit, my son. You call him God, we call him Ababinili or Chí-ho-wah...Those were the names for our God long before the white man came to these shores...Do you not see the similarity with one of the names you use for your God...Je-ho-vah in your Hebrew Bible, the Torah? Your God and our Great Spirit are the same...there is only one Lord God. No matter what name we choose to call him...and he watches over all of us."

"Never thought of it thataway...How is it you know about our religions, the Hebrews an' their Torah an' such?"

"Attended divinity school down in Shreveport in '70s...speak a bit of Hebrew too...and medical college at the University of Nashville in the 80s...but I feel closer to our own beliefs. I came back to the Chickasaw Nation to practice medicine and be a spiritual guide for my people. You pindah-lickyoee, as the Apache call you, or white-eyes refer to me a shaman or medicine man, but I just wear this medicine pouch around my neck for show." He grinned and held up the small ornately beaded leather sack hung on a thong just above his vest.

"What's in it?" Hank asked.

"Oh, some asafetida, hawk bones, cowrie shell and a small tin of Garrett's Snuff."

"Well, dang, who'd a thunk...You reckon I'll git my memory back?"

"Based on my examination of your head wound and my years of experience both as a shaman and a medical doctor...I don't have a clue. But it is healing nicely...and your side is too."

"Not knowin' who I am is gonna drive me to the drink...an' I don't like the stuff."

"Your memory may come back all at once or a little at a time, like remembering part of your friend's name...or it may never come back at all...Only time and Ababinili can tell."

THE PAINTED LADY

The Sartain brothers flirted with a pair of bar girls that would have been attractive even without the pancake makeup, rouge and dark eyeliner, not to mention the ruby red lip paint that was applied too copiously for a woman of higher character. Six of the gunmen's hired muscle were busy drinking up the five dollars that Rafe had advanced as part of their promised $50 pay to insure that the troublesome Irish woman was run off her Honey Creek allotment or maybe had a bad accident.

One of the men, a tall pocked-faced twenty-five year old named Jake Strong had his eyes on a cute nineteen year old saloon girl named Sarah Havercamp. She preferred to be called Jannelle as she thought it sounded much more alluring to the menfolk. She was a full-figured gal with an ample bosom that she showed off well with her low-cut dress.

Jannelle had been working the saloons and parlor houses of Commerce Street for two years and knew how to separate a man from his money as well as any old professional. Jake was hooked the minute she winked and slid the tip of her tongue over her sparkling upper teeth. The tall ruffian pushed away from the bar.

"What's yer name, purty lady?" he hollered out in the din of the bustling saloon.

She could barely hear the question but had become adept at reading lips as well as reading men. "My friends call me Jannelle," she said only an inch from his ear, then playfully nipped his earlobe, leaving a red lipstick stain.

The action worked as she had planned. His whole body shook with an almost electric shock and his knees nearly buckled. His eyes flared wide and he stared down at her hand unfastening the top button of his shirt. Looking down at her cleavage, he couldn't believe it when she asked his name.

"And what do they call a tall drink of water like you?"

"Jake...my...they...Jake...uh is what," he stumbled with his words.

"You got any money, big boy? We can go upstairs where it's a lot more...private."

He nodded. She mouthed the words, "Follow me," turned and headed up the stairs to the Chickasaw Parlor House. He followed her like a puppy on a leash.

Bass and Tobe watched the two climb the open stairs and exchanged a knowing glance.

Tobe noticed her rather broad bottom. "Looks like two pigs in a gunny sack."

"Uh, huh," Bass replied with a grin.

Gainesville was famous for more than cotton and beef in those days. The waitress returned with a shallow wicker basket filled with fresh baked yeast rolls, home-churned butter and a jar of local honey. Each took a roll and slathered it with butter, all but Tobe adding a golden dab of the bee's nectar.

"Marshal Bassett, you got sumthin' agin natural honey?"

"Not when I'm drinking, Jed...Not when I'm drinkin'. Messes with my enjoyment of this Canadian whiskey."

Jed just chuckled to himself. *White men have some crazy ideas, I reckon.*

Jannelle and Jake reached the top of the stairs and she opened the door into a small anteroom with a tiny sliding window about waist high. A hand-painted sign above the window read simply *Pecker Checker*. Jake glanced over at Jannelle with a quizzical look. The drunk from Corsicana had never seen the like.

"What 'n hell is this?"

"Do like the sign says, sugar, unbutton those pants so she can check you out for disease...House rules."

He begrudgingly complied as the Madame, wearing white linen gloves, checked out his privates for signs of syphilis or gonorrhea. Jake stared at the wall and tried not to look at what was going on down there. Her hands retreated behind the sliding window and it snapped close.

"See that weren't so bad...you checked out good!" she cajoled. "Lets go have us a little fun."

He stuffed himself back in his pants and followed her, his ardor having taken a turn for the worse. The cat house occupied the entire fifty foot wide area above the Painted Lady and the Red River saloons below. They walked into the twenty-two foot wide parlor with groupings of couches and chairs in several areas. Twelve-by-ten foot rooms lined both sides of the floor—girls of the line referred to them as their cribs.

She came to a door that was unlocked and pushed it open—he stepped inside the sparsely appointed tiny cubicle. A double bed with two sheets, two well-worn feather pillows, a wall mounted oil lamp, a small wood stove in the corner and a pine night stand with a wash basin, a pitcher of well water and a couple of towels filled the room. Pairs of hooks on the wall and the four-paneled wood door served as minimalistic clothing trees for the short-time occupants.

"Well, big boy. Why don't we get comfortable?"

Her alluring smile dazzled him again. She took both of her hands, pressed her ample breasts together enhancing her cleavage. "See any thing you like?" She winked again.

He began tearing at his shirt buttons then staggered as he tried to step out of his pants without taking his boots off first.

The steaks proved to be everything Selden had promised and more. Heaping bowls of fried potatoes, both Irish and sweet, boiled new potatoes and mashed potatoes were served family style. Everybody had a chance to taste some of Jed's dill pickle slices fried up golden brown in a buttermilk batter. All agreed they the best they had ever eaten.

"If'n I had to work here regular, I'd be as big as a house," Bass said in his deep voice. "Gotta say you know your steaks, Sel."

He smiled as the others nodded. Lindsey took in a deep breath and let it out slowly. "Wee doggies! Almost hate to take that train up to Ardmore and leave this den of inequity."

"Think I'll have me a smoke," Loss said as he took a five inch stogie from his frock inside pocket.

"Hell of an ide…"

Selden's comment was cut short by the sound of a young woman screaming. The lawmen all fell silent and looked up at the embossed tin ceiling panels. The next sound was obviously that of a body being thrown against the thin single plank wall between the cribs. Bass, Tobe and Selden all stood up, but Bass was first to speak,

"I'll handle this. Loss run and get Sheriff Wacker…Damn, I plum hate it when my after-dinner coffee an' smoke is interrupted." He tossed the white linen napkin on the table and headed up the stairs, two at a time.

Loss made his way though the crowd and out the front door. The other patrons in the saloon seemed to ignore the fracas upstairs, as if it was a regular occurrence. The piano player never missed a beat and the bartenders keep pouring liquor like there was no tomorrow.

"You reckon might Bass need some help?" Selden asked as he heard one more muted scream.

"I've knowed Bass near twenty years…don't think there's a man alive who can take him…Hell, you couldn't melt me and pour me on him," Tobe said as he sat back down and took a sip of whiskey and handed his steak bone to Boot under the table.

The lady in the big open parlor area between the cribs, pointed to the second door on the right as the big black man stepped up from the stairway. Bass heard the sound of a fist smacking against flesh and the sound of a body crumpling to the wood floor. He tried the white porcelain knob, but the door was latched with a tiny hook and eye on the inside. His size thirteen boot worked better than a key. The door flung open as Bass saw a tall, but scrawny drunk pulling up his longjohns. Jannelle's bloody body was sprawled part way across the bed, her nose obviously broken and her lower lip was split. Crimson dotted the cheaply papered walls and dingy sheets.

"So you like to hit women, do you boy?" Bass said menacingly through his teeth.

"Git yore black ass outta here, nigger! None of yer damn business…and who the hell are you, callin' me boy?"

Jake never got out another word. Bass sent a jackhammer right hook to his face—the blow sent the hard-case flying into the wall, a couple of his teeth dribbling out his slack jaw as he slid into a limp pile and wet himself.

"I'm Bass Reeves...yer worst nightmare...Boy."

He turned and placed two fingers on the young girl's neck. She still had a strong pulse, so Bass turned to the door and spoke directly to the Madam, "Git her to a doctor...she may be busted up inside, too."

The lady nodded and called to two other sporting girls that had come up to see what happened. One immediately took a folded towel and dipped it into the china wash basin.

"We'll take care of you, sweetie, don't you worry 'bout a thing," she said as she dabbed at the blood dripping from Janelle's nose.

Bass took a pair of leg irons from the outside pocket of his ever-present morning coat and locked them on Jake's bare ankles. "Excuse me, ladies," he said as he stood, hanging on to the eight inch length of wrought iron chain between the shackles and dragging the unconscious, bleeding woman beater toward the door.

The Madam and one of the girls moved out into the hall to clear the doorway. "The bastard will need these in jail," the young woman said as she handed him Jake's pants, boots and shirt.

"'Spect yer right, missy. Gits mighty cold in the steel hotel...I hear tell."

The Madam patted Bass on the chest above the silver crescent and star badge on his vest. "Thank you, Marshal. I won't forget this."

He grinned broadly, his bushy mustache spreading out and looking like a giant woolly caterpillar. "You know what?" he chuckled. "Don't think old slick here will ever forget this night neither." He slipped a silver dollar in her hand as he passed by her in the parlor and headed down the stairs. Jake's unconscious body followed behind, his head smacking on each of the hard wooden steps with a thump—thump—thump, all the way down.

She looked down at the silver coin in her hand. "My God, that was Bass Reeves."

Selden and Tobe grinned at the sight. Jed turned around and laughed out loud. Boot, underneath the table chewing on the bone from Tobe's steak, looked up briefly at Jed. But across the smoky bar, Raff Sartain noted the action and nudged his brother.

"Are you seeing what I am seeing?"

Rafe looked in the large center mirror behind the bar and caught the sight of one of their chosen assistants being dragged half-naked into the bar by some big black man. His well practiced smile and cultured refined demeanor disappeared in a flash. "That's not happening...I don't know what manner mischief Jake's gotten into, but nobody manhandles one of our men." He placed his half-full snifter of brandy on the polished bar top and pushed past the two women standing beside him without a word to either one.

Raff followed close behind as the two Beau Brummels elbowed their way through the drinking crowd and moved to intercept Bass before he dragged the pitiful-looking Jake out the front door. Rafe, his face flushed with anger, stepped into Bass' path as the big man was maneuvering between two round tables filed with locals drinking and playing cards. He saw the bloody face of his young henchman and how his body was sweeping the sawdust away from the wooden plank bar floor. It made him even madder. Then he spotted the US Deputy Marshal badge pinned to the black man's vest. The tiny letters IT stood for Indian Territory.

"What the hell you think you're doing with my man? You have no jurisdiction in this state!"

Bass looked at the shorter man and sized him up quickly...his experienced eyes went to Raff who stood almost shoulder to shoulder with his twin brother—their dark eyes burned back at him in similar disdain. *Twin peacocks. Not ones to get their hands dirty.* His eyes narrowed as he noted their crossdraw rigs with Colt Thunderers tucked under their frock coats.

"Now, you two boys run along and keep your noses out of my business. This here sorry-ass excuse for a man, done beat up a woman upstairs and he's going to jail...And just so you know, sweet-cheeks, the US on my badge stands for United States...I got jurisdiction anywhere I put my boots...from sea to shining sea."

Rafe's jaw muscles flexed visibly as he gritted his teeth. He could feel his brother's eyes as well as those of his men and several of the bar patrons bore into him. It was clearly his move and the noise level in the bar dropped significantly as many of the conversations stopped around them. Even the piano player noticed the confrontation and had stopped in the middle of his ragtime tune.

"Didn't you hear me, Nubian? I told you that's my man you are mistreating and I won't have it!"

Tobe, Jed and Selden made it to their feet and were already moving toward the front of the bar. Selden swept his dark gray frock coat back behind the bone-handled grips of his Single Action Army Colt.

"Son, I only warn once…you best step aside whilst you still have a chance," Bass said softly.

Rafe's temper boiled over. His right fist unclenched as his hand snaked across his midsection and wrapped around the birdshead handle of the .41 Colt. Bass caught the motion and dropping Jake's clothes, his massive left hand whipped out—a black cobra striking in the blink of an eye. His fingers closed around Rafe's wrist like steel bands, immobilizing his arm while his right hand let go of the leg shackle chain dropping Jake's legs to the floor with a thud. Bass surprised the immobile shootist by slapping him three times in rapid succession—hard. Rafe's hat flew off with the second strike—a backhand—and tumbled to the filthy floor.

The bar fell deathly quiet as the big man pointed his index finger over at Raff. "Don't even think about it peacock…I'll kill you where you stand."

Raff's hand was frozen above his belt. He had never seen anyone as fast as Bass and his low, soft voice unnerved him. The burly lawman had not backed down like others the two gunfighters had bullied before. His jaw moved, but no words came forth. The only sound that could be heard was the sound of a pair of Remington shotgun hammers being brought to full cock.

"I understand you have a prisoner for me, Marshal."

Bass looked left and saw Loss flanking a tall, well muscled man wearing a bowler hat and the Cooke County Sheriff badge pinned to his vest, standing directly behind Raff. He lowered his hand back down beside his own Colt as he crunched the wrist bones of Rafe's shooting hand. He heard a slight involuntary moan from the embarrassed gunslinger as his Thunderer fell to the floor. He locked eyes with Rafe as he spoke.

"That's right, Sheriff. I was just explaining to these two upstanding citizens how this one behind me earned himself a little time in yer hoosegow." He let go of Rafe's wrist, but never took his eyes off him. "Kindly step aside, gents and let the good Sheriff Wacker take charge of his prisoner...Oh, I think you dropped somethin'," he said to Rafe as he pointed to the pistol on the floor.

Rafe looked behind Bass and saw the three other marshals that had moved in close to support Bass. He rubbed his right wrist to get the circulation flowing again, reached down, picked up his six-shooter and holstered it, then wiped the trickle of blood from the corner of his mouth.

"Some other time...some other place," he said to Bass in a low voice.

"Look forward to it...Don't forget your hat...looks like *dandy* one," Bass said as the twins turned back to the bar.

Selden smiled and shook his head. "Cain't I take you anywhere without you getting into trouble?"

"Reckon not. Sometimes it seems to just find me, like a magnet...know what I mean?"

"Yessir, think I do...You know who those two are?"

"Don't know...don't care."

"The Sartain brothers...from California. Backed down Wes Hardin a few months ago right after he got out of prison."

"Wes was outa practice...seventeen years behind bars'll do that to a man."

"We ain't seen the last of those two, I'll speculate."

Bass just nodded.

Jake Strong began to come to as the sheriff and his deputy prepared to carry him outside to a waiting buckboard. They had him get dressed before they escorted him to the local lockup.

The Sartain brothers gathered their remaining men and moved next door to the Red River Saloon to try to drink off their embarrassment and plan revenge on their newly found enemy.

Bass and the others returned to their table, had another round of drinks and smoked cigars. When it came time to pay up, Selden called Ruth Ann over, "Hey there, young 'un. What's the total damage for this motley crew?"

She moved to the table and leaned in close to him. "Your bills been taken care of, Marshal." She pointed upstairs, "Miss Sadie is grateful for your friend's 'act of chivalry', as she called it."

"Tell her that her generosity is most welcome, certainly not expected," Tobe said with a smile.

"Yes, sir. I'll tell her. I always like to have real gentlemen here in The Painted Lady. Sometimes, it can get a little wild and woolly…if you know what I mean."

"We get the picture, missy," Selden replied.

After she left, Bass looked at the other lawmen. "Still think we need to leave little Ruth Ann a nice tip. She done us right and their cook made me want to slap my momma, it was so good."

His friends agreed and dug into their pockets for some silver to make her night special as well.

***

CHAPTER SEVEN

GULF & COLORADO RR
GAINESVILLE DEPOT

The morning sun was already high in the cloudless sky when
the five marshals boarded the Gulf & Colorado train headed to
Denver. With three passenger cars, plus a livestock car for
horses and an iconic red caboose, the train had originated in the
port city of Houston. It made a scheduled stop in Dallas prior to
reaching Gainesville where it took on additional passengers and
water. A diner car for the long trip to Denver would be added
when it reached Oklahoma City.

The lawmen moved down the aisle to two sets of facing
seats that were vacant, stored their long guns and saddle bags in
the overhead shelf and took their seats. They had enjoyed a big
breakfast at the Turner hotel and had their white shirts
laundered and their dark suits brushed and ironed by the
Chinese laundry next door to the hotel overnight.

"I feel almost decent in clean clothes, you Bass?" said Selden.

"Yup, bath, shave and clean clothes tend to perk up a man's attitude."

Other occupants of the spartan passenger car included cattlemen in big hats and rough clothing, duded-up drummers in flashy garb, farmers in overalls and ordinary travelers in street clothes, some with their women folk. Also included were a couple of blue clad soldiers on furlough. Some of the passengers were also going to Ardmore or Oklahoma City and some would be continuing their travel all the way to Denver.

Bass and Tobe were settled in the rear-facing seats on the right side of the car. Directly in front of them were Selden and Jed in the forward-facing seats. Loss sat across the car on the opposite side.

Bass looked up as the Sartain brothers and their men—sans Jake Strong who had been invited to spend some time in the Gainesville jail by Sheriff Wacker—made their way up the aisle. Rafe and Bass locked eyes. Raff grabbed Rafe's arm and pulled him past Reeves and the other marshals.

"Not now, brother, not now," he whispered into Rafe's ear. "Our time will come."

Bass smiled wryly at the five remaining hired guns as they moved past toward some open seats at the front of the car. The men had just sat down when the train lurched as the engineer released the Johnson bar—the engine belched a huge cloud of black smoke and began to chug its way north out of the Gainesville depot.

"Reckon where they're a headed, Bass?" asked Selden.

"Back of my neck says Ardmore, but, 'spect we'll find out in 'bout an hour and a half...we stop in Marietta fer water, don't we?"

"Yep, gotta jerk-water tank there...I'll put Loss on tail, if'n they git off in our town."

"Mind that's a good move...don't think we're done with that bunch of ass-eyed hooligans."

The Sartain brothers took the last rear-facing seat at the front of the car. Two of their gang, Carson Hatcher and Jude Miller sat opposite the twins.

"Just who in the hell is that big black marshal? Anyone know?" asked Raff.

"That would be none other than Bass Reeves. Been a deputy marshal fer the Hangin' Judge fer mor'n twenty years...Hear tell he's kilt most twice as many men as Wild Bill Hickok. An' ol' Bill was knowed to have kilt seven," answered Curly.

"Not one to have on yer tail, I'm told...Killed all of the Larson gang up in the Nations, 'ceptin' Ben an' they brought him in fer Parker to hang," added Jude.

"He's just a man...and he's not bullet proof, I can assure you," said Rafe as he turned and looked out at the rain-swollen Red River underneath the iron bridge that crossed the border into the Chickasaw Nation. The dark churning waters reflected his mood perfectly.

CHICKASAW NATION

The remaining members of the Dalton gang, Bill, Big Asa Knight, Jim Knight and George Bennett nudged their horses up the far bank of the Clear Boggy Creek south and west of Atoka.

"Damn good thang we stole these horses from that hostler at Smallwood last night. My feet wuz wore to a nub," said Big Asa.

"Don't know, 'siderin' this razor-spined nag I got. Son of a bitch may geld me 'fore we git to Elk," added George, who rolled over on his right cheek to ease the pressure on his sore crotch.

"Way I see it, if you hadn't a panicked when somebody lit that lantern in the house, we mighta got some saddles too…Jest quit yer bitchin', least we ain't walkin'.

"Sez you," George spat back.

Bill scowled at the two riders closest to him. "You two shuddup. We got a couple small ranches up ahead in the next four or five miles. If we play our cards right, we can pick ourselves up a saddle er two…Like takin' candy from a baby." He ducked under a low hanging branch and kicked his heels lightly into the buckskin mare's flanks. She responded by trotting up the switchback to the partially overgrown trail that connected the sparsely populated settlements.

The split-rail fence encircled the small farm's garden that adjoined a corral next to the barn some forty yards from the cabin—a four-room frame dog-run style house. Three sorrel mares grazed in a paddock near the garden. Bill took note of the layout and turned to Jim Knight, Big Asa's little brother.

"Jimbo, you think you can git yerself into that ol' barn and see if'n they got tack for them three?"

His face lit up at the thought of a saddle and blanket to put between himself and the black gelding he rode. His inner thighs already ached from trying to keep himself centered on its bare back. Horse sweat permeated his wool dress pants and longjohns and had chaffed his buttocks to a rash. "You betcha, boss. Good as done." He slid off the horse and tossed the reins to his brother. "Ya'll come a riding fast if I have to shoot my way outta there."

"Don't get yourself caught, now. The whole idea is to slip in there...kinda quiet like. We done lost two men on this job already," Bill said. "No shootin' 'less you have to...don't want to bring folks a runnin' from all directions. Still got a five or six day ride to Elk ahead of us."

"I hear ya," Jim nodded as he swept the smelly horse sweat froth from his inner thighs and flicked the excess off his hands. "Keep this shit up and I'm a gonna have to buy me some Boudreaux's Butt Paste next town we hit." He stretched his back out then took off down the shallow slope, keeping close to the edge of the woods. Jim moved quickly, covering the 200 yards to the back of the barn, taking care to keep low using the fence as cover where he could.

Once he reached the barn's rear wall, he stopped and listened for a minute. Hearing nothing that indicated a farm hand or hired help was inside, he cautiously raised the wooden latch on the large rear door and slowly pulled it open enough to enter. Luckily the big strap hinges were well aligned and oiled, and the movement made no noise. He slipped inside and pulled the door to, but left the latch open in the event he had to make a quick getaway.

Streaks of light filtered in though cracks in between the broad wooden slats that comprised the sides of the structure. Jim allowed his eyes to adjust to the relative darkness as floating dust particles danced in the sunbeams. He walked past empty horse stalls and well-stocked grain bins to the tack room. Lifting the one-by-four latch by the square horseshoe nail driven in the end, he opened the door and peeked inside.

Three well used saddles and an equal number of wool pads sat atop a single 4x4 rail. A broad grin crossed his face as he snatched up the first pad and dropped it over his right arm. He slipped his arm under the nearest saddle and lifted it off the rails. Moments later, he set them down outside the back door and went back for a second.

"Looks like yer plan is goin' like clockwork, Bill," George offered.

"Yep, musta been more'n one 'cause he went back in."

Picking up the second saddle, Jim turned and accidentally kicked a can of hand forged nails and sent them flying. He froze as the can clattered across the ground.

A yellow cur dog awoke under the porch at the sound from the barn, He scrambled to his feet and sprinted to the old building, barking loudly. Inside the house an elderly man pushed aside his lunch and stepped to the breezeway separating the two halves of the house. He saw the dog pawing at the closed barn doors and barking furiously. Without thinking, he grabbed the LC Smith shotgun he kept over the door.

Reaching the barn, the man grabbed the latch to the two wide doors and pulled the left one open. His dog charged into action, growling at the figure of a man silhouetted against the back wall and closed quickly with his fangs bared. The old man, alerted by the dog's aggressive action brought the side-by-side to his shoulder, but his aging eyes couldn't find a target in the semi-darkness…at least not until a pistol shot rang out and his dog yelped in pain. He fired a round of double-ought buck at the muzzle flash.

Jim knew not to stand still in a gunfight with a man holding a scattergun. The old man's shot went wide. Jim's did not. It hit higher than he aimed, but still tore a ragged hole in the old rancher's neck and spun him part way around as his arterial blood sprayed across the hard-packed ground. He inadvertently fired his last shot into the closed barn door as his muscles clenched the shotgun's pistol grip. Jim put another round into him as the old-timer brought his left hand up to try and staunch the blood flow from his neck. The 250 grain slug struck just under his armpit and tore into his spine. The impact knocked him over hard, never to rise again.

"God dammit!" Bill Dalton exclaimed as the sounds of the five shots echoed across the shallow valley. "Let's move!" The three bandits rode hell-bent-for-election down the slope as Jim exited the back of the barn with the last of the three saddles. They could see him waving them on as he nervously looked back at the house to see if anyone else exited the modest frame building.

"That yer idea of quiet? Mush for brains!" Bill barked at the smallest member of the gang.

"Sumbitch sicced a dog on me, boss. Couldn't be helped."

Bill tossed Jim a '92 Winchester carbine. "Git yer ass on the far side and give us some cover while we saddle up."

Jim opened the action partially to confirm a round was in the chamber. He lifted the lever up to close the bolt and then thumbed the hammer back to full cock. There was nothing else for him to say—he just nodded and followed the order. Running though the barn, he could see the spilled can of nails that had given him up. *Damn can...Had it made 'til you got in the way.*

He stuck his head around the corner of the barn door and looked back to the west. No one was coming on the road leading to the ranch. He checked the door and south facing windows of the house and could see no movement of the simple white curtains.

Blood pooled around the body lying almost at his feet. Jim could see the man's chest was no longer rising and falling after his two shots. His gaze fell upon the prized LC Smith double barrel. Impulsively, he reached down and pried it from the dead man's fingers. *Won't be needin' it no more wherever yer goin'.* He checked out the casehardened side locks on the hammerless two year old gun. It was a very good quality piece, the only scattergun the family had owned. *Finders keepers* Jim thought as he opened the action and dumped the empties on the ground.

"Time to go!" Bill hollered as he swung into the saddle. The other two men were already mounted when Jim ran out the back door and Asa proffered the reins to the bareback he had been riding. He didn't bother to complain about not being one of the riders who got a saddle. Jim jumped belly first on the horse's back, dragged his right leg over its rump and sat upright.

He nodded to Bill, who kicked his mount towards the timber to the south. All the others followed close behind, trying to put as much distance between themselves and whoever else lived at the small cattle ranch they had just robbed.

LOG CABIN

It was a little after noon when Winchester Ashalatubbi and Ben Sixkiller pulled the Murphy wagon to a halt by the barn—Ben was handling the reins to Angie's two red mules. In the back of the wagon was a bundle of stripped willow poles and a stack of sewn together and folded deer hides.

Hank, Angie and Boy came out the back screen door of the house and walked over to greet the two Chickasaw.

"So that's the stuff to make my punishment house..."

"Sweat lodge," Winchester interrupted.

"Right. Where you gonna built it?"

The shaman looked around. "That flat area down by the creek should do nicely."

"Need me to help?"

"Considering your lack of knowledge of what we're doing and since I don't want you stressing your stitches...No. Angie will help me while Ben finds suitable rocks for the fire."

"I'm already not likin' the sound of this."

"You have to trust the shaman, Hank," said Angie.

"Seems like I heard a story once 'bout a man tellin' his son to jump off the top of the barn...he'd catch 'im. The boy jumped. The man stepped aside...Splat, right on his tail. The man said, 'See, son, don't never trust nobody.'"

Angie and Ashalatubbi glanced at each other and grinned as they unloaded the material from the wagon.

Winchester put the final touches on the ten foot diameter lodge, which resembled an upside down bowl covered with deer skin and a loose hide flap over a small opening just big enough for a person to crawl through on one side.

Directly in front of the opening was a closely packed ring of round, stream-tumbled granite rocks, each at least the size of a muskmelon or cantaloupe. The circle was half again as large as a number three wash tub and had a roaring fire of cured split post oak from Angie's wood pile, in the center.

"When the fire burns down to just coals and stops smoking, we'll lift the lodge up and set it down over the circle of stone. I have already blessed the rocks from the Honey." Anompoli Lawa handed Hank a Chickasaw breechclout of soft, tanned deer skin. "Go in the barn and put this on. I must rub a special blessed ointment on your skin."

Hank held up the long, six inch wide strip of leather and the waist thong. "How do I git into this...thang?"

"Angie can help you, if you wi...?

"No!... I mean I mind I can figger it out...Ain't no front er back, is there?"

"No, there'd not be a front or back," Angie said grinning as she glanced at Ben walking up with a bucket of water from the falls. He also had a big grin on his face from overhearing the conversation.

Ben set the bucket next to the stone ring and Angie put a white porcelain dipper in the water.

The shaman glanced at the fire. "The fire will be down to coals by the time you come back out."

Hank walked out of the barn in the breechclout trying to cover himself, he just didn't have enough hands. Angie turned away and covered her mouth to keep from laughing at his discomfort. Boy laid down and covered his nose with both paws.

"I see that, Boy...It ain't funny, plus it's a bit chilly, ya know."

Anompoli Lawa took the lid from a jar of heavy salve and pulled out a handful of the viscous material.

"Turn around, I'll start with your back...Hold your arms away from your body."

Hank did as he was bid. "Smells like cinnamon and cloves."

"That's a start...It helps in the purification process, turn to the front so I can do it too."

"Don't draw flies, does it?" Hank asked.

"Hope not...Now stand there while we set the lodge over the stones and coals. I have to go inside and purify the air and ward off evil spirits with this sage wand." He held up a bundle of sage twigs, wrapped tightly with rawhide into a stick as big around as his wrist.

Angie struck a match and held it to the loose end until it caught. He let it burn for a moment and then blew out the flames. Dense white fragrant smoke curled up from the end. Anompoli Lawa got down to his knees and crawled inside the lodge, allowing the skin flap to close behind him. After a couple of minutes inside, waving the smoking wand around, he crawled back out.

"Now you," he said to Hank. "The bucket beside the stone circle contains water from the falls. Pour three dippers on the outer rocks, wait a few minutes and do it again. The lodge will fill with steam...Breathe deeply and slowly." He nodded and Hank crawled through the small entrance.

Inside, the only light was from the glowing red-hot coals remaining in the center. He could feel the heat emanating from the granite rocks. Filling the dipper, he slowly poured the water starting with the rocks on the far side of the ring. They hissed and popped as steam boiled upwards and began to fill the small dome. He repeated the process twice more until all the rocks had been covered and the lodge was completely full of the aromatic steam.

Hank held his hand up and could barely see it through the dense cloud of vapor. It seemed as if he instantly broke into a sweat while he breathed in slow and deep. After a moment, he repeated the process as the rocks had heated back up. The moist heat was stifling. Then there was a light.

"Here, drink this," said Lawa's voice through the mist.

He saw a shallow earthen bowl coming toward his hand resting on his knee closest to the entrance.

"What is it?" he asked.

"You don't want to know," came the disembodied answer. "Just drink…all of it…quickly."

Hank drank the pungent liquid, gagged, but managed to keep it down as the light disappeared. He dropped the bowl to the ground as the steam in the lodge began to swirl around his head. After a few moments, multicolored lights started to pulsate to the same rhythm as his heartbeat. He felt himself rise out of his body and float above it in the white cloud—he could no longer feel the heat.

Outside, Boy begin to pace around the lodge. Three times he circled, then lay down directly in front of the skin covered entrance.

Hank's movements were effortless as he turned toward what he felt was a light, but was not. It permeated the area and his entire being, but there was no source. A montage of images circled about his head—a red and white border collie, a pack donkey with prospecting tools, a twelve-man gallows, a Tumbleweed wagon, a stern looking man with a beard wearing a black robe slamming a gavel in a court room, a US Deputy Marshal's badge with *IT* and the number *5* on it—and then he saw something coming toward him through the bright swirling rainbow mists—It was Anna. She was holding Montford's hand.

"I brought your friend. He wanted to tell you something."

"Thank you, my white brother for avenging my death. I know you will return when you can and give my earthly remains the respect dictated by the customs of my people, he held up his hand…Chihoa-bia-chee."

Behind his form, standing with their heads bowed in shame, were his killers, Cougar, Ox and Bobo. Montford saluted and all but Anna, melted into the vapor as if they never were. In their place were two men he felt he knew, but didn't know. The younger looked much like him, but not as old as he was now and wore a US Deputy Marshal's badge pinned to his vest. The older man also bore a strong resemblance to the image Hank saw in the mirror when he shaved. *Is that me as an older man?*

"Keep your faith, son, and do what you know is right. Your brother and I will watch over you. Know that always."

"Father?…Who…who am I?"

"You will know all in time…when it is right. There is a time for everything," he said as he and his brother dissolved back from whence they came.

Anna remained. "I wanted you to talk to your friends and family and know that all will be fine."

"Anna, why are you restless? Why can't you help yourself as you helped me?"

"I can only help others until I am found and laid to proper rest. Only then will I know the peace Ababinili wants me to have."

"Where are you?"

She pointed back toward the falls. "There…Help me. Help me, plea…" she said as she faded away into the thinning vapor.

He looked down as his spirit hurtled toward his body still sitting beside the now dead darkened coals. His eyes snapped open as he jerked awake. Hank shook his head and crawled through the deer skin flap into the bright sun light only to be hit with two buckets of ice cold creek water by Angie and Ben as he stood erect.

"Jesus H. Christ and all his disciples!...That's freezin'! What'd ya'll do that for?"

"To cleanse your soul, my son and bring you back to reality. What did you see?" asked Anompoli Lawa as he handed him a blanket.

"How's 'bout I have somethin' to eat? Haven't et since yesterd'y...Then I'll tell ya'll what I seen, though you won't believe it...Not sure I do."

"The eye sees only what the mind is prepared to comprehend."

"Meby white-eyes should go back in the lodge and do vision quest again," said Sixkiller.

"No, no, pass...Think I got it worked out."

ARDMORE, I.T.
JASON BALDWIN'S OFFICE

Hillary opened the door to Baldwin's inner office. Rafe Sartain allowed his brother to enter first. He followed as the barrister's secretary closed the door behind them, but his dark eyes remained on the unattractive matronly secretary. She blushed as the attractive man winked at her before turning to face her boss.

Oh my gosh! Two of them look so much alike. How will I know which one has taken a shine to me?

Raff smirked slightly as he watched his brother toy with the older woman. He prided himself in being able to be subtle when called for. Rafe stepped up to the heavy carved black walnut desk and stood beside his twin.

Baldwin studied the two for a few seconds, trying to detect any physical difference between the two cocksure young killers. Aside from the color of their shirts and brightly contrasting cravats, they were mirror images of each other. Both smiled as they enjoyed the familiar routine, that they had been exposed to all their lives.

In unison they spoke, "Good morning, Mr. Baldwin, who may we kill for you?"

His jaw fell slack for a moment, and then he recovered his composure. "You men are quite direct and to the point, I'll grant you that."

"Life's too short to beat around the bush," Rafe said.

"You hired us for our reputation, did you not?" Raff asked with a sardonic grin.

"Yes, I suppose I did," he answered as he leaned back in his high-backed leather chair. The burgundy leather was fastened to the dark wood with round brass tacks. He seemed to be growing smaller by the second as the arc of shiny fasteners shone like stars in the light shining through the float glass window. "You boys have certainly managed to keep your noses clean. There are no warrants on you anywhere...I checked."

"We don't leave witnesses," they said simultaneously.

Baldwin grinned and nodded.

"Now, pray tell…"

"…what does this little excursion involve?" asked the twins.

After taking in a deep breath, Jason leaned forward and whispered a single word, "Gold."

Rafe and Raff turned to each other, their eyes searching for a clue as to what the nervous man had meant.

"Gold? Is this a payroll job?"

"Perhaps a bank…" they inquired.

"Nothing so plebeian, I assure you," Baldwin said as he stood and moved to a slender vertical wood cabinet. Opening the door, he pulled out a rolled up topographical map of the county north of Ardmore. He slid the rubber band off the chart, spread it out across the desk and placed a square glass ashtray on one side and an ink well on the other to help hold it flat.

"Right here is the Honey Creek property I'm interested in. The gold play along this area is the key to the kingdom, in my opinion."

"And the owner…"

"…refuses your more than generous offer…"

"Correct?" They said, sharing the question.

"You gentlemen are quick studies, I'll wager."

"What's his name?"

"And how big is his spread?"

"How many men does he have?"

"It's a she, one Angie O'Reilly. And she's sitting on 140 acres lying on both sides on the creek about here…and it's just her," Baldwin added almost sheepishly.

"You brought the seven of us up here…"

"…for one split-tail?"

"That 'split-tail' has killed three of my men in the last week."

The Sartain brothers glanced at each other and grinned.

"We do love…"

"…a challenge."

The five hired gunmen waited downstairs on the tree shaded sidewalk and eyed two young women entering the sundries store adjacent to the law office. Otha elbowed Jude.

"I'd give two day's pay to see what that yellow-haired filly has under all them crinolines."

"Hell, Otha, once she gets herself a look at that mug of yorn, you'd be lucky to see where she goes to church. Don't think that one is the like of them saloon gals you take a shine to."

"Meby yes, meby no. But when we get that other forty-five bucks due us, I'm gonna make me a run on her. Never let the word *no* get between me and a good time."

The rest of the roughnecks burst out laughing at the gap toothed gunman as Rafe and Raff descended the stairs and motioned for the men to follow. They crossed the bustling street and headed toward one of two new boarding houses that had been erected after the devastating fire that had torched most of Ardmore the previous year.

ARDMORE, I.T.
MARSHAL'S OFFICE

Bass, Tobe and Jed had pulled up bow chairs and were all nursing cups of coffee in Selden's office. Four hats were hung on the hat tree by the door. Boot was over in a corner, curled up next to the potbellied stove with the coffee pot on its top.

"Well, say one thing Sel, you make better coffee than Jed," said Bass with a grin.

"Guess who gits to make the coffee from now on, then?" replied Jed.

"Best I recall, Bass' coffee wadn't much punkin' neither," added Tobe.

"Now where 'n hell does it say in the book that everybody gits to pick on the big darkie?" Bass chuckled.

The door opened and Loss stepped in, hung his hat on the tree and made a beeline to the coffee pot. He stepped over Boot and poured a cup in his personal green ceramic mug.

"Well?" Selden asked.

"Deep subject there, Sel." Loss grinned, walked over to his desk, took his seat, had a sip of coffee and finally said, "'Spect ya'll 'er wantin' to know where our group of highbinders went, ain't cha?"

"Let me take a wild guess...Jason Alexander Baldwin, Attorney at Law's office...Close?" offered Selden.

"Well, God dammit, Sel. If'n you already knowed where they wuz agoin, why in Sam Hill did you send me traipsin' all over town follerin' 'em? Huh? Tell me that."

"Like I said, Loss, it was a guess. Needed to know fer sure."

"How long did they stay?" asked Tobe.

"'Bout thirty minutes, I reckon. Jest the twins went inside. When they come out, everbody went over to the Parker Boardin' House and got rooms."

"'Peers as though they intend to stay a while," said Bass.

"Yup. Reckon Loss an' I'll have to take turns tailin' 'em…If the Dalton gang is in fact headed this away…could take 'em as long as ten days if they stay shanks mare. Five if'n they steal some horses…"

"You can count on that, Sel. I figure we got six days at most…Tobe, Jed and me 'er gonna start scoutin' around fer Jack…Any suggestions?"

"Well, as you said on the train, Jack and the Chickasaw Lighthorse Montford Anoatubbi wuz goin' undercover as prospectors…The gold play is up along Honey Creek."

"How long is the Honey?" Jed asked.

"The part that's producin' starts up at the top of the mountain, meby three miles above the falls where the Honey comes out of the ground…"

"Out of the ground?"

"Yep, starts as a full-fledged creek gushin' right out of the mountain. Sweetest water you ever drank, too. Must run through several outcrops of gold bearin' white quartz that's part of the Tishomingo granite that forms the core of the Arbuckles…They's claims along the creek nearly all the way to Davis where she starts to flatten out. The biggest stretch is 'bout half a mile startin' from the falls. Owned by the widder lady that filed the complaint on Baldwin…Now if'n it comes a frog strangler, git the hell to high ground. With the Honey bein' underground fed, don't take much of a rain to turn her into a wooly-booger like it did a week ago...Ya hear?"

"We hear ya...Most likely Jack an' Montford found a good play above the falls, set up a camp an' got some equipment. Jack done some prospectin' up in Colorado as a young man...one reason he got the assignment. Nobody else knew their butts from a gin whistle 'bout lookin' fer gold," said Bass.

"You know Jack's disappearance, the Sartain gang and Jason Baldwin may all dovetail together, don'tcha, Bass?"

"My figurin' too, Sel...My figurin' too...We got a lot a ground to cover...Jest hope we're not too late...Reckon we'll start early of a mornin'...Need to git us a place to stay. Don't figger the Parker would be too good...Where's somethin' else?"

"That'd be Miss Willow's Boardin' House. Better'n where the Sartains is stayin'...She makes squirrel 'n dumplins to die for," said Loss.

"Well, hope it don't come to that," offered Bass.

***

CHAPTER EIGHT

HONEY CREEK

"Wouldn't recommend you boys twitch much," came the caution from between two western red cedar trees followed by the double click of two hammers being cocked.

"I'd pay real close attention to what the man says," said another voice from behind a large boulder on the other side of the trail. His warning was also just before the metallic sound of a round being levered into a Winchester.

Bass and Tobe exchanged glances.

"United States Deputy Marshals...You boys kin put down yer shooters, if'n you don't mind," said Bass as he slowly eased his coat away from his vest to show his crescent and star badge.

A grizzled old prospector stepped out from between the cedars. "Come on out Rube, I seen the big one's badge...All three of ya'll marshals, 'er ye?"

The other man stepped out from his hide behind the boulder and uncocked his rifle.

"You could say that," replied Bass.

"Sure glad the laws has showed up here on the Honey, Marshal. Been some fellers givin' folks a hard time 'bout bein' here. I'm a thinkin' they just want to take over our claim...such as it is," said the placer miner as he spit a stream of tobacco juice at a lizard and missed. "Ya'll like some coffee? Got some bilin' on the fire over to the camp through the woods towards the crick."

"'Preciate it, old-timer, but we're lookin' fer some friends. A kinda stocky white man...dark mustache, and a Chickasaw, might have a claim up here somewheres," said Bass.

"Ain't seen nobody in particular answerin' that kinda description...not on this side of the crick, anyways. There's claims on some of the feeder streams on t'other side, though...Gonna have to go all the way to the top and go 'round the headwaters to git there...too blamed dangerous to try to ford down here...Injuns say that water that's a bubblin' out of the side of the mountain comes all the way from Canady...Cold as all git out...'Magine that?"

"Don't say?...Well, much obliged," said Tobe as he touched his hat.

Boot ran along the well-traveled game trail in front of Bass, Jed and Tobe—sniffing at bushes and trees every few feet for squirrels or rabbits.

"'Peers as though Boot's found a second child...er puppyhood," observed Jed with a grin. "'Ceptin' fer his nose...Didn't sniff out them two miners."

"We was upwind...if'n you noticed," Tobe defended his best friend.

"Oh, you be right. Sorry Boot...How much further to the headwaters, ya think, Bass?"

"Well, lest the Honey runs over the top of that ridge up yonder, I'd say bout another two-three hunderd yards er so...You, Tobe?"

"My guess, too."

The side of the mountain had more grass and less trees and brush as it neared the crest. There were many outcrops of gray granite occasionally streaked with quartz, schist, gneiss or flint sticking up through the turf like so many misshapen gnarly fingers. The numerous deer, cougar, black bear, raccoons and other critters had worn a well-beaten path over hundreds of years that twisted and wound around the outcrops and boulders all the way to the top.

"I'm gonna say she comes out of the mountain in that pile of boulders up ahead where this here trail leads...Looks like that bigun is split right half in two."

"Noticed at least four other springs on the way up looked like they added to the flow," said Tobe.

"'Spect they's a bunch mor'n that on the other side as she heads down the mountain...ike the old man said.

In a few more minutes, they pulled rein at the big boulders. As they figured, the cold, clear water came right out of the ground and began its trek down the mountain, picking up speed as it went.

Bass dismounted, knelt down and got a couple handfuls of the cold water. "Great gosh amighty, but that tastes good. We oughta pour out our canteens and refill here...Don't git no better'n this..." He flipped a piece of white quartz into the crystal clear twenty foot diameter pool and watched until it disappeared from sight. "Must be couple hunderd feet deep. Goes straight down into the mountain ''til the light plays out...'Minds me of where the White River over to Eureka Springs in Arkansas comes outta the ground...jest not quite as big. Word has it that one comes from Canady too."

"Say, boys! Pert near noon time, what say we fix up some coffee and have a bite to eat?" said Jed. "They's some good grass over yonder we kin picket the horses in."

"Damn, Jed, you do come up with some good idees on occasion...You been savin' that one up, have you?"

"Now there you go, Tobe. Fixin' to pee in your beans...go ahead...jus' keep that up."

"Jest joshin', Jed, jest joshin'...Been in too many camps to not know the last man you want to bend outta shape is the cook."

"Uh, huh," Jed grunted as he grinned and dismounted.

LOG CABIN

"Angie, we appreciate your hospitality," said Ben Sixkiller as he and Winchester started down the steps of the front porch.

"Hank, it's my considered opinion, both as a medical doctor and a Chickasaw shaman, that those images you saw and told us about were fragments of your memories…"

"But, my pappy and Montford talked like they knowed what wuz gonna happen and wouldn't tell me 'zackly what…Now why is that?"

"Your mind is not ready to know some things, my son. It's still healing. That's why there remains a veil between you and your past…You must be patient."

"Ain't sure patience wuz ever one of my long suits, shaman…Don't seem like it anyways."

"Maybe it's Ababinili's way of teaching you maturity."

"What about Anna?"

"There will be a time for her also. It is you she wants to find her. That is why the Great Spirit sent Nashoba Tohbi to you when you came into the Chickasaw Nation. It is ever his way in his infinite wisdom to work wonders and miracles to perform."

"Wondered 'bout that…One thing I remembered after I come out of the lodge was 'bout how him an' me hooked up…Woke up one mornin' in my camp 'fore gittin' to Montford's house…an' there he was, lying right beside me. Like to scare't me to half-to-death to come out of a sound sleep an' have a wolf starin' me right in the face not three inches away…an' a white one at that. Then he licked me right across my mouth…Didn't know if'n he was jest taste testin' er what 'til he pushed his nose under my hand fer me to pet 'im…Figgered it was kinda an order, ya know? Them golden eyes jest seem to talk…"

"There is no question…he's the link to the spirit world," the shaman said.

Ben nodded. "The Nashoba Tohbi is the totem of our clan of the Chickasaw. Angie's husband, Towana, was my cousin. His mother, *Te Ata*, or Bearer of the Morning, was revered priestess and great storyteller of our people."

"Ain't real sure I'm the right person…or kin live up to all this that seems to be 'spected of me…" Hank shook his head and looked off to the creek.

"Think we give you Chickasaw name. *Oka'-bia-Lawa*, he who talks with the water," said Ben.

"Don't need another trip to that sweat lodge, do I?"

"We see…Leave lodge here for a while," Ben said with almost a grin.

"Cain't wait."

Anompoli Lawa and Sixkiller headed to their horses tied to the fence outside the gate. The shaman turned back to Angie and Hank as they reached the gate. "We do not choose, Oka'-bia-Lawa…we are chosen."

ARDMORE

Deputy Kyle Ratcliff watched as Sheriff Milo Cobb took a swig from the dark green patent medicine bottle and grimaced as he swallowed. The senior lawman set the bottle down on the cluttered pine desk and fumbled trying to replace the cork top with his left hand.

"Laudanum tastes purty nasty, don't it, Sheriff?"

"Yer grasp of the obvious is a pure caution," Cobb said as he wiped the last reddish-brown drop of the opium-based concoction off his lower lip with the backside of his hand.

"Thanky, boss. That means a lot, comin' from you."

Cobb said nothing, just shook his head and reached for his timepiece nestled in a small pouch sewn into his plain linen dark gray vest. He flipped open the embossed cover of the nickel-plated watch and glanced at the time, *12:42*. Snapping the cover closed, he looked down at the plaster-of-Paris cast on his throbbing right wrist, and was again reminded of the mission set for later that afternoon. "All right, now. Them boys Baldwin hired should have their bellies full by now…You and Horace git on over to the boardin' house and git 'em saddled up. It's high time we take care of that little Irish hellion once and fer all."

"You ain't coming with us, Sheriff? We jest supposed to show them the way up to Honey Creek by ourselves?"

"Dammit man! Do I need to find you a sugar tit?…You know how much it hurts to ride with a broke wrist?"

"Bet hurts a whole lot…'member how much you moaned and carried on after that wolf bit you? I thought…"

"Don't pay you to think! I pay you to foller orders! Now get yer ass in motion before I find out if I can shoot with my off hand."

The anger in Cobb's face was readily understood by anyone, even the intellectually challenged Kyle Ratcliff. He sprang from his ladderback chair and scrambled for the door, keeping an eye on the sheriff the whole time. Once outside, he approached

Deputy Horace Jones, who was planted in a wooden chair, leaned back against the unpainted plank siding of the new jail with a double barreled shotgun cradled in his lap.

"Mount up...Cobb's got a job fer us."

"Hope it's more interesting than sittin' here watchin' folks do nuthin'. I'm about bored half to death...er is it half bored to death?..."

Fifteen minutes later, the two deputies led the Sartain brothers and the five hired guns north on the red brick Main Street. Their steel horseshoes clicked and clattered as they passed by townsfolk in open topped buggies and nearby farmers bringing in crops of onions, radishes, and an assortment of fresh spring greens in heavily laden buckboards or Murphy wagons. Rafe and Raff tipped their hats to the ladies and reveled in the double-takes that the chivalrous demeanor from identical twins generated.

ARDMORE, I.T.
MARSHAL'S OFFICE

Loss burst into the office almost making Selden spill his coffee.

"Dadgum, Loss, you gotta bust through the door like you's headed for the dinner table?"

"Sorry, Sel, but that Sartain bunch and those two no-'count deputies just rode out of town...headed north. Thought you'd wanta know."

"Yep, damn shore do. Let's saddle up. Got a purty good notion as to where they're headed."

ARBUCKLE MOUNTAINS

The four remaining members of the Dalton gang skirted Ardmore to the east in their trek toward Elk, north and west of the town some nineteen miles. They were mounted on horses they obtained near Mannsville in the dark of the night.

"Mighty nice of you to leave those wore out nags in trade fer these boys at that stage station, Bill. You must be gittin' soft in yer old age," said Big Asa.

"Hated to take a man's working stock…needed to leave him somethin'. Ain't like he was a banker er nothin', 'sides a few days of rest an' good grain, an' them horses'll be fine to hitch to a coach."

"Shhh!" cautioned George Bennet. "Hear horses…bunch of 'em behind us back around that bend."

"Clear the road…over to that bunch of cedars. Quiet now," Bill ordered. They eased over behind the large evergreen grove and dismounted. "Put yer hands over their muzzles…they'll want to talk to them other horses."

Deputies Ratcliff and Jones led the Sartian brothers and their men at a slow trot along the wagon road in the foothills of the Arbuckles north of Ardmore. Each of the twins was smoking a long dark cheroot.

Bill parted the branches of a cedar to watch the group ride past. When they were out of sight he turned to his men. "Mount up."

154

"Looked like a posse, Bill, them two in the front wuz wearin' badges...Think they're lookin' fer us?" asked Jim Knight.

"Don't think so. None of 'em was cuttin' fer sign. 'Peered to me as they was goin' some place in particular...No need in takin' chances though. We'll stay off'n the road an' head to the west now, in 'ny case...Be to Elk by this afternoon."

"Dang, them cheroots those two dandies was a smokin' looked good...kin even smell 'em...We been out of tobaccer fer three days..."

"You gonna whine all the way to Elk, George?" Bill interrupted.

"Naw, Bill, just sayin' is all."

"Well, you kin ketch up to 'em and ask fer a drag, if'n yer of a mind."

"Damn, cain't a man say nothin' 'bout wantin' a smoke without you gettin' all pissy?"

"Ain't gittin' pissy, we been outta food fer almost two days too and yer bitchin' 'bout a smoke?...Me, I'd druther have somethin' to eat."

"Got a point there. My stomach is wonderin' if'n I still got a mouth," added George.

Fifteen minutes later, Marshals Lindsey and Hart rode easy along the same wagon road the Sartains were traveling—almost a mile behind the hired guns.

"Ain't tryin' to hide their tracks none," Selden said as he periodically glanced at the road.

"Bit too cocky fer their own good...an' I'm glad," added Loss.

"Hello! What have we here?"

"What?"

"'Nother set of tracks...make it four horses...cuttin' the road, headed west, after the Sartains passed."

"Dalton?"

"My guess. Just as I figured...Headed to the Wallace place over to Elk...Damn I'm good."

"Reckon we oughta switch trails and track the Dalton gang?"

"Nope, know where to find 'em...Give 'em a few days to settle in and git comfortable. Won't be near so wary...They'll be edgy for more'n a week...Need to stay close to the Sartains anyways. They're up to no good...no question 'bout it. Up to no good," Selden surmised.

HONEY CREEK

The nine riders bunched up as they cleared the rise overlooking the wagon road leading back west and down the valley to the center of the O'Reilly allotment. The tracks of horses and steel rimmed wagon wheels bore witness to the scant traffic that had passed by earlier in the week. Deputy Kyle eased up on his reins, allowing his chestnut gelding to graze on the six inch high winter grass. He pointed toward a limestone bluff that ran parallel to the creek.

"See there? That's the outcropping that her old man built their house up against...Ya'll can ride all the way to the house without being see'd…but danged if'n I know how to get down from there."

Raff nodded. "Why don't we just ride up and knock at the door?…I have a thing for the ladies."

"As do I, brother…but something tells me this little lassie is not feeling real romantic just right now." Rafe chuckled.

"So what do you suggest?"

"How far is it down to the farmhouse and barn?" the twins asked together.

Kyle looked at Horace, who merely shrugged. "Reckon it's a good four…meby five hunerd yards…See them tall cottonwoods? I remember a couple big'uns down by the crick not too far from the barn. Don't see the house proper from here…Their place ain't all that big, but is kinda long an' skinny."

The twins nodded.

"If we can't see them…"

"…they can't see us. Spread out, gents…"

"Otha, you, Curly and Jim Bob take it up on top of the bluff. Circle around and come back down behind her…"

"According to the map, the bluff plays out up by the falls…"   "Can't be more than three quarters of a mile," the Sartains gave orders—they had that unusual connection that identical twins often have of thinking alike and completing each other's sentences.

"Our pleasure," a scar-faced thug replied as he reined north and urged his mount into a lope.

"Carson, you and Miller…"

"…ease on down by the creek. Take it slow and easy…"

"The whole idea is to spring a big surprise on the lady…We'll work our way in close on foot."

"She'll never know what hit her." The brothers glanced at each other and grinned.

"What about us? You need us to be ready to arrest the woman?" asked Deputy Kyle.

"You two stay close to us. Keep your trigger fingers ready, boys…"

"…cause she's armed and dangerous," Rafe finished as he winked at Raff.

The two brothers shared another knowing glance, then nudged their mounts down the wooded incline and veered off the roadway—in short order, all six riders disappeared into the brush.

Working slowly and weaving through the available openings, they closed the distance to the cabin. Carson Hatcher and Jude Miller pulled up when they could see flashes of the red barn though the trees.

"'Bout as far as we go mounted," Carson whispered.

"First one to get a bullet in the bitch gets five bucks," Miller said, stroking his black-waxed handlebar mustache.

"Says who? You ain't got five to yore name."

"Says Rafe…'er meby it was Raff…last night…at the Golden Garter…You don't remember?"

"Hell that must'a been when I wuz outside takin' a piss behind that black walnut tree…Didn't hear him say it, but damned sure sounds good to me." Carson swung down and tied the reins to a dogwood sapling and moved off through the woods in the direction of the cabin…

HONEY CREEK HEADWATER

"Dang, but that coffee was good…guess that water makes all the difference," said Bass.

"An' guess I had nothin' to do with it…that what yer say'n?" countered Jed as he put away the pot in his saddlebags.

"Ingredients make the pie."

"Do not."

"Do too."

"Well, who puts the ingredients together, huh?…The cook, that's who. Think they come together all by themselves like a bunch of magnets?"

"Alright, children, settle down. Takes both a good cook *and* good ingredients…so there," said Tobe. "Now how's about we fork our saddles and see if'n we kin find Jack's camp?"

"That's a plan," agreed Bass.

The three lawmen tightened their cinches back up, mounted and headed down the mountain in the direction of the falls. There were well-worn trails on the north side of the creek identical to the ones on the south side. Game trails, by their nature were narrow, only rarely over two feet wide, necessitating they travel single file with Boot usually leading the way. Due to the undulating terrain, sometimes the trail was almost flat and sometimes it was steep enough the riders had to lean back in the saddle.

"Jed, why don't you slip up that feeder stream yonder an' see if'n you find anythin'?" Bass said. "We'll ease on down the main creek. You kin ketch up to us if'n it's clean."

Jed nodded and headed off to his left, working back uphill. Bass and Tobe forded the small feeder with Boot splashing behind, snapping at a small school of bream in a shallow pool.

"Come on, Boot, you couldn't cook 'em if you caught 'ny," Tobe admonished his dog, and then laughed at his own joke.

"If'n they was any dog in the world that could learn to cook...it'd be Boot...I'd wager," offered Bass.

"That's a fact...Yessir, that is a fact."

Jed joined back up from his unproductive trek back up the hill. "Nothin', boys. Couple a places looked to have been panned, but they weren't no eddies where a feller might find 'ny color."

"Looks like the Honey is bendin' back to the right. Be some slow water or gravel bars 'fore she heads back down the moun...Whoa...looky down there!" Tobe exclaimed. "Ain't them bones?"

"Think yer right, Tobe," Bass said as they eased down the embankment.

"Damnation! 'Peers like they's two horse skeletons," Jed said as he and the others dismounted and ground tied their horses.

"I'd say that there is what's left of a man, too...God rest his soul," said Tobe as he walked over, squatted down and began to study the bones. "Shot in the head while he was trapped under his horse."

Bass moved closer to the other equine skeleton. His keen powers of observation came into play as he nudged a hoof over with the toe of his boot. The leg flesh was long gone, but traces of hide and ligaments with some longer hair remained around the fetlock. The shoe, still nailed to the hoof, had a metal bar hammer-welded across the arms. Recognition of the familiar sight brought a lump to his throat. "This horse over here belonged to Jack," called out Bass.

The news caused Tobe's spirits to drop considerably. "You sure? How kin you tell?"

"Bar shoe, front left. Jack's geldin' cracked a hoof...been wearin' a bar shoe most of the last three months."

Jed knelt beside Tobe at the human remains beneath the first horse skeleton. He spotted the broken quill and bead hat band and gingerly picked it up and held it for the others to see. "Looky here what I found! This ain't Mr. Jack's body, I don't suppose."

"Wrong horse, Jed. That's a Chickasaw Lighthorse hat band. Seen 'em a'fore," Tobe said solemnly as he moved up closer to Bass and studied the remains of the second horse. He gazed around for a couple seconds before he spoke, "All this proves is that his horse is dead...They got themselves bushwhacked from over yonder there cross the creek."

"I mind yer right. Check out the area and let's make sure he's not layin' nearby...Remember what happened to his brother? Those Larson bastards murdered the whole bunch of them at once," Bass said angrily.

Tobe nodded. He had heard Hank McGann's dying words after the gut shot marshal was carried into his Sand Springs office ten years before. The lawman's final words were forever seared into his memory, *They kilt us, Tobe...Kilt us all.* "Ya think they's any chance he made it down to the creek?"

"Wish I knew, Tobe...Wish I knew. Fixin' to try an' find out," Bass said as he worked his way down to the creek bank. He glanced around and his eye caught some gouge marks on the small boulder, then a glint flashed at the edge of his vision. He squatted down and picked up three brass cartridges, two on the bank and one just under the water in the eddy. ".44 Russians." Bass looked up the bank at Tobe and Jed. "Jack carried a matched set of New Model Number 3 S&W Russians....44 caliber. My guess is he went into the creek...Whether shot er jumped, cain't tell...They was 'ny blood, it's washed away."

"Good God, Bass! If'n he went into them rapids, be no stoppin' ''til the falls...he wouldn't stand a chance in hell...not one...shot er not," Tobe offered.

"Reckon we oughta move on downstream...jest in case. Need to tell the Chickasaws 'bout their man," said Bass dejectedly.

LOG CABIN

Hank sat down hard in a slat-back chair at the dinner table. He steadied himself by putting his forearm on the table. Small beads of sweat appeared on his face and ran down his chin. Angie glanced up from kneading bread on the other end of the

162

table just in time to see a bead of sweat drip to the pine top—his face was flushed.

"Oh, Lordy. It's the fever again!" She wiped the flour from her hands onto her red and white checkered apron and rushed to his side. Placing her hand upon his forehead, she shook her head. "Just like a man...not saying a word when he's bad off! Now get your carcass up and over to the bed with you."

He started to protest, but the sudden onset of dizziness, exacerbated with the nausea that often accompanies a severe concussion overcame him. Hank stood up, then almost toppled to the unpainted plank floor. Boy looked up from his spot near the fireplace and whined. Angie placed an arm around his waist and pulled him tight.

He winced as the pressure on his side wound reminded him of the attack that left him with only partial memory.
"Ah...Ah."

"I'm so sorry, my sweet Hank...I'll surely be taking care, I promise. Now lay yourself down."

He followed her gentle lead and sat on the side of the bed, and then sank onto his back. Angie grabbed his scuffed brown boots and lugged them off, one at a time. She took a corner of her apron and gently wiped the sweat from his brow.

"I'll be heading down to the creek and gathering some young willow to make more of your medicine."

Hank nodded weakly and laid his head down on the feather pillow. He looked into her green eyes and mouthed the words "Thank you." He tried to smile, but it didn't convince her a bit.

"You close those brown eyes and get a rest, I'm saying...Doctor's orders...I'll be back in two shakes of a lamb's tail."

She grabbed a pair of heavy curve-bladed kitchen shears she used for cutting chickens apart from a drawer in the counter, put them in her apron pocket and started to pick up her shot gun as she opened the door, *No, shouldn't be needing this today.* Boy was on his feet and out on the porch before she could close it.

"Are you saying you wanted to go outside too, white one?"

He woofed and danced on the front porch as she stepped down the risers to the ground.

"Well, come on then. You can be taking care of your business while I cut some willow branches. He turned, jumped the fence and headed toward the barn.

"Now why would he be going to the barn?" she mumbled. "There'll be no figuring that one. He has a bit of an agenda of his own, he does."

Angie went out through the gate at the front of the cabin and headed down a path toward a bend in the creek where she knew a thick stand of willows had established themselves. She glanced around at all the budding trees and listened to the songs of the birds as they flitted through the branches, *My, but a fine spring day it is*—she was wrong.

***

CHAPTER NINE

HONEY CREEK

Bass, Tobe, Jed nudged their horses back up the incline toward the main trail that ran along the ridge line to the falls. Boot ran on ahead in his usual scouting mode.

"Reckon we oughta stop down to that widder woman's cabin, downstream of the falls, Bass?" asked Jed.

"'Spect so. She coulda heard er seen somethin'. Ain't gonna be satisfied 'til we find Jack...er his body...I owe him that."

"My hopes are we'll find Jack all safe and sound sittin' somewheres havin' his own self a hot cup of coffee...but ain't puttin' much stock in it...Not a man alive could survive goin' down those rapids and over the falls," offered Tobe.

"Jack's special...Lost count of how many times he's been shot er stabbed...just heals up an' hairs over 'fore you kin say scat...Like he's always had a guardian angel er somethin' watchin' over 'im."

"That angel was watchin' a bit closer, wouldn't a been shot 'n stabbed all that many times…I'm thinkin'," added Jed as he looked at the turbulent water.

Downstream a mile or so, three riders descended through the boulder-strewn broken escarpment and worked their way back north. Otha gained experience at tracking men when he was a scout for the Army and had done a considerable amount of bounty hunting in the days before he signed on with the Sartain brothers. He pulled rein and dismounted as the three came across a well-worn path that paralleled the west side of Honey Creek.

He squatted down on the trail and studied the ground. "Well, well…guess this here 'splains how the bitch kilt them others," he said pointing at the large male boot prints in the red dirt. He let fly a stream of brown tobacco juice and watched it hit beside a small circular depression in the ground. Comparing the two boot prints, he detected one was slightly lighter than the other.

"Haw! Her man is a gimpy sumbitch…whoever he is. See them regular little holes?…Uses a cane to get hisself around."

"That bein' the case, meby he's an old man…meby her grampa. Rafe said she wuz a widder woman…" Curly surmised.

"Gonna bet your life on it?" Jim Bob asked.

"What'er you sayin'? Even if they's two of 'em, hell, we still got 'em outnumbered nine to two…Them's purty good odds, I calls it."

"That may be, Curly, but that extra five bucks could be the hardest you ever earned...'Sides, them two deputies ain't much punkin'."

Curly shot him a look. Jim Bob just grinned as Otha swung back into the saddle.

"You two can sit and ratchet-jaw all day, if'n yer of a mind...Me, I'm gonna get me another day's pay with just one little ol' bullet." Otha spurred his horse down the path leading to the farmhouse.

Thorny barbed wire-like greenbriar vines—*whoa-vines,* as they were called—bristling with needle-sharp growths on all sides, ripped through the once well-creased worsted wool pants and tore into Raff's thighs. Blood trickled down both his legs from numerous painful previous encounters. "Blast these damnable briars," he muttered as his forward progress was once again held up by thigh-high vegetation.

"I seem to remember one of us said something to the effect that we should wear chaps. But someone else said, 'Why bother?'" Rafe said with more than a drip of sarcasm in his voice. "Mirror mirror, on the wall, who's the smartest one of..."

"Shut up, brother! Isn't it bad enough that I already ruined these pants? We had them shipped special from St. Louis, remember?"

"Button it up...we can't be more than a hundred yards from the cabin. We should have just ridden in...What a waste of time and effort."

"Let's split up, then. That way, at least one of us should find a clear path."

"Now you are talking some sense. Besides, we'll make enough from this job to buy us fifty pairs of custom pants."

Raff nodded and backed out of the almost impenetrable thicket. He moved to the left as Rafe took off right, closer to the vertical bluff—each of the deputies followed closely behind one of the brothers.

Carson Hatcher moved silently through the brush, avoiding carefully the random growths of the same thorny greenbriars that proliferated much of the south. His partner, Jude Miller, had gone another direction as the two spread out looking for a trail leading to the house from along the creek. Only sixty yards or so separated the two, but the creek side near the farmhouse, barn and corral was heavily wooded. It was obvious why the O'Reilly's had planted their crops up on the flatter plateau above rather than waste time clearing the brushy creek bottom. Hatcher froze when he heard a melodious voice singing an Irish tune and stepped behind a large cottonwood near a willow grove next to the creek.

"O Danny boy, the pipes, the pipes are callin'. From glen to glen, and down the mountain side…"

Angie continued humming the old Gaelic melody as she stepped to the edge of the grove, pulled the heavy shears from her apron and began to snip the new growth from the young willows.

Hatcher moved slowly across the forty yards separating him from the woman's back. He started to slide his hand down to the worn Colt Single Action riding high on his hip, but her silky Irish voice and hourglass figure in the blue gingham house dress gave him another idea. *If she's half as pretty as she sounds, it would be a waste of womanhood. A roll in the hay and nice payday sounds real good to me.* He watched as she snipped a couple more slender willow branches and stashed them in her apron. He closed to only five feet of the still humming Angie; he swore he could smell the faint scent of lilac water on her, and his pulse raced…

Marshal Lindsey reined up as he and Loss Hart reached the spot where the Sartains and their band of cutthroats began to split up. The tracks told the story.

"Three of 'em went high and plan to circle around the south side," Selden said with a concerned look on his face.

"What's our play here?…Don't cotton too much to splittin' up," Loss said as he looked down the road into the heavily wooded valley.

"Me neither…but cain't be helped. We go a ridin' down this wagon road and they'll bushwhack us sure as I'm sitting here…Time to earn our pay, pard. Tell you what…tie up in those trees down by the creek…I'll work my way in close along the bluff. If'n we're lucky, meby we can catch 'em with their pants down, while they are busy lookin' at the house."

"Gotcha," Loss said as he focused his attention on the direction Selden had pointed.

The older marshal reached back and grabbed the buttstock on his '86 Winchester and tugged it free of the worn leather scabbard. He silently levered the action partially open and confirmed the chamber was loaded. He then pulled the lever up flush, closing the bolt, making sure the blued steel hammer rested on the safety notch. Selden laid the rifle across his lap, and then extended his gloved hand to Loss. "Good luck, ol' son…Let's get 'er done."

The two shook hands firmly then urged their mounts off the ridge as they went their separate ways.

The striking redhead selected and cut the last willow branch she planned to strip and boil for Hank's elixir. She dropped it and the kitchen shears in her burgeoning apron pocket when Hatcher's right hand snaked around her right shoulder and clamped firmly over her mouth. His strong left arm wrapped around her ribcage, lifted her off her feet and pulled her tightly against his chest. She struggled mightily and kicked her legs trying to get a foothold, but without success. The terrified woman tried to scream, but the man's gloved hand cut off any sound.

"Easy there you hot-tempered little filly. You and me are gonna have us some fun right here and now…and you ain't got no say-so in the matter. So's you jest as well lay back and enjoy it."

Angie's eyes flew open wide with fear. *How could I let this happen? Hank! Hank!* She tried to turn her head to scream, but the brutish man was much too strong. Her hand went instinctively to her apron and wrapped around the black painted handle of the shears. In a flash of silver, her hand brought the curved razor-sharp blades up and plunged them back at her unseen attacker. Missing the protective leather chaps by only a half-inch, she buried the four-inch long blades almost to the hinge until the man's pelvic bone stopped their penetration at the hip joint.

Carson Hatcher's right leg buckled as he screamed out in anguish at such pain as he had never experienced. He fell backwards, landing hard with her still in his grasp. His grip across her face moved slightly, allowing his index finger to fall across her mouth.

The taste of dirt, grime, and horse sweat almost made Angie vomit, but she kept her wits. She opened her mouth, then bit down with all her strength, until she heard a gross cracking sound and the man howled out with pain once again. His left arm eased its vice-like grip and actually pushed her away. But she didn't ease up with her teeth clamped firmly on the finger and commenced kicking his shins with her heels. She rolled clear of her unknown attacker, the single riding glove still in her mouth.

"God damn you, shanty Irish bitch!" Hatcher yelled out at as blood spurted from his stub of a trigger finger. He pulled his Colt, but struggled to make it fire as the panic-stricken woman scrambled to her feet. She was almost twenty yards away when he finally realized his finger was no longer there and switched the revolver to his off hand.

He cocked the hammer and was almost lined up with the back of the running woman when a mass of white terror sprang onto the small clearing. The wolf-dog bowled the man over as the single action fired wide of its mark, the shot echoed up and down the wooded valley. The wolf latched onto the man's throat and shook him violently like a cat playing with a rat.

"Hatcher! Hatcher?...You alright?" Miller called out before he caught a fleeting sight of the blue dress passing through the trees. He fired once, splintering a dogwood tree just behind her—he thumbed the hammer back. "Damn whore runs like a deer," he said as his aim was interrupted by an oak tree. He tried to lead her, but his bullet clipped the bark off a sweet gum.

"Hank! Hank!...Help me!" she yelled as she neared the barn.

Jude Miller stepped out from behind a large sycamore and lined up the slender front sight of his six-shooter on the woman's head. He pulled the trigger just as a 405 grain slug from a .45-70 lifted him completely off his feet and caused his shot to go high.

Bass, Jed and Tobe had made their descent half way down the escarpment north of the falls to the big pool on Honey Creek. Reeves signaled a halt when he heard the first shot echo off the bluff behind the house.

"Hold up...ya'll hear that?"

"Ain't deaf yet, well meby not completely...six-gun," Tobe replied.

The sound of three quick pistol shots, followed by a large caliber rifle shot were unmistakable.

"Down there! That last one was from Jack's .45-70. Bet money on it."

He quickly spurred his buckskin down between the broken boulders. Tobe and Jed followed close behind. They took the steepest, but shortest way down to the trail that ran by the pool. The experienced riders all were leaning so far back, their shoulders were almost touching their horses croups as they ran, bounced and slid down the hill. The horses two-stepped and hopped with their front legs while their back legs were tucked under—haunches literally dragging the rocky trail—acting as a break against the momentum of going downhill at breakneck speed. Boot stayed just back of the horses, knowing instinctively not to get in front of the thousand pound animals as they scrambled down the slope. They pulled to sliding stops at the bottom next to the falls—the sound of water tumbling over the falls behind them was all that could be heard.

Inside the cabin, Hank wiped the sweat from his brow as a wave of nausea almost took him to his knees. Adrenaline coursed through his veins as he glanced to the corner and spotted the double barreled shotgun exactly where Angie had placed it before making her trip to the creek. *Why did she go unarmed? Hard headed woman...who does she think she is, anyway? Where are you girl?*

"They stopped firin'," said Tobe, standing up in the stirrups to try and detect the exact location of the shots that had echoed off the slightly curved bluff.

A fusilade of six-gun fire began again.

"Wrong," stated Bass. "Fan out. Go towards the shootin' meby 'nuther two hunderd yards, then on foot...an' we go in quiet. Nobody shoots 'til we kin see what we're shootin' at...no tellin' what's goin' on down creek," said Bass.

Otha also heard the shots in front of him and spurred his horse toward the sounds. The animal managed to cover only fifty yards when Boy launched himself from the top of a boulder on the left side of the trail, striking the galloping horse where the shoulder joined the neck. The horse screamed as it and rider tumbled violently to the ground, turning a complete somersault. Luckily for Otha—at least temporarily—he was thrown clear of his thrashing mount. He rolled to his knees, drew his side arm and fanned three shots directly at the charging, snarling creature.

"What the hell?" *I couldn't have mis...*

The last thought Otha Heinler would ever have, ended incomplete and in disbelief as one hundred and forty pounds of fury hit him at nearly twenty miles an hour. It was only a passing snap of the powerful jaws that ripped out his throat, slinging his body into the swift rapids to be swept away.

Hank's last question was answered when a flurry of hastily aimed shots rang out to the left of the cabin. Angie suddenly appeared just past the corner of the barn—her hands holding her house dress bunched up on both sides as she ran for her life. He blinked twice to clear his eyes and levered another cigar-sized .45-70 round into the rifle's chamber. He picked out a small patch of brush where several tell-tale puffs of black powder smoke had emanated. He couldn't see the shooter, but experience told him everything he needed to know as he lined up the shiny brass front sight in the buckhorn rear sight and squeezed the trigger. Hank hardly noticed the big gun's recoil—the smoke from his own shot partially obscured the view out the cabin window.

Blap! The unmistakable sound of a big soft-nose bullet striking flesh rang out amidst the din of six-gun shots. Ardmore deputy sheriff Horace Jones tumbled out of his hiding place and lay still. A second shot from the house sent a well-dressed shootist's hat sailing.

"Mother-of-God!" blurted Raff as he realized just how close he had come to meeting his maker. He slunk back into the woods to try to circle the house and steer well clear of whoever was in there with the big rifle. Rafe and Kyle emptied their guns at the woman who was running past the barn. Hot lead slugs flew dangerously close, kicking up spurts of dirt and splintering the weather-worn red painted doors and siding on the other side of her. Two more shots made soft *whap* sounds striking and passing through the medium weight cotton of her skirt as she screamed at the house again.

"Hank!"

He moved to get to the door as Jim Bob and Curly appeared in the trail leading down to the creek. Both men opened up as Angie cleared the four steps to the porch in a single leap, falling to her knees in the process. The fall was fortunate as two rounds impacted the thick door where she would have been had she still been on her feet. She reached for the latch, but the door flew open as if by magic as Hank yanked it wide.

"Stay down!" he yelled as more bullets smacked into the door frame and one shattered a picture of her father in his Sunday best next to the fireplace. He literally jerked her inside and slammed the door closed as she fell to the floor and rolled under the kitchen table. Hank dropped the latch in place and limped back to the window. He threw the Marlin up to his shoulder and snapped a shot at one of the two men, catching him as he turned slightly to the side to reload his empty six-gun. The round hit the square brass buckle on his gunbelt and tumbled, laying his belly open and spinning him around before he sank to the ground.

Curly was shocked at the sight of his own intestines splayed out over his thigh. He sat up and yelled to his companion, "Help me, Jim Bob!...Get me back to my..." His words were cut off by another round from the house. This time, the bullet tore into his head, exploding it like a ripe watermelon and slammed him to the red Indian Territory dirt for good.

"Hell with this!" Jim Bob exclaimed and turned to run. A third shot from the house passed though his leather chaps, leaving a bloody burn mark on his upper right thigh, but not doing much damage. Forty yards down the trail he almost ran into a black man with a marshal's badge on his vest. Jim Bob threw up his Colt and pulled the trigger as the black lawman brought his Henry up toward his shoulder. The bounty hunter's hammer fell on a empty cartridge before the well-used 1866 fired.

Jed's heart was in his throat as the expression on the paid assassin's face turned perplexed. The man stared at the marshal for a couple seconds and then glanced down at his own chest, where the .44 rimfire slug had cleanly punched a hole where the fourth button on the center of his shirt had been. Crimson began to spread across the yellowed cotton material and Jed watched as the man's eyes rolled upward and his legs turned to jelly.

Jed took in a couple deep ragged breaths and suddenly remembered to chamber another round. He threw the lever out and back—a short, stubby soot-covered spent brass flipped up lazily and landed at his feet. Jed tried hard to process what had just happened, but knew he still had to support the other marshals and whoever was trapped inside the cabin. He kicked the empty shooter out of the man's hand, picked it up and stuck it in his gunbelt.

Bullets tore into the window frame close to Hank's head. He ducked clear of the opening and moved to put his back against the thick cabin wall. His head hurt, the wound in his side and his banged up knee all ached, but he turned to Angie who was still panicked from her ordeal. "Are ye shot, darlin'?"

"I don't know…I don't know…" she panted. "He came out of nowhere…"

"You got blood on yer face…did he hit ya?"

"I'm thinkin' no…I bit him for all I was worth, then stabbed him with me shears."

Hank couldn't help but smile, even under the circumstances. *Angie O'Reilly yer a spitfire if ever I saw one.* "Good…For a minute, I thought you might have had some trouble out there."

Her eyes flashed anger for a brief second. Once she saw him smile, she couldn't help but laugh. "Oh? So you're not above pulling a woman's leg are ye? You think it's fun and games were havin'?"

"I'm glad you're safe, Angie. Don't know what I'd do without you to nurse me along."

"You're doin' fine by all I see…what's that? Is that blood on your leg?"

Hank looked down to see a damp red stain seeping down his left thigh. "Aw, Christ! And that was my good leg! Never felt it hit me."

"They must have nicked you when you opened the door for me."

"Got 'ny clothesline cord?"

"I do."

"Cut a length an' wrap around my leg above the hole and slow the bleedin'," Hank said as he shoved the last three of the .45-70s past the loading gate on the side of the Marlin's receiver. "We're almost out of rounds for the rifle. Better grab yer shotgun. Don't know how many more sidewinders are out there."

Angie pulled a length of cord from a coil hanging on the wall and cut a two foot length with a butcher knife from the table. She looped the line around his leg twice, pulled it tight and tied a knot. "It was only the one I saw, but it seemed like half of the Nations was shooting at meself. Never thought the creek was so far away before."

Hank nodded. "Purty sure I connected with three of 'em."

Tobe scanned the area around the back of the barn. The corrals were wide open and save for a couple scared horses dancing around, nothing else moved. Off to his right, he caught sight of Bass and Jed moving to the edge of the clearing surrounding the barn and hitching post in front of the cabin's fence.

Bass signaled Tobe to move in to the side of the barn. He nodded and slowly moved to the south side. Bass motioned for Jed to remain hidden and then he and Boot moved over to join him. Together they began to work their way back into the woods and circle around the clearing on the creek side of the house.

Rafe eased over to Deputy Kyle, who was seated with his back to a large oak tree some forty yards from the house. The not-too- bright lawman had reloaded his six-gun and was not taking any more chances. He had seen what the big bore rifle had done out the front window.

Rafe knelt down close to Kyle and smiled. "Well now, looks like the pot of gold is gonna get split three ways instead of seven."

"What pot of gold?" an incredulous Kyle asked.

"You didn't expect us to just announce it in the saloon did you? Everybody in town would have been out here trying to cash in."

"You mean it's not about the claim?"

"Who needs a claim when the work's already been done? Word is...she's got over sixty pounds of gold inside the cabin, just ripe for the picking."

"Sixty pounds?"

"Twenty pounds apiece...Swear on my mother's grave. You could live high on the hog with twenty pounds of gold, couldn't you, Kyle?"

Rafe could see the wheels turning inside the deputy's head.

"No more answering to Sheriff Cobb...Live where you want. Women, whiskey, you'd live like a king..."

"Three way split? Just you me and yer brother?"

"Absolutely. All I need you to do is sneak up and take a peek inside that side window. We have to know how many are inside and where...You do the easy part...Raff and I will finish 'em off."

Kyle hesitated. Rafe knew exactly how to play him.

"Now if you don't need twenty pounds of gold, I suppose you can just sit here behind this tree. Raff and I can collect thirty pounds each, but I was just being generous, since you rode all the way out here and all."

The thought of losing out on a fortune was more than he could stand. Kyle's head began nodding even before he began to speak. "I'll do it, I'll do it…all I got to do is look in that window and tell you what I see, right?"

"Absolutely, you have my word as a gentleman."

Kyle fought off his fears and let his greed take over. He crawled though the lower vegetation until he was close to the bluff, reached the side of the cabin and then inched up to the window.

Angie had stuck a wooden mixing spoon under the knot and given it a twist above Hank's leg wound, effectively creating a tourniquet—it was lucky the bullet had not struck his femoral artery. The venous bleeding would soon stop. He snuck a peek out the front window as Angie picked up her ten gauge.

"Do you think there's a chance they pulled out? They haven't fired a shot at us in several minutes."

"Not likely," he replied. "I think what they came after is you. Nobody knows I'm here exceptin' yer uncle and that Sixkiller fellow." Hank turned just in time to see Angie's eyes fly open wide with fear. The shotgun rose to her shoulder in the blink of an eye. The blast was deafening inside the cabin.

"What the hell was that all about?" he shouted as his ears rang.

"The window…It was a face I saw in the window!"

Bass turned toward the house at the sound of the shot. In the distance, he could see a body slump to the ground along the north wall. *Bastards almost got in.* Movement caught his eye. He spied the outline of a man crouched behind a tree. He motioned to Jed and pointed in the direction they would move. Jed nodded. Boot took off to the north. Bass let him go and kept his eyes on the well-dressed man as he closed the distance without a sound. Lessons he had learned years earlier living with the Creeks as an escaped slave had not been forgotten. He eased the hammer back on his Winchester '92 until it caught at full cock.

"Freeze, mister. Don't move a muscle."

Rafe was startled by the booming bass voice. His first instinct was to try to use his lightning fast speed to defeat this unseen enemy, as he had always done in the past. But the voice was from behind him and he knew the man already had the drop on him.

"Now stand real slow and turn around...Keep yer hands where I kin see 'em."

Rafe complied—he could not believe his eyes. The very same black marshal that had embarrassed him in front of his men back in Gainesville was glaring at him over the sights of rifle from only ten yards away.

"You be under arrest for attempted murder, and anything else I kin think of before we get yer sorry ass to Fort Smith."

"You'll never live long enough to get me to trial, nigger."

Bass grinned a bit. "You got any idea how many times I heared that one? Here you is...all dressed up fancy and trying to be one of them comedy actors...That is kinda funny, I do declare. If you didn't have another pressin' engagement, you oughta go on the Chautauqua circuit."

"You talk real big when you got the drop on a man. I'll bet you are too yellow to face a real man like me in a fair fight."

"Git your hands up, slick, and keep 'em there...Jed, git over here and make yerself useful, if you would."

"What you want me to do, Bass? Take his gun?"

"Nope, I'm gonna show this here cracker what a man can do in a fair fight...Hold my rifle."

"You ain't gotta do this, Bass. He ain't worth it."

"I know...and that's exactly what I aim to prove to 'im ...directly."

Bass started singing very softly to himself, the old Negro spiritual, Swing Low Sweet Chariot written by by Wallis Willis, a Choctaw freedman before the war. Anyone who knew Bass Reeves was aware of his penchant of singing quietly when he was about to do some shooting and just naturally got ready for it. He pulled the trigger on the rifle and eased the hammer down to the safety notch, then handed it to Jed, butt first. He never took his eyes off the shootist with his hands held high. Jed leaned Bass' rifle against a tree and kept his own '66 pointed at the man with the fancy duds.

He stopped singing. "What's yer name, slick...fer the coroner's record?"

"You should be proud to know, that the man who killed you was called Rafe Sartain...nigger."

Rafe stared up at the taller man and smiled broadly. *No way in hell I can miss something that damned big.* He slowly lowered his hands until the right hovered only inches above the cross draw rig. He tried to make out any expression from the big marshal, but could not detect any emotion whatsoever. His gaze went down to the massive black hand hovering over the worn walnut handle on the single action Colt.

The big man's voice boomed out again, "Make your play Sartain…If'n you got the guts."

Something in the way the man said his name set the blood boiling in the dark-haired man. His hand streaked for the birdshead handle of his six-gun as Bass did the same. Rafe's thumb cocked the hammer before he cleared leather, but a .38-40 cal slug dug into his forehead before he could comprehend what had happened. His eyes went wide and he fell backwards into the greenbriars as his .41 Colt blasted a hole in the bottom of his holster.

"Good God Almighty!" Jed blurted. "I ain't never seen the likes."

Raff Sartain had been running for his horse and was almost to it when he heard the shot. A sharp pain hit him and he stumbled, almost falling to his knees. Somehow, he knew he had not been hit. The pain subsided and suddenly he felt different. He could not explain it, but for the first time in his life, he felt—alone. He heard a low growl and turned to see an old red and white dog with its teeth bared. Raff pulled his revolver and shot the dog in the chest—the wounded animal yelped and fell over. The last living member of the Sartain family grabbed his reins and swung into the saddle.

Selden Lindsay stepped from a thicket and called out, "Bass! You alright?"

"Right as rain. Just gittin' here?"

"Been caught up in the damned briers. I could hear you, but I couldn't get through fast enough."

Just then, Loss came up from the creek trail and looked back up the wagon road leading into the farm from the ridge. He spotted Raff making his break. "Damnation! One of 'em's gittin' away!"

Bass snatched up his rifle from the tree and ran to the roadway. It was clear the rider was close to 300 yards away and would be over the rise in mere seconds.

"Too far," observed Loss.

"Take him, Bass," said Selden calmly.

Reeves thumbed the hammer back and took a fine bead on the small bouncing target. He held over what he estimated to be the correct Kentucky windage and fired.

"Aw, hell…missed," Loss groused as the man continued his escape.

"Nope," Bass said mater-of-factly.

The rider's neck suddenly cocked to one side and then his head started flopping back and forth in an unnatural manner. He tumbled off the horse as it reached the top of the hill.

"Told ya," Bass said with a hint of pride. "Let's go see how the folks in the house are a doin'."

***

CHAPTER TEN

LOG CABIN

"Hello, the house," Marshal Lindsey shouted from the grove of cedar trees on the south side of the yard. "United States Deputy Marshals."

"Show yourselves and keep your hands where I can see them," Angie called back from inside the house. "Easy to say you're marshals…It's some proof I'm needing to see."

Selden, Loss, Bass and Jed walked from behind the trees toward the front gate in the slat board fence. Lindsey opened it and they entered the yard.

"Ma'am, we're lookin' fer a man," said Lindsey.

Angie and Hank exchanged nervous glances.

"Is it wanted by the law ye are?" she asked.

Hank shook his head and shrugged. "No idea."

"Stay put." She took a deep breath and lifted the door latch.

Angie, still holding her shotgun, stepped out on the porch. "That would be far enough. Let me see some badges, if ye will."

Selden was first to remove his hat and open his coat to show the shield affixed to his vest. He was followed by Bass, then Jed and Loss.

Hank stepped out and stood beside her. "Ain't my nature to hide...It gaulds me," he whispered. He had one of his Russians in his right hand and his left held the shillelagh to support himself.

"Jack!" Bass exclaimed.

He stood erect, got a puzzled expression on his face for a moment and then said, "Bass? Jed?...Damn! Good to see you boys. What'd er ya'll doin' here?"

"You know these men?" Angie asked. "He called ye 'Jack'."

"Shore...Bass Reeves, Jed Neal, Selden Lindsey, as I recall and I do believe that'd be Loss Hart. United States Deputy Marshals all...And yes ma'am, I'm Jack McGann, United States Deputy Marshal...goin' on twenty-two years."

"Why didn't ye tell me?"

"Didn't know...'til I seen Bass there. Then everthin' come back in a rush...like it had never been gone. Kinda like a dam bustin'." He looked at Bass and grinned. "Got shot in the head." He pointed to the bandage still protecting the wound. "Fergot who I was, 'til ya'll walked up...Did ya bring Tobe with you?"

Bass looked around. "He was with us just a little bit ago ago. Meby he went lookin' fer..."

Tobe rounded the bend in the road and walked up toward the house. He was carrying Boot's limp body cradled to his chest. Tears stained his face.

"Aw, Boot, no...no..." Jack said.

Tobe came in the yard, walked to the porch and laid Boot down carefully, close to the edge. Boot's brown eyes looked up at Tobe's face with pure unconditional love.

"Bastards shot him..." He stroked his head. Boot licked his hand, his tail thumped twice and then once more on the wooden planks and he was gone. Tobe gently stroked his head again and then looked up at Angie for what seemed like an eternity and finally said to her, "A part of my heart...just died..." His voice cracked and he took a deep breath. "He was my best friend...hung on 'til I found 'em...He knew I would..." He looked back down and continued softly stroking Boot's head. "Wasn't just a dog, you see...He was...he was...Boot...He was Boot." Tobe's body shook with silent sobs.

Bass, Jack and the other marshals, each in his own style, looked away or at the ground in respect for Tobe's sorrow—and maybe to hide their own tears from each other.

Angie knelt beside Boot's body, reached over and embraced Tobe. He tried to choke back the anguish—but to no avail. There was something about a woman's hug.

"I'm so sorry for your loss..." she softly said. "I wasn't blessed to know your Boot, but I can tell he was a wonderful companion," Angie said as Tobe wept unashamedly into her bosom. "I have a sweet-smelling wooden apple box. I'll wrap him in a quilt and we can bury him over by the big oak near the barn. There's some nice flat limestone rocks ye can be making a marker with, if ye wish...I know there's a place in Heaven for the likes of him...Ye'll be seeing him again one day, ye'll see."

Tobe nodded and softly said, "Thank you."

She got up, went inside and came back with a quilt. She helped him carefully wrap Boot in the covering and stood as he patted it.

Bass walked up and put his arm around his shoulders. "I'd consider it an honor to help dig his grave, Tobe."

"I'll make the marker," Jed offered.

Selden and Loss continued to stare at the ground uncomfortably. Each had tears filling his eyes too.

Tobe nodded again. "I need a little time...ya'll don't mind." He turned, walked to the gate and headed down toward the creek. He disappeared around some cottonwoods in the direction of the falls.

"Should someone be with him," Angie asked.

Bass shook his head. "No, ma'am, he needs to deal with this himself. Tobe's a strong man...Boot was like a son to him. He just has to find a place in his heart to store the memory...He'll be alright."

Angie looked over to see Winchester Ashalatubbi and Ben Sixkiller ride up from the road to the fence. They dismounted and came in the yard.

"Sheeah, Angie...Guess we're late. Passed a body on the road coming in. Shot through the neck," said the shaman.

"They came back, uncle, with..."

"We make it eight, Winchester...good to see you and Ben again," said Selden. "Loss an' I were a bit late too. Marshals Reeves, Neal and Bassett took care of business...'long with Angie and Jack."

"Jack?"

"Hank got his memory back all of a sudden when he saw his friend, Bass Reeves. He's Jack McGann, United States Deputy Marshal," Angie answered.

"Hank was my older brother...a marshal too. Saw him in my vision. He was killed near ten year ago...That's why I had that reaction when Angie suggested the name...It was too close to home."

"Bass Reeves? Well, we are in austere company," said Winchester as he shook Bass' hand. "A real pleasure to meet you sir, I'm Anompoli Lawa, Christian name is Winchester Ashalatubbi. Most folks call me Win..."

"The pleasure is mine, 'he who talks with many'. I have great respect for the medicine of the Chickasaw."

Ashalatubbi looked at him with only slight surprise. "You speak our language."

"Close enough. Lived with the Seminoles and then the Creeks for two years."

"Looks like we need to borrow wagon again, Angie...I'm assumin' Marshal's Service will take jurisdiction, Marshal Lindsey?" Sixkiller asked.

Selden nodded. "Save a lot of confrontation, I 'spect. I'll jest deputize you, Ben, to make everythin' legal...If'n it's alright."

"My thought exactly."

Winchester noticed Jack's blood-soaked pant leg. "Looks as though Hank, I mean Jack, managed to collect another bullet."

"Yep, 'fraid so…This 'un is still in there, Doc."

"We'd best go inside…I'm going to have to remove it."

"Somehow I knowed you were gonna say that…"

"Ben, would you get my medical kit from my saddle?"

"Jack, when we git inside, yer gonna have to tell us how you survived that trip down the rapids."

"Bass, that's another story all together…You won't believe it…not sure I believe it my own self."

Tobe walked up the path along Honey Creek until he came to the falls. He found a couch sized boulder on the edge of the large pool, climbed up and took a seat—his dusty boots dangled inches above the crystal clear water. A light breeze blew down the valley, causing a slight ripple to dance across the placid pond. The sound of the water cascading over the distant rocks could barely be heard and soon he was lost in thought.

The elder lawman's tears ran freely as he reminisced about his beloved border collie. He thought about how sad Molly, Nellie Ruth, John L. and the grand children would be to learn of Boot's passing, and the pain seemed to deepen. Tobe pulled his feet up close to his body, crossed his arms over his knees, rested his chin on his arms and slowly rocked back and forth.

After a few minutes, he wiped the tears from his eyes with the back of his hand and a motion out of the corner of his eye caught his attention. He glanced to his right and saw a young blond-headed girl in a faded calico dress standing beside a huge white wolf-dog, watching him from only ten feet away. She had her arm across the big animal's shoulder and looked at Tobe with soft blue eyes for a moment, and then said, "Your puppy is in a better place now...where there is no pain or want. He is forever young and happy...You must let your heart be at peace. He wants it to be so."

He brought both hands to his face to clear the residual moisture from his eyes that seemed to be blurring his vision. When he removed them, she was gone—the white wolf was still standing there. He froze for a second, until he looked into the animal's huge golden eyes. Somehow, he sensed the mighty canine was not a threat. The wolf sat down, cocked his head and raised a paw as if to say hello.

"Hello, there, big boy. What's your name and where did your friend go?" Tobe said as he straightened out his legs and held out an open hand.

Boy responded to his voice by moving closer and jumping up on the rock beside him. He took a massive paw and placed it in his hand. Tobe smiled as the animal lay down beside him and put his head in his lap. Together, they sat in silence and watched as two Red Tailed Hawks circled slowly by overhead, searching for their next meal. *Don't know if this is a dream or what...but, I'm just goin' to sit here and enjoy it...Mayhaps I just imagined the little girl...There's somethin' spiritual about this place,* he thought as he glanced over at the falls tumbling down the side of the mountain to pour into the pool right next to a huge boulder.

"Angie, I'm going to need a sizable amount of boiled water to clean the wound site on Ha...uh, Jack's leg. Would you take care of that for me?" Winchester directed.

"Should I make up the willow elixir for his fever and pain as well?"

"Sure, that's a good idea. He's gonna need something besides this laudanum after it wears off. I've only a partial bottle and we'll need all of it just for the surgery."

She grabbed the porcelain bucket and headed out to the well.

"Jack you'll need to shed those bloody pants before we can get started."

"Guess you want the union suit as well, huh, Doc?" Jack replied.

"Here's a kitchen towel to cover your privates if you tend towards the bashful type."

"Sometimes, a man can use a little privacy," Jack said as he struggled to get his boots off. "Make yerself useful," he said to Bass as he sat down in one of the ladder-back chairs around the table.

"Happy to oblige, partner...you've had yerself a string of bad luck lately," Bass said as he straddled Jack's right leg and pulled on the tight fitting boot.

Jack moaned slightly as the boot came off, as his knee was still a bit sore. "Got that right. Easy on the other one...might be a little blood in it. Angie will be all over us if we get her floor messy."

"It'll clean it up, me knight in shinin' armor...If it weren't for yourself...never would I have made it to the house," Angie said as she came in the back door with the pail of water.

"You were really cuttin' a chody across the yard. Them bushwhackin' buzzards played hob trying to pick you off."

"Be that as it may, I know to thank ye and the good Lord for me blessings today."

Angie poured half the water in a cast-iron Dutch oven and the rest in a tea kettle. She took a couple sticks of split firewood and added them to the firebox on the side of the stove. "Marshall Neal, would ye be so kind as to fetch me a few more sticks of kindling? Don't know how much water the good doctor here might be needing."

"Be my pleasure ma'am," he said as he headed for the door.

Ben Sixkiller stepped in as Jed walked out. "Selden, got team hitched up. Can you and Loss give me hand with bodies? Looks like we have ourselves a wagon full."

"I already sent Loss out to start collectin' their horses and gear. He'll be back in fair soon, I 'spect, but we may as well get started on the ones close by...It's a ways back to town and those stiffs ain't gonna keep. Need to talk to the sheriff and see if he has local paper on any of these ne'er-do-wells. If so, there's the matter of the reward money."

"Not to mention the fact that two of them were wearin' deputy sheriff badges...I smell a rat about this whole business," Bass said.

"Deputies?" Jack asked. "We never saw no badges. It all happened so fast."

"I had never before seen the first man who attacked me," Angie said as she shuddered at the memory of him grabbing her.

"I don't trust that potbellied sheriff any further than I kin throw 'im. Don't need eight people to execute an arrest warrant on a single woman," Selden said. "This looks like a hired killin' to me, plain and simple. Them deputies most likely served as guides to bring the Sartain gang here...And don't forget we know the twins spoke with that shyster lawyer Baldwin yesterd'y...They came to town on a purpose."

Ben nodded agreement, and then headed for the door, followed by Selden. Jed came back in with an armload of firewood and dropped it in the small wooden box next to the stove.

"I'll be out helpin' 'em load up the bodies, Bass. Four folks makes it short work," Jed said as Bass gingerly slipped the second boot off Jack' foot, exposing a bloody sock.

"Good idea, Jed...From the looks of this, Jack, don't think you lost too awful much blood."

"That'd be a first."

Angie turned to see what they were discussing. "Get those socks and pants off! How in thunder do you think I can get them clean once that blood sets?...And the drawers along with 'em."

Jack protested. "But not while you are..."

"Poppycock! Would ye be forgettin' that I've seen your naked self already?...Now off with them, before I do it meself like I did before!"

195

Bass, Jed and Doc all chuckled. Jack tried to protest.

"But I was asleep er unconscious!"

Angie suddenly realized what she had said, and in that Victorian age, women of virtue generally did not see men naked unless they were married. Her hand went to her mouth as she and Jack both turned slightly pink in the face.

Bass broke out in his booming hearty laugh. "You know, in all the years we rid together, don't recall ever seein' you embarrassed afore."

Jack stood up and shucked his suspenders and shirt. He unbuttoned his pants, sat back down and turned to Bass. "A little help here?...While yer restin'."

Bass grabbed the cuffs of the bloody wool pants, tugged them free and handed them to Angie to soak in cold water. Jack began unbuttoning his union suit, and wriggled out of it. He stood there stark naked, with his wounds—both new and old—showing.

"Now is everybody happy?"

Bass grinned. "Is it me, er you jest gettin' grumpy in yer old age?"

Jack threw the kitchen towel at him. His partner caught it and smiled broadly.

"Now what you gonna use to cover up with?"

Winchester interrupted, "All right, all right...let me get to work here. Jack, take a spoonful of this and swallow."

Jack did as he was asked. He grimaced at the taste of the reddish-brown tincture of opium. The liquid contained both morphine and codeine and was extremely bitter. Although it

196

was highly addictive, Doc Ashalatubbi didn't have enough to get the wounded lawman hooked. He poured the last spoonful and signaled for Jack to finish it off. He did, but shook his head, stuck out his tongue and almost gagged.

"My God! Can't see how anybody in their right damn mind would take that crap to get themself giddy."

Bass returned the towel, and Jack sat back down in the chair, draping it over his lap. Angie offered a glass of water from a ceramic pitcher on the counter and a teaspoon of honey.

"Here ye go, ye big baby…it should help wash away the bad taste."

"As soon as the water is hot, I'll clean the wound. May take a while to probe for the bullet. It didn't come out on the inside of your thigh," Doc said as he glanced at the entrance wound. The site was puckered in with dark clotted blood filling the depression. The flesh around the entrance was already bruised and swollen.

"Hey, that's luck for you, Jack," Bass said cheerily.

"How you figure?"

"If the shooter had been any closer, it woulda passed on through…and we'd be diggin' it outta yer other leg an' you'd have three new holes in ya, 'stead of jest one. Haw!"

"Bass, if I wasn't so banged up and you wasn't so dammed big, I'd whup your butt right here, right now."

Bass just grinned and winked at Angie. "Well, meby you'll be good enough to feel up to it in a couple days, but right now, you couldn't lick yer upper lip."

Loss entered the house carrying an armload of rifles and a bunch of gunbelts recovered from the bodies they had found. He stacked the long guns in the corner one by one and piled the gunbelts and six-shooters next to them. "Selden thought you might be needin' 'em more'n the men who brung 'em here...Ben done told us about the other yahoos that tried to blow ya'll up."

"'Preciate it. It's been real...interesting 'round here lately," Jack said as the medicine began to take effect. "I'm smooth outta ammo for the Marlin. If they's any extra for them carbines, I sure would like to borrow it."

"I'll check out their saddle bags...see what I can rustle up. They's some six-gun cartridges left in their gunbelts. What caliber you shootin'?"

".44 Russian...Bet they ain't none of 'em using it."

"You go out of yer way to make it hard on yerself?...Tell ya, what...I'll see if I can scrounge together a couple hoglegs and as many rounds as we can lay our hands on. I 'member the twins both used matching .41 Colts..."

"Didn't do 'em much good...did it, Loss?" Bass interrupted.

"From the looks of things, I'd say no."

"Cocky little roosters. All hat an' no cattle," Bass added.

"Tell me, Jack. Are you starting to feel woozy?" asked Doc.

"Dunno...I've been kinda woozy off and on for the last week er so... ain't I Angie?...Kinda hard to tell the difference."

She turned from her task of peeling the bark off the handful of willow branches and lay down the paring knife. "Aye, he took a mighty clout to that thick noggin of his."

"Good thang it was his head...any other place an' it might of killed him." Bass grinned.

"Ain't nothin' I'd wanta repeat, I kin tell you that...And all this time, I thought you liked me, lassie."

"Oh, but I do, Hank...I mean, Jack...I do." She smiled.

Doc frowned. "Have you already forgotten that I treated you a few days ago? Ready for another vision quest in the spirit lodge?"

"Oh, no...I'm doin' fine...but now that you mention it, I may be gettin' a little...what'd you call it?"

"Woozy...Let's see how your pupils are doing."

"Ain't got no pupils. Never been no school marm." Jack smiled at what he thought was a joke.

Doc pulled back one of Jack's lids and looked at the fairly dilated center, followed quickly by checking the other eye. "Coming along nicely...About four minutes to go. How's the water, Angie?"

She lifted the lid on the kettle with a oven pad and set it aside. "Starting to bubble...we would be close."

"In that case, I ask you other men move outside. We don't want to risk infection and this is no hospital, after all...I'll need all the lamps you have, Angie. I'll also want a wash pan to sterilize my tools in, too when the water is at full boil."

She nodded and started collecting all the coal oil lanterns in the house to bring close to the bed.

"We'll help Ben and Jed finish loadin' the wagon," Loss said.

"Take it easy, pard...looks like yer in good hands," Bass said as he placed his big hand on Jack's shoulder.

Jack smiled a crooked smile as he sat back, slightly slumping in the chair. Suddenly out of nowhere, he began a rousing rendition of Stephen Foster's classic song, "Waaay down upon the Suwanneeeeee river...far, far awayyy..."

Bass winked at Doc and whispered, "'Bout as close to bein' drunk as he'll ever get as a teetotaler."

"Before you go, help me get him into the bed before he's completely out."

Each got on either side, helped him stand with considerable effort, and shuffled him over to the bed. Doc laid him on his right side as Jack kept on singing. The Chickasaw shaman and physician nodded knowingly and grinned. Bass and Loss headed outside, both of them chuckling at the off-key rendition.

Once outside the whitewashed slat fence, the two saw Ben and the wagon coming out of the woods past the barn with Selden following. He was mounted on a horse they did not recognize—two other horses were trailing behind. Lindsey led the riderless mounts into the open corral by the barn and turned them loose before closing the gate. Ben stepped down from the wagon seat and started to walk over to Deputy Kyle's body next to the house.

"Where'd you find them cayuses?" Bass asked Selden.

"Up the creek a ways."

"Musta been the three we trailed from up by the falls," Bass said as he climbed over the hand-hewn rails in the enclosure to help Lindsey strip the tack from the horses. "Recognize the owners?"

"Naw. Prob'ly came from down south…One thing kinda strange…there were three horses, but only two bodies out past the barn."

"You think one got away?"

"Unlikely. There was a mess of blood down by the creek. Seen some big tracks there that dang sure weren't human…Wadn't no cat, neither. Musta been wolf."

"That's odd…Lone wolf sticking around here with all this commotion goin' on? Better keep our eyes open, boys."

"I'm heading up to the north end of the valley to pick up my horse and see if I can catch the one from the Sartain you picked off…Still cain't git over that shot," Selden said, shaking his head.

"Jesus, Mary and Joseph…speak of the devil," Bass said as he spotted Tobe coming from the direction of the falls, being trailed by a giant white wolf. He drew his pistol and said softly, "Tobe, freeze right where you are and don't move a muscle." Bass eased his six-shooter to eye level and aimed just past Tobe's elbow.

"No!" Tobe said as he moved over in front of Bass' line of fire and held up his hands. "He's friendly."

Ben was headed back toward the wagon with Kyle's body over his shoulder and took in the scene. "That is Nashoba Tohbi, Jack's wolf-dog, Bass. He Chickasaw sacred spirit animal. Jack call him 'Boy'."

"Huh…didn't know Jack had a dog. Didn't have one when he left Fort Smith."

"Mister Jack told us spirit wolf took up with him when he first hit Arbuckles. Been with him ever since."

"Why is he a spirit wolf?" asked Loss.

"He sees and talks with spirits of dead…All white animals sacred to Chickasaw because of this."

"Right," said Loss with a look of disbelief.

"Oh, my sweet Jesus," remarked Tobe as he stared at Ben.

"What?"

"Seen a little blond-headed child beside him when I first saw 'im, Bass…leastwise thought I did…She even talked to me. When I looked again…she was gone. Figured I musta been dreamin'."

"That would be Anna. Angie's child lost in falls near two years ago," said Ben.

"Come again?" asked Tobe.

"She restless spirit…save Jack's life. He see an' talk with her several times…You must be special person too, Tobe Bassett. Only special people allowed to see spirits. She must have sensed anguish in your heart over loss of Boot and sent Nashoba Tohbi to be with you."

Boy looked up at Tobe for a moment, then padded toward the cabin, jumped over the fence and laid down on the porch.

"Well, reckon they done a good job…I'll always miss my Boot, but she told me he was in a wonderful place now and not to grieve."

"She'll be ridin' six white horses when she comes…She'll be ridin' six whi…" Jack paused again in his serenade as the potent mixture of medications took their effect. He fell back on the flattened feather pillow and his eyes rolled up in his head again.

The shaman tied a folded layer of white cotton bandage across his nose and mouth and motioned Angie closer. She held a lamp close to Jack's leg as Anompoli Lawa wiped away the excess blood and began to fish deep into the wound with his surgical probe.

Jack suddenly raised his head and said with a big grin, "Whooo boy, that smarts." He passed out again, still with a silly smile on his face.

"He seems mighty happy, considerin' all ye are doing to that open wound."

"Be grateful his is a gentle soul," the doctor said as he gingerly took the slender steel probe and attempted to follow the path of the gunman's bullet. The rounded end of the instrument prevented it from digging into undamaged tissue. He skillfully manipulated the handle to follow the path of least resistance in the ragged channel torn in Jack's thigh. Suddenly the probe struck something solid with a muted *click*, and the experienced country physician knew it was not the femur bone.

"Found it," said Winchester without moving the probe or looking up. "Hand me those forceps, Angie."

She reached over with her other hand, pulled the long needle-nosed forceps from the sterilizing pan and placed them in his palm like he had shown her how to do.

He followed the probe down deep into Jack's leg until it also touched the bullet. Winchester slowly pulled the bloody probe out, opened the forceps and then closed them down, locking the jaws around the projectile. Very slowly, he backed the instrument out of the three inch deep puncture until the .44 caliber ball came into view. He looked at it carefully under Angie's lamp, turned and dropped it into the pan with a *clang*.

"Well, we're, or should I say, Jack was lucky. The ball didn't fragment and no major veins were cut...Just going to be sore as hell for a while." He washed the leg down with rubbing alcohol, then wiped the entire area with tincture of iodine. "You know, Angie, let's pack the wound with some of your turpentine and tallow balm. From what I've seen on his other wounds, that stuff works better than anything I've got in my kit."

"It was me grandmother that taught me how to make it back in Castletown, Ireland. Works on everything from cuts to insect bites, it does."

"You'll have to make up a batch for me. I often question the apothecary companies' product efficacy. They seem to want to confuse the results with the price."

She nodded as she handed him the jar and then laid out the bandages to wrap his leg.

"Already seems to be clotting well, but if the bandages do start to soak through, go ahead and change the dressing. Otherwise, don't do anything for forty-eight hours. That will give the clot time to set."

"Uhhh…Say, Doc, when you gonna start?" Jack said as he raised his head.

"Finished, Jack. All done."

"All done?…All done? I wanted to watch…never seen a bullet bein' dug out afore…Shoulda woke me. Dang! I wouldn't do that to ya'll…" He glanced up at Angie. "You shore are purty." Then he looked hard at Winchester. "But yer not." He shook his head twice before he passed out again.

"Methinks he'll be apologizing when he wakes up for such rude talk."

"Not very likely, I would surmise. He won't remember a thing from the time we laid him on the bed until the laudanum wears off…Trust me," Winchester said with a grin.

Ben Sixkiller bent over and filled his hands with some loose topsoil and rubbed it briskly across his bloody palm surfaces as small black and green blow flies circled around, trying to get access to the sticky red mixture. "Miz O'Reilly said there's another one down by trail to creek. First man that attacked her…can you men give me hand?…Too tight for wagon."

"You bet," Tobe said.

He and Jed fell in behind him to pick up the last of the bodies lying close to the cabin. A minute later, they came upon the bloody body of Carson Hatcher—Angie's kitchen shears still embedded in his hip joint. Jed placed his boot on the dead man and grabbed the black enamel handles. With considerable effort, they came free. He wiped the blood from the curved blades on Carson's shirt.

"Still good as new...*waste not, want not,* the good book says."

"Still need to wash 'em off and oil 'em good or they'll rust up. Sumthin' 'bout blood and steel that jest makes things want to rust," Tobe replied.

Ben picked up the man's six-shooter and stuck it in his gunbelt. He noticed the jagged canine teeth marks on his throat and the unnatural position of his head. "White man anger Ababinili...send spirit wolf to protect woman."

Tobe noted the animal tracks leading to and from the body. "All I have to say is, Jack should be thankful for that Boy of his. Angie, too...He's special, all right."

Jed, the largest and strongest of the three lawmen, grabbed Carson up under his arms. Ben and Tobe each took a leg and they moved him up the hill and stacked him inside the wagon bed.

Jed spoke as the pair of mules began to fidget, "That team don't take to kindly to the cargo."

"Nope." Tobe chuckled. "Reckon they're used to a better class of people."

Sixkiller, who normally didn't show much emotion, grinned at the small joke.

"We still gotta round up our horses," Jed noted.

Tobe looked up the road to the silhouettes of Seldon and Bass riding the opposite direction to do the same. "Yep, it's about all over but the shoutin'...as the sayin' goes."

The three turned and headed back up the trail toward the falls.

Bass exited the woods leading four horses—the back three tied to the tail of the one in front in Indian style—to the wagon road. Selden led three mounts, including his own.

"Gonna have to ask the Judge for an extra allowance for wrangler duty."

"Really think he'd spring for it?" Bass laughed.

"Sure...there's always a chance..."

"Slim and none, by my estimatin'," Bass replied as he moved to tie off the lead horse.

"You know Parker well as me...hear he can squeeze a nickel 'til the buffalo craps."

"Sounds more likely than a wrangler allowance, I'd wager."

Both men mounted up and rode past the fly-covered body of Raff Sartain. His dark eyes were open, blankly staring sightlessly at the clear blue sky overhead—his head was cocked at an odd angle. Neither man stopped, as the wagon would be along to pick him up for transport to Ardmore.

"All dressed up nice for his funeral," Bass noted as he let fly a stream of tobacco juice that landed near the man's dusty boots.

Selden nodded. "I stopped wonderin' a long time ago about what makes men do what they do."

"Makes no damned sense to me...how many men died trying to get that young widder off her place. An' that's not countin' her husband...Somebody got a heap of greed in 'em...all I got to say."

"Uh huh…Just like those Dalton scum we're after. If they worked as hard tryin' to earn a livin' as they do tryin' to steal…"

Bass smiled and nodded. "An' we would both be out of a job!"

"Got a point there, Marshal Reeves…Hold on there…think I see somethin' up a hunderd yards on the right…Looks like a sorrel mare down by the creek. Five'll git you ten it's the dead man's pony."

"She didn't run far with him off her back."

"Probably hungry and thirsty."

"I could use me a drink myself…and this canteen is about dry, anyhow."

The two men closed in on the mare, then split up, one on each side. Selden sidled up to the grazing horse talking softly to her then casually reached for the reins.

"I got her if you want to get that drink."

Bass dismounted and pulled the canteen off the saddle horn. He eased closer to the creek, keeping a sharp eye out for water moccasins. Uncorking the cloth-covered galvanized canteen, he poured out the remaining tepid water and submerged it into a clear eddy behind a boulder. Once it filled, he stood and took a long draw of the cold refreshing liquid. He refilled the container and replaced the cork.

It was then he noticed the dark figure of a body wedged between two large rocks downstream about forty yards. He almost spit out the last couple drops of water lingering on his tongue. *Jesus! What the Sam Hill is that?*

He turned and walked back to the horse and looped the canteen strap around the horn. "Sel, hate to say it, but there's another body in the creek down by the causeway."

"Any idea whose?"

"Nope...guess I gotta get my boots wet and see."

"Want me to hold your coat?"

"Be all right. Creek shallows out some here 'bouts. That's how come the body got hung up on those rocks."

Selden untied his lariat tied to the front of his rigging. "Here you go...we got three ropes, don't need but two. Should be able to drag the body out."

"Good idea," Bass said as he pulled the rope off of Sartain's saddle and tied the two ends together with a square knot.

Selden walked his horse downstream and up to the creek bank. Bass handed him the honda and noose end of the joined ropes and Lindsey slipped it over his saddle horn, and then pulled up the slack.

The tall black man fed out a little coiled line at a time as he waded out into the spring-fed water. *Damn that's cold.* Bass thought as the water topped his boots and ran inside. Luckily, the creek was wider there and, therefore, relatively shallow though still swift. In short order, he made it to the body and slipped the lasso over the man's arm and neck and then jerked it taught.

"You got it!" he called back to Selden.

Lindsey bumped his reins and the own son of Black tucked his nose to his chest and backed away from the creek in a straight line until he had pulled the man up on the near bank as

Bass waded ashore. Selden relaxed the reins and nudged Dan forward, creating some slack and quickly removed the running noose from the horn. "Any idea who it is?" he called to Bass.

"Don't know the name, but he was one of the galoots on the train comin' up from Gainesville with the Sartain brothers…Recognize the skinny chin and pencil mustache?"

"I do. Reckon he makes it nine…Don't recall the throat being all torn out like that, though."

Bass untied the two ropes and slipped the lariat off the body and examined the man's wounds—although torn and ragged, the moving water had washed away the blood. He simply shook his head. "That wolf of Jack's musta been real busy today."

Selden pulled in his rope, looping it in eighteen inch coils to tie back onto his saddle. "As the preacher man says, 'The Lord works in mysterious ways'."

"Amen to that, brother…Amen to that."

***

CHAPTER ELEVEN

ELK, I.T.

Bill Dalton, Big Asa, Jim Knight and George Bennet rode their tired and flagging mounts past the small hamlet of Elk, known after the turn of the century and statehood as Poolville, Oklahoma. Houston Wallace's log cabin lay some three miles north in the deep woods on the southern edge of the Arbuckles. It was difficult to tell who was the most tired, the horses or the men. They were out of water and hadn't eaten in two days.

"Damn, I'm so hungry I could eat the ass end out of a leather duck," moaned Big Asa.

"'Spect the womenfolk will be able to rustle up a feed when we git to Houston's. It's jest over that rise yonder in front of us...Reckon you kin hold out for another twenty minutes er so without fallin' out of the saddle, Asa?" said Bill.

"I'll manage," he answered with a forced grin.

"Me, I'm worn to a frazzle. Think I could sleep fer a week," muttered an exhausted Jim.

"Well, 'fore I lay down an' 'fore I eat, I gotta doctor my butt. Even my blisters got blisters," said George.

Bill just shook his head. "Don't think I've ever seen a more whiny bunch of peckerwoods in my life. Here we got a satchel full of money an' all I hear is…"

"Looky there! Kin see the smoke from the chimney over the trees yonder," interrupted Jim as he pointed excitedly at the ridge line.

The four men crossed the plowed ground south of the homestead that laid alongside Russell Pretty Branch Creek and rode into the clearing with a small unpainted barn and the Wallace brother's log cabin. Three pre-teenage children playing in the yard noticed the riders approaching.

"Daddy!" a skinny twelve year old girl yelled, and then jumped up from her game of jacks and started running toward the men.

Bill slid from the saddle and swept the brown-haired girl in his arms. "Hi, baby girl, miss me?"

The youngster wrapped her arms around him and squeezed him as tightly as she could. "You know I did, Daddy…and don't call me *baby* no more. I'm almost growed."

"I kin see that. You musta grown two inches whilst we wuz gone…Gracie."

"Oh, Daddy."

Three women in faded cotton house dresses rushed out of the cabin. Two of them ran toward the men—a pregnant one in her early thirties stayed on the porch, the back of her hand to her mouth and her eyes began to fill with tears.

Bill put his daughter down, removed his hat and slowly walked up to the woman on the porch. He could not bear to look the her in the eyes, but delivered the grim news staring at his feet.

"Erlene, I'm real sorry...Jim...well, he didn't make it. He... uh, got shot in Longview. He wa..."

Erlene Wallace screamed in utter despair and sank to her knees, sobbing. Houston Wallace's wife, Maude, ran to her sister-in-law to offer comfort.

Jennie Dalton, Bill's wife, walked up next to him, her arms crossed around her bosom. "Well, Bill Dalton, I hope it was worth it," she said as she watched Erlene sob.

"Honey, we done got enough to git us back to California...an' then some."

Houston Wallace came striding over from the barn—he was a big man, over two hundred and fifty pounds with a full dark beard. He noticed Erlene being comforted by his wife and quickly guessed the reason. "Where did Jim git it?"

"Longview," Bill answered solemnly.

"Quick?"

Bill nodded. Houston's weather-worn face changed little. He was not the kind to go for any visible show of emotion.

"Imagine ya'll 'er hungry..." He turned his back to Bill and spoke to the children, "You kids go on and see to them horses.

Looks like they could use some grub too…Give 'em a good brushin' down, they need it."

"Ya'll come on in the house, got some squirrel stew on the stove. I can fry up some hot water corn bread. Coffee's on too," said Jennie. She turned and walked back toward the house. "I'll fry up a chicken for supper. But, we're almost out of everything."

"Honey, you, Maude and Wallace can go into Ardmore tomorrow and pick up some supplies. Got a list of things I need you to git, too," Bill said. He stepped back to his horse and retrieved the canvas bag from his saddle that had First National Bank of Longview printed on the side, and then followed his wife and the others into the house.

LOG CABIN

Ben and Winchester sat on the seat of Angie's wagon out in front of the fence, their horses tied behind—Ben was on the reins. On horseback to the rear of the two Chickasaw ponies, Selden and Loss were nearest to the house.

Jack sat in a rocker on the porch, flanked by Bass, Jed, Tobe, Angie and Boy.

"Wish we could stay fer supper, Angie. Need to git these bodies to undertaker Appollas' so's Doc Gibson kin look 'em over 'fore they git too ripe. Danged blow flies 'er already gittin' some kinda fierce," said Selden. "We'll come back out tomorrow and get Montford…It would be disrespectful to put his remains in the wagon with these highbinders an' curly wolves…Ya'll need 'nythin'?"

"Need a couple boxes of .45-70 fer my Marlin an' I'm needin' me some chaw. Plum ou…"

"You can bring him his bullets…but I'll not have that nasty stuff in me house, Jack McGann." Angie tapped her foot as she looked down at Jack who ducked his head.

"Yessum…don't know what I was thinkin'. Musta temporarily lost my memory agin."

Bass, Tobe and Jed nudged one another and grinned.

"You can bring him some stick candy if he has to have something…I said me piece…Now I'd be needin' a jug of turpentine to make me healing balm for Uncle Winchester."

"We kin do that, ma'am…Ben, let's head thataway." Selden tipped his hat, wheeled Dan about and led out to the north, followed by Loss.

Ben snapped the reins across the rumps of the mules. "Come up there, boys." They followed the two marshals out to the road.

"Remember, Jack. No walking on that leg for two days," Anompoli Lawa yelled over his shoulder as the wagon disappeared behind the trees shrouding the road.

"Well, you heard the good doctor, boys. Reckon ya'll will have to carry me and my chair back in the house…Over to the fireplace, you don't mind."

Bass and Tobe looked at each other, picked up Jack, chair and all and turned him facing the wall next to the door.

"We'll come back out and get you 'bout supper time…meby," said Tobe.

Angie grinned, opened the door and led the procession inside. Jed closed and latched it when they were all in.

"Hey, come on now. This ain't right...Uh...my leg is startin' to pain some...Ahhh..." He waited a moment. "Hello...Kin ya'll hear me?"

"I mind you'll jest have to cowboy up 'til supper time, Jack," Bass yelled through the door.

"Damnation!"

"How long should we leave him out there?" asked Tobe.

"'Til he quits whinin'," answered Bass.

"Faith and it's glad I am you are all friends. It's not on your bad side I'd want to be."

"Jack and I have been partners for nigh on to twenty year, Miss Angie...He would do the same to me, he had the chance...If'n we didn't leave him out there fer a spell to stew, he'd go to pettin' his self...Ain't inclined to put on 'ny pity glasses."

Jack looked down at Boy sitting beside his chair. "Looks like it's just me and you, son."

Boy got up, jumped off the porch, cleared the fence and headed to the barn.

"Well, if that don't kill the corn ankle high."

Ben pulled the mules to a stop at the body of Raff Sartain. He, Selden and Loss got down and walked to the body, Ben at the head with Selden and Loss at the feet.

"Hell of a shot…Hell of a shot," said Loss as he looked at the exit wound that took out the center of Raff's throat.

"Hold on. Let me go through his pockets 'fore we throw him on the pile," said Selden as he knelt down and started going through Sartain's clothing. He handed Loss the Colt Thunderer that was still in the holster. "Hmm, wad of paper money…ten Double Eagles…watch…hello."

"What is it, Sel?" asked Loss.

"Telegram," he said as he unfolded the yellow flimsy that was in the upper inside pocket in the man's frock coat. "Well, well, well, talk about the pot at the end of the rainbow…"

"What's it say?" asked Winchester.

"Let ya'll read it in town. Let's git him atop the rest of 'em an' move out…Stink is gittin' worst by the minute. We kin go through the rest of the bunch's pockets at the undertaker's."

"I see some wild mint around that seep down by the creek," said Winchester as he pointed. "Why don't ya'll gather a bunch and throw it on top of the corpses? Won't last all the way to town, but we can keep a handful to crush and rub under our noses."

"Dang, never thought of that," said Loss. "Learn somethin' ever day."

ARDMORE, I.T.

The sun was dipping low in the sky as Selden pulled his timepiece from his vest pocket. He touched the well-worn spring release on the pocket watch cover. *Already 4:45,* he

thought as he glanced at the face. "Loss, better go ride ahead
and make sure Doc Gibson knows we're comin'."

"I'll drop by the undertaker's place as well. These boys are
already in purty bad shape."

"They'll sure enough be earnin' their fee on this bunch of
cutthroats…Kinda glad I'm not in that line of work."

Loss nodded, and then spurred his horse into a gentle lope.
He soon passed the first houses on the northern outskirts of
town, leaving the slow-moving wagon well behind. Town's
people waved as he passed by, and hurried to get to the office
before the doctor disappeared in some unknown direction.

He reined up outside and quickly dismounted as a young mother
left the front door of the frame building—her eight year old son
sporting a new cast on his left forearm and a white cotton sling
tied around the boy's neck.

"Just wait 'til your father gets home, you hard-headed smart
aleck. How many times have I told you to stay out of that tree?"

Loss noticed the puffy eyes of the youngster and figured the
pain of the boy's fracture would likely have sufficed as a
punishment. He tipped his hat at he passed them on the new
boardwalk. "Evening ma'am. Doc's still inside, I take it?"

"Why, yes he is, Marshal. But he's fixin' to head home for
supper directly."

"Got some business that might make his dinner have to
wait."

She looked at him curiously and watched as he entered the
building in a bit of a hurry.

Several minutes later, a crowd had gathered around the wagon being driven down Ardmore's Main Street. Word had spread rapidly about nine bodies being brought in at one time by the US Marshals. Curious onlookers ran alongside and tried to make out who the bodies were. Riders followed behind and gawked at the grotesque scene. Several young boys called out to Selden.

"Hey, Marshal! Are them desperadoes? Where did you git 'em? Are they famous outlaws?"

He motioned for them to stay back. "Go on! Ya'll don't need to be a seein' this…Stay back."

His protests went unheeded. Finally, Ben pulled up in front of the undertaker's office. Loss, Doc Gibson and Marston Appollas, the undertaker, were already standing near the door. Behind the trio were Marson's assistants—two young colored men in long white coats.

"Whoa up there, boys." Ben set the brake and looped the reins around the lever.

"Well, gentlemen, I suppose we should get started," Appollas said to the two behind him.

LOG CABIN

"Ya'll woulda left me out there all night if Angie hadn't a made you bring me in, wouldn't ya?" grumbled Jack just before he took a big forkful of mashed potatoes.

"Naw…had to have the room on the porch…that's where Bass, Jed and I 'er gonna bed down. Angie said she was gonna

219

make us up some pallets." Tobe picked up his glass of tea and took a sip.

"It's being so mild out, thought you might sleep better on the porch."

"That was some fine fried chicken, Miss Angie. You need to give me your breadin' recipe so's I kin give it to my Nellie Jennie. She's always lookin' fer new ways of cookin'," said Bass.

"I expect it's the same as hers, except that it would be buttermilk and eggs instead of sweetmilk and eggs I use to soak in before rolling in flour and spices."

"Lawdy, lawdy, Miss Angie, it does a man's innards good, to have fixin's like this," Jed said as he started to push away from the table.

"Now, you'd not be getting up before you've had a slice of me pecan pie, would you?"

Jed instantly pulled himself back up to the table with a big grin. "Alway kin make room fer pecan pie…that's my favorite."

"Mine too," said Bass as he sopped up the last of the sawmill gravy on his plate to make room for a slice of pie.

"Think I've put on a pound er two in the short time I've been eatin' her cookin'," offered Jack as he too cleaned his plate for a slice.

"Think it's been mor'n a pound er two, Jack. Believe I threw my back out of whack pickin' up you an' yer chair…You best git well in a hurry if'n you think we're gonna be a carryin' you around…better think agin," added Tobe.

"While you gentlemen are having your pie, it's your pallets I'll be making out on the porch...I've put a fresh pot of coffee on for after dinner," she said as she headed to the door with an armload of quilts, blankets and pillows. There was a scratching sound just as she reached for the latch.

"Bless Paddy, that would be Boy back from his roaming... know his scratch anywhere...Got better manners that some people I know." She glanced over her shoulder at the men as she let him inside and stepped out on the porch. "You'd be giving him some of the table scraps, I'm askin', while I lay out your bedding," she said through the open door.

"Yessum. We can handle that," said Tobe.

ARDMORE, I.T.

Doc Gibson stepped back from the last body, Deputy Kyle Ratcliff, pulled down the peppermint oil anointed white cotton surgical mask he had over his mouth and nose. He turned and nodded to Marston Appollas that he and his assistants could prepare the final body for burial. Marshals Lindsey and Hart were adding Kyle's personal effects to the basket and making notations in a notebook.

"Well, that should do it, Marshal. Other than the two that expired as a result of blood loss from massive trauma to their throats by some wild animal, all the rest were the result of various types of gunshot wounds," Doc Gibson said as he walked over to the basin to wash his hands.

"'Peers as though we need to have a little come to Jesus meetin' with Sheriff Cobb in the mornin' 'bout his deputies," observed Selden.

"I'm betting we kin ketch him at Sally's Restaurant 'round eight er nine. He goes there ever mornin' fer breakfast, coffee and politickin'," said Loss.

LOG CABIN

Sometime just after midnight, the sky started flashing back to the southwest with jagged streaks of lightning followed by rolling peals of thunder in seven or eight seconds. Bass rolled over, opened one eye and caught glimpses of towering thunderheads silhouetted in the inky sky as the lightning started arcing across the heavens continuously. The anvil of the mature cumulonimbus spread out like a gigantic mushroom in the stratosphere. Suddenly, an onrush of cool air from the outflow of the storm cell down-draft whistled through the trees and ruffled the top blanket on his pallet. A brilliant white bolt of energy crashed into a tall oak tree near the top of Turner Falls, splintering the three foot thick trunk and sending a clap of thunder rolling like a cannon shot down the valley. Bass abruptly sat upright, his eyes flung wide open by the sight and sound.

"Uh oh," he said. "Looks like we got us a real doozy a comin', fellers."

Tobe raised up on an elbow and looked to the southwest. "Damn, Bass, yer gittin' observant in yer old age. I mind we're gonna have to head to the bar…"

Lantern light from inside suddenly streamed out onto the porch as Angie opened the door. "Methinks ye gentlemen should bring your pallets inside. I know this kind of storm and outside is not a place ye'd be wanting to be."

"Yessum, you don't have to ask twice. Think this is goin' to be a real frog strangler," said Jed as he got up and rolled up his bedding.

"There'll be room by the fireplace next to Boy. He'll not be minding...I hope."

They had decided to wait out the storm with coffee and some scones Angie had baked earlier and listen to Jack's accounting of events since he came into the Arbuckles on his undercover assignment. The racket made by the rain pounding on the tin roof and the frequent crashes of thunder made sleep impossible. Sitting around the fireplace—as the extended rain storm put a decided chill in the air—seemed to be the wisest decision. The fire would occasionally hiss with water dripping past the flue down onto a burning log.

"...an' so that's purty much the story of the bushwhackin' an' Montford gittin' killed, an' then my little excursion down the rapids."

Bass interrupted Jack, "You knew the falls was comin' up then?"

He nodded his head and looked incredulously at Bass. "Oh, hell yeah...Meant to worry about it, but didn't have the time...Seems like it all kinda run together, leastwise what I kin remember of it...an' then me lying there talkin' to Anna." He turned and gave a gentle look to Angie. She extended her hand and Jack took it tenderly in his.

"Gotta say she and Boy saved my life...Still don't understand what she meant about not bein' allowed to say who she was...er do anythin' more'n help," Jack finished the story and took a sip from his cup. "Even the vision quest in the sweat lodge didn't help none on that part...Never believed in haints, ghosts er spirits...'til now."

"That makes two of us...I got the sense when she talked to me, that everythin' was gonna work out all right...She seemed powerful attached to Boy," Tobe offered.

Boy looked up at Tobe and cocked his head, then looked at Jack.

"It's almost as if he could talk," Angie said.

Boy immediately gave a short woof.

"Mayhaps he can," said Jack with a grin.

ARDMORE, I.T.

The sun broke bright and clear as it often does after a good nighttime rainstorm. The numerous red and white oak trees that lined the streets of Ardmore still dripped with moisture and the constantly changing repertoire of the mockingbirds and other feathered songsters dominated the sweet smelling air.

Marshals Lindsey and Hart made their way from their office to Sally's Restaurant just a little over a block from the courthouse—Selden carried a small brown paper sack.

Loss opened the glass-paned door, ringing a small brass bell attached to the header. The room was crowded with mostly business men in suits, eating breakfast or drinking coffee—a few farmer or rancher types in town for supplies were scattered around. Four middle-aged waitresses scurried about from the kitchen to the tables with either coffee pots or steaming trays of freshly cooked bacon, thick slabs of ham and eggs with biscuits or stacks of pancakes. Selden spied Sheriff Cobb—with a clean white hospital-type sling for his right arm—at a large round table near the center of the room holding court with some of Ardmore's more affluent merchants. Cobb set down his coffee cup.

"Gentlemen, as I see it..." He noticed Lindsey and Hart moving toward his table. "Marshals! Good morning, you're out and about early...Have a seat and join us for coffee...Lorraine." He motioned to one of the servers.

"Think we'll pass," said Selden as he reached in the paper bag and pitched two nickel plated deputy sheriff badges on the table beside the sheriff's plate—one was almost half covered with brown spots. "Recognize these?"

Cobb glanced up at Marshal Lindsey then back down at the badges before he picked one up with his good hand and held it out in front of his face. "Appears to be a couple of my deputy badges...don't know about the speckles. How did you come about with them, if you don't mind my askin', Marshal?"

"Took 'em off the bodies of Jones and Ratcliff over to Marston Appollas' undertakin' parlor...at least we think it was Ratcliff...Most of his face had been blown off with a ten gauge...Messy business, very messy business..."

"Oh, them brown spots on that one badge yer a holdin'…'er called blood spatter, Sheriff," Loss added.

Sheriff Cobb's face turned a pasty white as he quickly dropped the badge back on the table and several of the business men also paled, got up and hurriedly excused themselves. The remaining men glanced at each other then at Cobb.

"I'm, uh, sure I don't understand, Marshal."

"Well, it seems that your deputies were killed along with seven ne'er-do-wells *all the way* from down Fort Worth way out on the widder O'Reilly's place. Seems they were harassin' the widder agin'. Seems they run into a buzz saw an' all got themselves kilt. An' seems that meby you'd learn to leave the good widder alone 'fore you run completely out of deputies…an' hands," Selden said as he looked at the Sheriff's broken arm.

"An' seems a bit strange that yer deputies were consortin' with hired killers from a hunderd miles away…don't it?" offered Loss as he picked up a biscuit from Cobb's plate and took a bite.

Milo cast a disparaging eye on Hart as he continued to eat the biscuit. "As I said before, Marshals. I'm sure I don't understand…What my deputies do on their own time is no affair of mine."

"Oh…so they were both off duty *all* day yesterd'y, were they?" asked Lindsey.

"An' wearin' their badges, were they?" chimed in Hart. "Off duty?"

Cobb began to turn beet red. "Are you accusing me of impropriety of office or somethin', Marshal?"

"Oh, certainly not, Sheriff…If we accuse you of *anythin'*, I guarandamntee you that you'll know about it," said Selden loud enough that everyone in the restaurant heard it.

"Oh, yes, sir, you'll know about it all right. Yesindeedy, you'll know about it…No question," added Loss with a big grin.

Marshal Lindsey scooped up the badges from the table and put them back into the bag. "Evidence." He smiled at the stunned Cobb, turned and headed back toward the door. Marshal Hart grabbed another biscuit from Cobb's plate and followed.

The two federal marshals headed back in the direction of their office. Selden turned to Loss when they were out of sight of Sally's. "Loss, why don't you step inside Marquis Furniture store here and tail the good sheriff when he leaves the restaurant?"

"Dollar to a donut, he goes straight to that shyster's office."

"No bet. 'Spect we'll all want to know how long he stays in there though."

Marshal Hart nodded, turned and opened the door to the furniture store and stood just inside watching through the big plate glass window as Selden continued toward the office. He didn't have long to wait as no more than three minutes later, Sheriff Milo Cobb passed by on the sidewalk. Loss waited a short minute and eased out of the store behind the still agitated lawman.

Three blocks further down Main Street, Cobb entered the downstairs lobby door of the two-story Baldwin Building. Loss stayed in the opposite side of the street and sat down on a bench in front of the Parker Boarding House. *Uh huh, that wasn't much of a stretch...come straight here.* He unfolded the morning newspaper he had picked up and started reading—keeping one eye on the front door of the building.

Hillary Kerry opened the door to Baldwin's inner sanctum and stuck her head just inside. "Sheriff Cobb to see you, Mr. Baldwin."

"Send him in and bring us some coffee, would you?" He spun his chair around and picked up the crystal decanter from the credenza behind his desk.

"Right away, Mr. Baldwin...You may go in now, Sheriff," the dowdy woman said as she opened the door wide.

"Well, Cobb, I assume everything went as projected with our little project," the lawyer said as the door closed behind the sheriff.

"I, uh, I'm afraid you assume wrong, Baldwin. I just found out that that hell cat out there sent nine bodies back to town in a wagon...including both my deputies and yer hotshot shootists last night. They're all over at Appollas' being prepared fer burial as we speak...by my count, that makes twelve altogether."

The affect of the news on Baldwin was immediate. His eyes narrowed to mere slits as the veins on his temples began to

228

throb. "My God! She's starting to make Lizzie Borden look like a Sunday school teacher."

"Not only that, but I had a little visit from Marshals Lindsey and Hart this morning trying to tie me to all of this! Yer scheming is about to get my ass in the fire and I'm not going to have it!...You understand me? You're not paying me enough for me to spend the rest of my life in the penitentiary or swing from Judge Parker's gibbet...I'm not God's own fool."

"Idiot! You come straight over to my office? You are God's own fool! Lindsey is no bumpkin, he probably had you watched to see what you would do."

Cobb got up and walked over to one of the seven foot tall double-sash windows, eased the curtain back and looked out on the street. He couldn't see Loss Hart sitting on the bench in front of the boarding house because of a large white oak tree blocking the view on the other side of the street—then again, Loss had known the foliage would hide his spot on the bench from anyone looking out the second floor. "Don't see nobody."

Hillary pushed open the door with her ample hip and came into the office carrying a tray with two coffee cups, a small pitcher of cream and a bowl of sugar. "Here's your coffee, Mr. Baldwin."

"Not now! God dammit woman, can't you see we're busy? Now get out!"

She glared at him for a moment, then turned and went back to her own office.

"Women...God help us." He turned to Cobb. "All right, let's look at this logically. If the marshal had prima facie evidence, he would have used it. It would appear to me that anything they might have is purely circumstantial. I think we should lay low for a while, keep our eyes and ears open...A solution will present itself...always does. Patience, my dear Sheriff, patience." He lit one of his Cuban cigars and blew a cloud of blue smoke over his head. "Hillary! Where the hell's that coffee?"

***

CHAPTER TWELVE

ARDMORE, I.T.

Houston Wallace snapped the reins over the rump of the bay mare pulling the buckboard. "Haw up there Bonnie."

She dutifully turned left off Broadway onto Scott Street where many of the town's wagon yards were located. With Ardmore approaching five thousand in population, plus the outlying area with farmers and ranchers—wagons on the main downtown streets were discouraged. Except for loading or unloading, wagons, buckboards, drays, buggies and the occasional curricle preferred by the upper crust were expected to tie up at the conveniently located wagon yards that were just off the main downtown business district. The lots also reduced the amount of horse and mule droppings on the newly installed brick streets that required a full-time city crew of two men to scoop them up on a hourly basis.

Houston drove into Reese Farmer's Wagon Yard and Livery, stepped down, turned and helped his wife Maude, and then Jennie Dalton to the ground. The ladies straightened their full ankle-length town dresses to better allow the wrinkles to fall free.

"Like me to feed and water 'em fer ya, mister?" asked Reese as he untied the lead rope from the mare's harness. "Just fifty cents extry."

"Sure, she's had a bit of a drive this mornin'…We'll be back in a spell." He turned and walked toward the street with the women and said in a low voice, "Now, let me git this straight, Maude, honey, you 'er Miz Pruitt an' Jennie, you'd be Miz Brown? That it?"

"Do we need to write it out for you, Houston?" asked Jennie.

"Naw, I kin remember…Just checkin', that's all…I'm gonna go down to Big Buck's Gun Shop an' see if'n he's got that ammunition Bill wanted, then go by the mercantile fer some new duds…What the boys wuz wearin' when they come in were purty threadbare an' don't think you ladies would ever git the stink out."

"We'll be headin' over to May's General Store and fill our grocery list…our cupboard is pretty threadbare, too," said Jennie.

"Meet ya'll back here in say…two hours?" he said as he started to walk away.

"Stay out of the parlor house, Houston Wallace…You don't want me to come there lookin' for you," warned Maude as she shook her finger in the big man's face—she was every bit of ninety pounds soaking wet to his two-fifty.

"Yessum...er no, ma'am," he said and mumbled when he was out of earshot, "You know that...Ol' biddy damn near snatched me bald headed last time."

BIG BUCK'S GUN SHOP

Houston opened the door to the small gun shop just off Main on Hinkle Street. The small brass bell attached to the header tinkled his arrival. Racks of new and used rifles and shotguns lined the twelve foot high walls. The room's ceiling was covered with embossed galvanized tin decorative panels. Polished oak display cases held handguns of all sorts—small derringers and pocket pistols, as well as center-fire wheel guns from .22 to .45 caliber. An enameled tin sign advertising Annie Oakley shooting one of Winchester's pump .22 rifles was mounted on the central support column just above another one with John L. Sullivan in his famous fighting pose advertising Hohenadel Beer. The place smelled of gunpowder, gun oil and leather.

"Come in the house, pilgrim. Whatcha lookin' for today?" called out a big gray-haired man with a full matching mustache. The proprietor—wearing a gray three-button, open collar shirt and a full length tan leather apron—stepped from behind the counter. "I'm Buck Steiner."

Buck had driven an ammunition wagon during the war of Northern Aggression as southerners were want to call the conflict back in the 1860s—a very dangerous job in the heat of battle. A stray shot into one of the wooden kegs of cannon powder would have left little to none of him to bury.

He had decided to use his experience with arms and ammunition to become a gunsmith after the war. Luckily for him and the residents of Ardmore, the shop had been spared from the recent conflagration that destroyed most of the downtown. Had it reached the stacked canisters of black powder stored in the back room, the resulting blast would likely have taken out the rest of the block.

Houston handed Buck a slip of paper with what he needed. "You got all this in stock?"

Buck got out his pad and added up the total number of rounds in the three different calibers listed on the note. "Well, now, looks to be a little over a thousand rounds all together...Whatcha gonna do, start a war?"

"Naw...jest thought we, uh, I might git a better deal if'n I got a bunch at one time."

"Well, yes and no...Yes on the deal, but no, I ain't got this much on hand...Got a shipment comin' in tomorra on the train from Dallas. Kin let you have four hunderd rounds of the .44-40 and three boxes of 12 gauge buckshot with the rest after the delivery...how's that?"

"Reckon that'll have to do." Houston handed him a ten dollar bill. "This cover it fer today?"

"Close enough," Buck said as he put the eight boxes of Winchester ammunition into a cloth flour sack. He turned and pulled three boxes of Union Metallic Cartridge shotshells off the shelf below the rifle rack. "We can settle up for the rest when you come back in."

"Sounds like a deal," Houston said as his eyes found a nickel plated Colt New Navy model 1889. "Whoa...whatcha got there?" he asked, pointing at the shiny revolver on the second glass shelf.

"Which one ya talkin' about? That new style double action?"

"Double action? Yeah...lemme see it."

Buck slid over the mirrored wooden panel that covered half of the back of the eight foot long case. "Now this here one just come in last week. Colt cain't hardly make 'em fast enough for the demand." He pulled back the L shaped release and rolled the pristine cylinder out as he laid the revolver on his left hand and stuck two fingers through the open frame. The highly experienced gun dealer spun the cylinder slowly with his thumb. "You can load six rounds at once, and dump all the empties with just one press of the ejector rod...Lot faster than the old Single Action." He pressed the knurled button atop the ejector to show how it functioned. Closing the empty cylinder, Buck pulled back on the trigger, causing the hammer to cock and fall on an empty chamber. "Double or single action...a man can fire it as fast as he pulls the trigger."

"Well I'll be dipped. I heard of these newfangled guns, but that the first one I ever laid eyes on," Houston said as he nearly drooled on the counter.

"Like the way it feels?" Buck asked as he handed the new gun to him, butt first.

"Yeah...feels a little lighter than my old thumb buster," Houston said as he pulled the hammer back and sighted down the six inch barrel at a cigar store wooden Indian across the street.

"A little bit. Try the trigger pull."

He let the hammer fall with a reassuring metallic click. A smile came to his face.

"Like the way she handles?"

"I do, I do. Man can always use himself another fine handgun, I always say."

"That's what keeps me in business, my friend. Would you like to take it with you today?"

"Reckon I would. What's the damage with, say...four boxes of ammo?"

"Today, I can let it go for...twelve dollars...and with the ammunition...make it an even fifteen."

"Sound fair to me," Houston said as he dug another two crumpled tens out of the top front pocket of his bib overalls.

Buck handled him a five in change. "I'll get the box from the storeroom," Buck said as he turned.

"No need...I'd just throw it away anyhow. Jest put the rounds in the bag and I'll carry the shooter out in ma pocket."

"The customer is sometimes right," Buck said with a grin as he pulled four boxes of Western brand .41 Colt off the shelf and set it on top of the buckshot in the bulging sack. "You gonna need another sack? Thisun's gitting mighty heavy." He gathered the neck together and tied it off with a length of cotton twine.

"Ain't no hill for a stepper…What time that shipment come in?" Houston asked as he slipped the handgun down inside his deep back pocket. "What mama don't know won't hurt her."

"Heard that one a time or two…Be after three or so before the shipment gets off-loaded and the delivery wagon makes its run."

"Well if that be the case, we'll plan to come in the day after tomorra. Cain't get back home 'fore dark."

"Must have a purty good drive, Mister…sorry, I didn't catch your name."

"Houston, uh, Benton Houston. I'm up towards Davis a ways."

"Nice to do business with you, Mr. Houston. Have everythin' all boxed up for you when you come back."

The customer touched the brim of his beat-up brown fedora. "Better go round up the womenfolk before they spend me into the poorhouse."

Buck nodded and chuckled. Houston lifted the heavy sack of ammo as if it weighed nothing and headed for the door. As he reached it, an equally tall, but not quite so heavy, man stepped inside.

"Mornin' to you," the stranger said. "Let me hold the door."

"Mighty nice of you, mister…uh, I mean Marshal." Houston tried not to show his nervousness at the sight of the shiny silver badge on the man's vest. He held onto the sack with both hands to keep from dropping its contents as he made his way outside and disappeared down the boardwalk.

Selden slowly closed the door and walked across the gun shop to the counter. "Hey there, Buck…He new in town? Don't recall ever running into that one."

"Said he's from up near Davis. Name's Benton Houston. Just bought up all my .44 Winchester and ordered more."

"That so? Benton Houston…Don't know that name."

"And he picked up a new .41 Colt revolver and some buckshot. Nice way to start out my day…What can I do for you, Selden?"

" Need to see if you have any .45-70 Government."

"Going after buffalo, are you?"

"Seems to me, they've been pretty much shot out…Nope, not for me…a friend needs some for his varmint gun."

"Hate to see the size of those varmints!"

"Well, my friend is…a little different. When he has to shoot sumpthin' he expects it to stay shot."

"Can't argue with that logic. Four hunderd and five grains of hot lead will do it 'bout every time. Got five or six boxes of Peters…how many you want?"

"Better give me all of 'em. Never know how many varmints he might run into out there," Selden said as he pictured the bearded bear of man who had just left.

MARSHAL'S OFFICE

Selden walked in and sat the sack of ammunition and the jug of turpentine he had picked up from May's on the corner of his pine desk. "Got Jack all fixed up. At least for a while…Angie's turpentine too."

"Well, we was right 'bout Cobb...Went straight as a dose of salts through a goose to Baldwin's. Stayed there fer near thirty minutes, then went back to his office. 'Spect he's seein' to hirin' some more deputies," said Loss as he poured himself a cup of coffee from the pot on the stove in the corner. "Need a cup?" he asked Selden.

"Don't mind if I do," he said as he grabbed his cup from the desk and held it out while Hart filled it.

Loss returned the pot and took his seat at his desk, propped his feet on top and leaned back. "I mind they'll slip up somewheres along the way...we give 'em enough rope."

"My thoughts...Oh...had Bart over to the newspaper print up a dozen notices fer some of the local merchants to keep an eye out for those twenty dollar bank notes Dalton stole from Longview National Bank. Telegram from Sheriff Brownlow said none of 'em was signed...so they would have to be forged. Be President Joseph Clemmons er bank treasurer Clyde Magee signatures on the note...One er t'other." He took a sip of the strong black coffee.

"You know they ain't gonna be able to resist spendin' some of that money...probably burnin' a hole in Bill Dalton's pocket already."

"My gut tells me we should start seein' some of them bills just about 'nytime...Finish yer coffee and let's go pick up those flyers. They oughta be ready by now."

239

MAY'S GENERAL STORE

Jennie opened the right side of the big double doors to May's General Store and allowed Maude to enter first.

"I just love to come in here...there are just so many *things*. Mr. May always has the latest patterns of cloth...Just look at that table over there, stacked five high with new bolts of material and there, a whole area of just kitchen things," Maude said in a low voice and pointed.

"He's gotten so big, he'll soon have to separate the store into departments."

"Do you think? Would he still call it a *General* store?"

"Might call it a *Department* store or something like that."

"That sounds so odd...May's Department Store...I don't like it."

"Not for us to say...Grab one of those baskets and start filling our list. I'll go over and tell the clerk what we need stacked outside at the loading area that's too heavy for us to carry," Jennie said and walked over to the counter.

"Such a wonderful place," Maude mumbled as she approached the dry goods area and began going through the table of fabric.

"Good morning, ma'am, welcome to May's. How can I help you?" the clerk in a white shirt, black bow tie, sleeve garters and a long white apron behind the counter asked.

"Good morning. Here's a list of bulk things I would like for you to take out to the loading dock, if you would," Jennie said as she handed him a scrap of paper.

"Yes, ma'am..." He glanced at the list. "...fifty pounds of flour, ten pounds of sugar, ten pound bucket of lard, two sides of bacon, five pounds of salt, twenty pound sack of pinto beans, case of canned peaches, hunderd pounds of chicken scratch and two hunderd of whole oats...Yessum, we'll have that out there in a jiffy. Will there be anythin' else?"

Jennie, glanced around and leaned over closer. "Do you have any...uh, spirits?"

The clerk also looked around—the selling of whiskey in Indian Territory was a federal crime—and lowered his voice. "I can have you some by day after tomorrow...How much would you like, ma'am?"

"Can you get, say...a three gallon keg of Kentucky bourbon?"

"Not a problem, Miz...?"

"Brown."

"Miz Brown. Yes and what time would you be coming in?"

"We'll be in by noon. That all right?"

"That'll be fine, ma'am...Just a moment and I'll have your bill figured up..."

"Not yet. My friend over there, Miz Pruitt..." She pointed at Maude. "...is getting some other things. Spices, sundries and apparently has her eye on some dress material."

"You two ladies make yourself to home. Anything too high for ya'll to reach, just let me know...we got a step ladder and will be right proud to help you out."

"Thank you kindly," she said as she turned and moved over beside Maude. *Sure is nice to have some spending money for a*

241

change. A woman could get used to this, and that's a fact. "Oh, Maude, that color of gingham just matches your eyes. Let's get enough and I'll make a dress for Gracie too."

"I'm also out of thread and backing...Be so nice to have some new things, won't it?"

"Yes, it will...I also ordered some whiskey for the boys as a surprise."

"Wouldn't mind havin' a touch myself," Maude said.

Jeannie nodded. "Let's go check out, if you have everything."

"I'm ready."

They walked over to the counter and laid the bolt of blue gingham, thread, backing and basket of the other items next to the big brass cash register.

"You can total all this up now," Jennie said to the clerk.

"Yes, ma'am." He added the new items to his sales ticket pad and added it all together. "Comes to twenty-eight dollars and thirty-two cents, Miz Brown."

Jennie opened the draw strings on her small cloth purse and pulled out a twenty dollar bank note with a ten dollar bill and handed them to the clerk. "Here you are."

"Yes, ma'am and your change...sixty-eight cents makes twenty-nine and a dollar makes thirty. There will be someone outside to load when you bring your wagon around. We appreciate your business...and we'll see you day after tomorrow when you come to pick up your, uh, other item. Ya'll have a nice day." He nodded at the ladies as they turned and walked toward the front door.

REESE FARMER'S WAGON YARD

The ladies rounded the corner onto Scott Street. Maude was carrying her bolt of material and backing wrapped in brown paper and tied with white cotton string while Jennie carried the spices and sundries in a paper sack. The entered the gate to the wagon yard and looked around.

"Guess Houston hasn't finished his shoppin' yet," observed Jennie.

"That had better be it...I'll peel his head like an onion if he's over to Miss Sadie's havin' a drink," groused Maude. She called over to the slender young man standing near the fence close to the livery building. "Mr. Farmer, you can go ahead and bring our wagon up, if you would...I'm sure he'll..."

"Yessum, I see yer husband yonder."

Jennie turned around to see Houston walking through the gate, his arms full of packages and carrying a heavy flour sack. "Not mine, hers." She pointed to Maude.

"One buckboard, comin' right up." Reese headed to the back side of the yard.

"Bend down, Houston," Maude said, tapping her foot.

"I ain't been..."

"I said bend down!" He bent over and she smelled of his breath. "Alright...it's a good thing." She smiled and kissed his nose.

"We'll go over to May's and load up, then head toward Elk. Should get home in time to fix up a nice supper," said Jennie.

"Got to come back in town day after tomorra. Buck didn't have all the ammo Bill wanted," Houston said.

"Good, have something else to pick up at May's anyway," added Jennie.

Reese Farmer pulled the mare to a stop by Houston and the ladies—he stepped down. "Wellsir, that'll be six bits. She's a nice mare…Check that right front shoe when you git home, though. Seemed just a touch loose. I re-clenched the nails fer ya…no charge."

"'Preciate it, Mr. Farmer. We'll be back in a day er so." Houston handed the man three quarters and then helped his wife and Jennie up into the wagon. He clambered into the seat, nodded at the hostler and popped the reins. "Come up, Bonnie." She moved out of the yard into the street, turned right and headed toward May's.

Selden exited the tobacco store with a handful of flyers—across the street, Loss was entering the front door of Sally's cafe. A buckboard with a man and two women aboard slowly passed by, the iron wheel rims clacking noisily on the red bricks of Main Street. Lindsey casually studied the three for a couple of seconds, memorizing the features of their faces—recognizing the man as the same one from the gun shop. He noted one of the two women wore a wedding ring, but the other's hands were clasped together in her lap and he could not discern the presence of the telltale jewelry.

He averted his eyes as the wagon drew abreast, to keep his true interest in the three from being quite so obvious. The buckboard, the back laden with feed and supplies, turned west onto the major cross street that eventually became the dirt road to Healdton. It disappeared around the corner. *Now that's interesting. Buck said the man claimed he was from up by Davis, but they's leaving town in a differ'nt direction. Wonder why he would make that up?*

LOG CABIN

Angie set the platter of smoked ham slices and fresh baked bread on the table next to the large mason jar filled with homemade dill pickles. The aroma of the bread filled the room as the four lawmen sat around the table, exchanging grins as they anticipated the tasty noon meal.

"Help yourselves, and eat hearty lads," Angie said.

"Sweet lady, aren't you gonna join us?" Jack asked.

"In due time, my dear. I'll be a puttin' the finishin' touches on the potato salad."

"Man, oh man…if we stay here any longer, I'll be needin' a draft horse to ride me home," Bass added.

"I'll be havin' a few chores for ye menfolk afterwards, if ye are of a mind," the red headed dynamo said with a lilt in her voice. "I'm most out of firewood…for the kitchen and the fireplace." She handed the ham bone to Boy under the table.

"Now, you know I'm not supposed to be walkin' yet," Jack muttered, with more than a small frown on his weathered face.

"Wasn't talkin' to ye, was I now?" Angie shot back. "I'll find something for ye to do inside…like me silver needs polishin'." She whisked up a mayonnaise dressing using fresh eggs, olive oil, cider vinegar, homegrown herbs and dried mustard. She folded it into her boiled potatoes and stirred the pot to mix it well, then added generous pinches of salt and pepper. After one more good stir, she moved the pot to the table and scraped the tasty mound into a waiting blue and white hand-painted ceramic bowl. "Me mother liked her potatoes this way. Hope ye'll be enjoying it as well."

Jack motioned for her to sit down beside him. "Have a seat, darlin'. This ain't no restaurant, ya know."

"Better'n most I've visited, Miss Angie," Bass said.

"Aw, go on with your blarney now." She blushed.

Jack noticed the flash of color in her fair skin. His frown melted instantly. *God she's a beauty. Man would be a fool to let one like her slip outta his hands.*

Boy, with the big ham bone in his mouth, padded to the door and whined. Bass got up and let him out. "I 'spect you want to go bury your bone, huh?" The big animal jumped off the porch and headed to the barn. "He must have a hellova stash out by the barn somewhere...Seems like he's always takin' his bones out there," he added as he closed the door and went back to the table.

"He likes to gnaw in private, meby," said Jack.

Bass took his seat and noted Jed was unusually silent. He thought back and remembered that the normally talkative man had not said much at dinner or during the late night storm that kept everyone awake. "Jed, cat got your tongue? You be especial quiet."

Jed looked up and dabbed at a spot of potato salad on his lower lip. He looked around the table as everyone's attention had suddenly fallen on him. He swallowed hard and looked

Bass in the eye. "Remember yesterd'y when we rode in and things went all to hell in a hand basket?"

"Kinda hard to forgit...got a bit dicey as I recall."

"Well that's the thing...I'm kinda stuck on what happened when I run into that first fella..."

"Somethin' we don't know 'bout?" Jack asked as he swallowed the last of his pickle.

"Couldn't even talk 'bout it...the man had me dead to rights. I thought...I thought..."

"Go on, Jed...get it out of your system. Do you good," Tobe said as he set his goblet of tea on the table.

"Well, all happened so fast...like I said, he done gone and got the drop on me...wadn't five feet away," Jed said as he looked around. "By the time I got my old Henry up to shoot, that bore of his Colt...looked most bigger than a stove pipe..." He paused for a moment. "I heard his hammer fall 'fore I pulled the trigger."

"Did he jest miss ya...at that range?" Jack asked.

"Nosirreebob...His gun...Well, his gun was just smooth outta bullets, er else I'da not be here sitting with ya'll."

"It's what we call luck of the Irish...even if you're not Irish," Angie interjected.

Bass nodded as he and Jed locked eyes. "And you been thinking 'bout your family, and what they woulda done with you gone...Am I right?"

"How did you know?"

"Been there, Jed, been there...You ain't the first man to look the devil in the eye and walk away."

"'Spect we all have…a time er two…Goes with the territory, as the man says," added Jack. "…even though I don't have a family." He stole a quick glance at Angie.

"You do remember, I been doin' this a right smart longer than you have," Bass continued.

"That's how we met, as I recall…you treated me fair and square, even as yer prisoner…Never forget that."

"Ye, a marshal, were his prisoner?" Angie asked.

"One and only time, ma'am…Guess I was in the wrong place at the wrong time."

"And ye became a marshal after ye were found to be innocent?"

"Yess'm. They found out it was Ben Larson who really done the murder and turned me loose. Even put good word in for me with Judge Parker when I went to ask him for a job of work."

"Jed's being a little shy…he saved my life from that killer. Took a bullet in the neck as a re-ward. Cain't say enough about his good character," Tobe said with a big smile.

Angie nodded. "I never took the time to think about what ye lawmen go through, dealing with such riff raff as we have been plagued with of late. Putting your very lives on the line…all in the name the law." She slipped her hand into Jack's under the table and gave it a firm squeeze. "Makes me so proud to call ye men me friends."

***

CHAPTER THIRTEEN

HONEY CREEK

The wagon jolted from the new washed road cuts on the main road before the turn off to the cabin following the previous night's heavy rains. Winchester Ashalatubbi bounced upward with the jolt, landing hard on the unforgiving bench seat. "Ow," he grunted. "This would be a good place to build a road. Be close to the cabin if they wanted it to be."

"Sorry, I try to find smooth parts," Ben Sixkiller apologized.

"Not your fault, son. The Great Spirit made the rain…the rain made the ruts. Who are we to complain?"

Ben shot an admiring glance at the older man. *Shaman always has way with words that make a man think.* "We be there in few minutes. Think your niece'll have something for us to eat?"

"I would say so. She knew we were coming back for Montford…Angie is a good woman."

Ben nodded.

Ben pulled the wagon—with his and Winchester's saddle horses tied behind—into the turnaround in front of the house as Bass and Jeb were walking out the front door. Both lawmen waved at the two men, who returned the greeting.

"Afternoon, Anompoli Lawa…Ben," Bass called out. "Ya'll almost missed lunch." He grinned broadly. "But I think she saved enough for you gents to sneak a bite."

"We smelt bread baking for last mile," Ben said without a hint of a smile.

"Hope ye don't mind ham sandwiches, Uncle Winchester," Angie said from the open doorway. "Sure and baked several fresh loaves and got plenty of ham and potato salad. Figured it would be more company we'd be having."

"Always a pleasure to visit. Your smile brightens the very day," he replied as Ben reined the mules to a stop and set the foot brake. He slowly eased to a standing position and steadied himself with a hand on the back of the seat.

"Need a hand?" Bass offered as he stepped off the porch.

"Not yet," Winchester replied. "Getting a little long in the tooth for these wagon rides. I think they are made for younger backsides."

"Cain't argue with you…oughta hear them folks in the back of the Tumbleweed Wagon. They complains to high heavens 'bout that there green devil," Jed said as he nodded.

Ben hopped down and removed his driving gloves, placing them back on the seat for the return trip. "Meby so they not commit crime, not ride in wagon."

"Gotta point there," Bass agreed. "Come on in, 'fore we throws it to the hogs, as my daughter Mame always says...Well, looky here," he added as Marshals Lindsey and Loss Hart trotted their horses up to the fence and dismounted. "Got two more for the table, Angie."

"Faith and also looking for the good marshals, I was."

Selden and Loss came in through the gate just as Winchester and Ben were climbing the steps. Selden carried a cloth sack tied at the neck.

"Brought your turpentine, Miss Angie...and Jack's ammunition for his Marlin."

"Beware of Greeks bearing gifts," said Tobe as he walked out onto the porch with a steaming cup of coffee in his hand.

"Who you callin' a Greek, Tobe?" Lindsey said with a grin. "Hope ya'll left us somethin'. Poor Loss here ain't had nothin' to eat since breakfast...Gonna dry up an' blow away."

"Bless your hearts, there's plenty. Just need to put on a fresh pot of coffee," said Angie as she took the sack from Selden.

"Jest as soon have buttermilk, you don't mind, Miss Angie." said Loss.

"Got that too."

"Bring travois to carry Montford down mountain. No get wagon up there," said Ben between bites of his sandwich.

"The ladies of the tribe made a beaded doeskin burial pouch and I brought red ocher to paint his face in accordance with Chickasaw custom before we seal him inside," added Winchester.

"Where are you goin' to bury him?" asked Jack.

"As you may or may not know, the Chickasaw are a clan of the Muskogean and as such, are mound builders from back thousands of years ago. We have a secret burial mound site that no Pindah-lickoyee or white-eyes are allowed to see. We will bury Haklo Oka' there after I have sanctified his earthly remains," said the shaman.

"Haklo Oka'?"

"Montford's Chickasaw name, Jack. It means 'Hears the Water.'"

"Didn't know that...Wish I could go back up there with you...I feel I owe him..."

"You can pay your respects when we come back down. I don't want you walking around, much less riding a horse. Your wound is healing nicely. Don't clabber the milk."

"Yes, sir...but I ain' happy about it."

"Tobe, Jed and me will lead you up there, Winchester."

"We appreciate that, Bass...We're ready when you are."

Boy got to his feet and stood waiting by the door.

"'Peers Boy is goin' with ya'll. Wouldn't recommend you argue with him none."

"Thought never crossed mind, Jack," said Sixkiller.

Bass' buckskin stallion picked his way around the numerous outcropping of rocks and boulders followed by Tobe, Jed, Winchester and Ben bringing up the rear with the travois as they neared the location. Boy led the way down the declivity to the scene of the ambush.

"Here we are, boys. Best we leave the horses up top. Be a bit crowded down around the site," Bass said as he dismounted and tied his mount to a scrub oak.

The others followed suit. Ben tied off, retrieved the sacred burial pouch from the travois and headed down the embankment.

"Spread out and look for human bones. I'm sure the critters have scattered them about…if you have a question, go ahead and bring it to me. I'm reasonably certain I can identify it," instructed Winchester.

The men scattered out and began to collect what they felt were Montford's remains—they brought every piece to the shaman for verification. Anompoli Lawa checked each bone then cleaned and carefully placed it in the pouch. Even Boy brought bones from further out. "Thank you, Nashoba Tohbi," he would say.

The shaman sat cross-legged on the ground next to the pouch and from the medicine bag hung from his neck, he took a small hog-bristle brush and began to clean the debris from Montford's skull preparatory to painting it with the ocher. The bright red clay and grease based mixture was the same the never-defeated Chickasaw used in their war paint in days gone by. He returned the brush to his bag and respectfully coated the front of the skull with the red pigment using only his finger tips. Finished, he place the skull in the center of the burial pouch and added the rest of the bones as they were brought to him.

Ben found what was left of Montford's Lighthorse quill and bead hat band—this was placed next to the skull.

"Think we've found everythin' that wasn't carried off, Anompoli Lawa," Bass informed him as he and the others all removed their hats and bowed their heads.

Winchester nodded, closed and tied the sacred doeskin and got to his feet. He pulled out a small beaded pouch from his medicine bag, opened it and took a pinch of sacred dogwood pollen—similiar to the hoddentin or piñon pine pollen used by the Apache and Navajo in their ceremonies—and scattered it to the four directions. He took another pinch and sprinkled it over the burial pouch and yet another straight up into the air to sanctify the journey to the happy hunting grounds. Anompoli Lawa then pulled from his medicine bag, his personal totem carved from a piece of lightning riven oak and waving it above the remains, he chanted in the Chickasaw tongue, "Ababinili hoyo aboha ona, Haklo Oka'…Chihóa-bia-chee…May the Great Spirit guide you, Hears the Water, that you may achieve your rest…go with God."

The others repeated, "Chihoa-bia-chee, Haklo Oka'."

Ben carried the bag back up the embankment, placed it on the travois and secured it. He mounted his pony and led the procession back down the mountain. Bass and the others followed at a respectful distance as was the Chickasaw custom.

MARSHAL'S OFFICE

Selden and Loss walked in the office from having lunch at Sally's, Lindsey nonchalantly pitched his hat at the tree, catching one of the hooks. Hart tried to duplicate the feat and missed, sending his hat to the dusty floor.

"How is it you do that? You don't never miss," he said as he picked up his hat and slapped it against his thigh to knock most of the dust off before he hung it up.

"Don't think about it...just flip my bonnet in the general direction...See, Loss...what I been sayin'...you think too much. Gotta go with yer instincts."

"Well, easy fer you to say...you ain't wearin' my head."

"Hummf, don't know if'n thats a curse er a blessin'...Think I'll pick the blessin'...You gonna fix up some coffee while yer still up?" Selden said as he sat down and started going through the stack of papers on his desk.

"Durn yer hide. You like to broke yer neck hurrin' across the room so's you could sit down 'fore me. Didn't cha?"

"Why I'm sure I don't know what yer talkin' 'bout, Loss," he answered with a grin.

"Jest as well...yer coffee don't have no more bite than a white pine dog with a poplar tail," he said as he was putting a handful of ground coffee in the pot.

"Loss, you cain't tell nobody nothing that ain't never been nowhere...an' you kin write that down," Selden said as he perched his gold-rimmed reading glasses on his nose.

"Say what?"

The door opened and a stout man with short mutton chop whiskers, in a three piece suit and high starched collar—Marcus May, owner of May's General Store—entered in an excited state.

"Come on in, Mr. May. What kin we do fer you?"

"Those flyers you dropped off at my store yesterday?" He reached into his pocket and pulled out a white envelope and handed it to Lindsey. "Was doing my books last night and going through the paper money and the note in that envelope caught my eye...Twenty dollar bank note from the First National Bank of Longview and it didn't have either signature your flyer said to look for...I came by earlier this morning, but there wasn't anyone here."

"Sorry about that Mr. May, we had business up in the Arbuckles and stopped fer lunch. Jest got back." He opened the envelope and took out an invoice, and a bank note. Selden glanced at the front then the back of the note. "Loss, take a gander...what do you think?"

Loss walked over and looked closely at the bill. "No question, ain't neither President Clemmons ner the treasurer Magee's signature. Best I kin make out it's somethin' like Sherrilford 'er Shacklford."

"No matter...either case, damned shore ain't what it's supposed to be...Know who might have passed it?"

"I asked all my people...Best we could figure, it was a woman by the name of Miz Brown. Not from Ardmore. She bought a considerable amount of supplies, including a special order to be picked up tomorrow."

Selden sat up straighter in his chair and smiled, the corners of his unruly mustache turned up. "They have a buckboard load of supplies?"

"I would say so, looking at that invoice."

"Were she travelin' with a man?"

"Actually, Marshal, I'm told by our swamper at the loading dock there was another woman and a man...a big bear of a man."

"Damnation! Think I seen 'em leaving town yesterd'y." He paused for a moment and considered his next step. "We appreciate all this, Mr. May. Now here's what you do..."

JASON BALDWIN'S OFFICE

"Sheriff, my client has sent a couple of friends from over at Lawton to replace your two deputies...He's suggested that we need to take a different approach to the widow O'Reilly situation." Baldwin paused to take a puff on his cigar and blow a blue cloud of smoke toward the ceiling. "You boys can come in now," he directed his voice toward a side door to a small anteroom.

Cobb turned to see two expressionless Apaches enter. They stood side-by-side, their arms folded across their chests, wearing similar garb—loose earth-tone cotton pants and shirts with a red sash tied around the waist and knee high deerskin moccasins. Red cloth bands were wrapped about their heads and each had a Colt revolver and a large butcher knife stuck in their sashes.

"This is Múh-Jaune and Dalaa-Goshe. You can call them Yellow Owl and One Dog. They are of the Be-don-ko-he clan of the Chiricahua Apache. Both served as scouts for General Miles when they tracked down old Geronimo and forced his surrender...Oh, and Yellow Owl is the grandson of Cochise."

"Well, what the hell am *I* supposed to do with 'em? The Chickasaw will raise hob when..."

"They won't know anything about it. Send these two out to watch the O'Reilly place...it's what they do. They're like wraiths. I procured a warrant for her from Judge Graham as well as a couple of John Doe's in case there's anyone else out there with her."

"We bring pindah-lickoyee woman in. Meby so you see by and by. Yellow Owl speak truth." His black eyes burned into Cobb's causing the man to turn away. The Apache's flinty demeanor was enhanced by a long scar that ran from the corner of his eye to just below his mouth, giving him a permanent lopsided frown.

"Trust me, Cobb, these men know their business...When the time is right, they'll make their move just like they did with Geronimo...You'll see. Now deputize them...They'll slip out of town for the Arbuckles."

MARSHAL'S OFFICE

"Well, I was right," Selden said as he walked in the office. "I checked back with Buck on the off idee that that big man mighta ordered more ammo when he was in yesterd'y...He did, purtnear a thousand rounds all told."

"Lordy, lordy...Cain't let 'em git hold of that."

"Right. Since they's comin' back in town tomorra...Hair on the back of my neck tells me his name is Houston Wallace, not Benton Houston. Him an' his brother...the one that got kilt in Longview...got a cabin west of here over near Elk...Looks like it's all goin' to come to a head, Loss."

"'Spect so. Mind we oughta be at May's an' Buck's waitin' when them women and that feller come in to pick up the rest of their stuff."

"That too. Believe I'll ride out to the falls and git Bass an' them. Gonna need a good posse. They's the only ones we kin trust 'round here."

"I see you, Sel...That sheriff's so crooked you could pull a cork with him...Want me to come along?"

"Why don't you stick around and keep an eye on our erstwhile sheriff. We'll be back in sometime 'round dark thirty."

"Works fer me."

"Tell Miss Willow she'll have the marshals as guests agin' at the boardin' house tonight."

"I'll tell her. Was gonna have supper there anyways."

LOG CABIN

"Now, I don't have a clue as to who them women are. If'n they 'er kin to anyone in the Dalton gang 'er not. Howsumever, they's passin' stolen bank money an' had to have contact with 'em somehows. That Houston Wallace...whole 'nother story altogether. He's the brother of Jim Wallace who got hisself shot down outside the bank in Longview," Selden said as he pushed back a little from the table and wiped his chin. "Mighty good lunch, Miss Angie."

"Go on with ye, Marshal. It was just left overs."

"How much ammunition you say he wuz gittin' at that gun shop, Selden?" asked Jed.

"Buck…the shopkeeper…said right at a thousand rounds."

"Oooh gollies!"

"We'd best stake out both places tomorra, I'm thinkin'," said Bass. "Don't figger we'll have any trouble with the women, but like to take that Wallace feller without gunplay…If'n we kin."

"Then meby they'll tell us fer sure if'n the gang is out to the cabin, 'er not," offered Tobe.

"My money says that's exactly where they are…Well, ya'll 'er through pettin' yerselves out here on Miss Angie's cookin', what say let's head back on into town?" Selden got to his feet. "Say, where's Boy? Ain't seen him since I got here."

"He's off roamin', I 'spect. Stays gone a lot since things settled down a mite…meby he's found a girlfriend," Jack said. "Damnation! Wish I could go with ya'll…"

"Ye blatherskate! That would be an asininity if I ever heard one. Just because you've been able to get to the privy and back by your ownself and now it's wanting to fight bears, is it?" Angie swatted Jack's shoulder with her dish towel.

"Now, darlin', didn't say nothin' of the sort…Just wish I was able to go is all."

Bass and Tobe glanced at each other and grinned.

"If wishes and wants were wings, a frog wouldn't bump his butt ever time he hopped...says I." Bass patted Jack on the shoulder.

The quartet of law officers grabbed their hats and headed out the door.

"Now there goes a fearsome group...Don't think I'd much want to be in Dalton's shoes," Jack said as he watched the door close.

Bass, Tobe, Jed and Selden mounted up and nudged their horses into an easy trot north toward the main wagon road back to Ardmore, unaware of two sets of black eyes watching them from the deep woods south of the cabin...

ARDMORE, I.T.

The bright morning sun streamed through the windows of Miss Willow's dining room. Bass, Tobe and Jed were enjoying her bountiful breakfast of ham, eggs, grits, biscuits and gravy when Selden and Loss came in from the front parlor.

"Glad to see ya'll waited on us," Selden said. "Mornin', Miss Willow."

"Didn't want it to get cold...Thought you an' Loss might be a sleepin' in," Tobe piped up between bites.

"Mornin', Selden, Loss. Ham an' eggs or pancakes?"

"Yessum, both will be fine," said Loss.

The portly, gray-haired proprietress rolled her eyes. "Marshal Hart, if you ever missed a meal, I swear I would expect to hear a pig sing."

"Well, Miss Willow, you know the old sayin', 'Never try to teach a pig to sing…it wastes yer time and irritates the pig', don'tcha know."

"Just biscuits and gravy and a cup of your wonderful coffee, ma'am…If'n you don't mind," Selden said as he shook his head and cut his eyes at Loss.

"Ain't never seen nobody in my life eat as much as Loss here and still look like a gutted snow bird," observed Bass.

"Wellsir, in our business…as you're aware…ya never know when you might git to eat agin'…So I ain't takin' me no chances," Hart commented as he pulled out a chair at the long dining table and stuffed the cotton napkin in the top of his vest.

BIG BUCK'S GUN SHOP

The store's owner was taking inventory of his various stocks of ammunition and perusing the racks of leather belts hanging along one wall. He jotted down notes on a legal-sized yellow pad as he identified shortages for a new order he was creating. Hearing the small bell attached to the front door, he looked up to see three men enter—two white and one black—all sporting the distinctive US Deputy Marshal badges on their vests.

"Mornin', Selden. Back for more ammo already?"

"Not today, Buck. I'm good…but you cain't ever have too much. This here's Marshal Tobe Basset and Marshal Jed Neal," Lindsey said as he introduced the men.

"Marshals, it's a pleasure." He shook hands with both men.

"Buck, Jed and Tobe er gonna hang out across the street an' keep an eye out for that feller you know as Benton Houston. We think his real name is Houston Wallace. He's wanted fer aidin' an' abetting. Aim to arrest him when he comes fer that ammo you just got in..."

Buck frowned as he nodded. "Aidin' and abettin'? That the same thing as accessory after the crime?"

Selden looked perplexed. "I reckon it is...you do lawyer work on the side now?"

"Naw. I jest read a lot when things are slow here in the store...Dime novels, Police Gazette and the like."

"Sorry it's gonna cost you a sale, Buck, but we have reason to believe that ammunition was gonna wind up in the hands of one Mason Frakes, aka Bill Dalton. An' we jest cain't have that," Selden said. "If the wheels come off this little shindig, get on down behind the counter...No need gettin' yerself hurt."

"Understand completely...Bill Dalton, huh? Who'da thunk it? Anythin' ya'll need me to help, just let me know," Buck offered. "Always go armed in the shop here...just in case." He patted the leather shop apron on his right hip, then lifted it to display a Colt Single Action Army revolver in his deep front pants pocket. "A little .45 caliber persuasion always goes a long way."

"Got that right...Hope it won't be necessary...we plan to take him peaceable...but, it'll be up to him," Tobe added.

"Appreciate yer help," Jed said as the three turned for the door.

ARDMORE, I. T.

Houston Wallace pulled rein on the mare pulling the farm buckboard just as she drew near the Hinkle Street intersection with Main. "Whoa up there, Bonnie." He turned to Maude, sitting between him and Jennie Dalton. "I'll walk from here over to Buck's an' then meet ya'll over to May's...Shouldn't take long." He handed the leather ribbons to his diminutive wife and stepped down. She clucked at the horse and they continued toward the general store—Bonnie's steel shoes clicking on the red bricks.

Maude skillfully backed the buckboard up against the loading dock at May's, set the brake and both women stepped down.

"Kin I help you ladies?" the young swamper asked.

"We're going inside to settle up. Won't be but a moment," Jennie replied.

She and Maude entered the open double doors from the loading dock and stepped inside.

Over in the garden tools area, Bass was examining a four tine pitchfork while Selden was going through a pull drawer box of squash seed in the feed and seed section. Both men watched the women enter and approach the counter from the corner of their eyes. They each touched the brim of their hat as the signal to move in.

"We forgot to get corn meal the other day, and need to add that to our, uh, other supplies," Maude said.

"Yes, ma'am...Oh, you're Miz Brown. In for your, ah, order I see," the clerk replied.

"Yes, and I need to add twenty-five pounds of meal, too."

"Yes, ma'am, here's your order of…medicine," he said as he set the three gallon keg on the counter. "I'll git your corn meal…That'll be nine dollars and twenty-two cents."

Jennie pulled out a ten dollar bill from her purse and laid it on the counter. "Here you are, my good man. Would you be so kind as to take the keg and meal to the loading doc…"

"Excuse me ma'am. I'm US Deputy Marshal Selden Lindsey," he said as he stepped up on the left of the two women. "And that's US Deputy Marshal Bass Reeves on yer right there."

Jennie and Maude turned first to look at Selden, and then turned around to look up at Bass. Both women put their hands to their mouths, their eyes wide with surprise and apprehension.

"Ladies," Bass said as he tipped his hat and opened his coat to show his badge. "Are you aware that traffickin' in liquor in the Nations is a Federal crime?"

"I don't understand what you mean. What is trafficking?" Jennie asked.

"Buyin' er sellin' alcohol, ma'am," said Selden. "I'm afraid ya'll will have to come with us. Yer under arrest."

Bass grabbed up the keg of whiskey from the counter. "We have to confiscate this liquor fer evidence," he said to the clerk who had been joined by the owner, Marcus May.

"Perfectly all right, Marshal. We're happy to cooperate with the law," May offered.

Selden and Bass escorted the ladies over to the Parker Hotel just off Main Street. The owner, Ben Parker, was manning the check-in desk.

"Mornin' Selden, how can I help you?"

"Is Miz Parker about?" Lindsey asked.

"Fact is, she's in her sewin' room. I'll fetch her for you."

Ben walked through the door behind the desk that led to their living quarters. In a moment, he escorted his wife back out front.

"Marshal Lindsey, how nice to see you. How's Annie?"

He and Bass both whipped off their hats and he answered, "She's fine, Pearl, real fine. I'll tell her you asked…This here's Marshal Bass Reeves from Fort Smith."

"Nice to meet you, sir." Ben held out his hand. "Your reputation precedes you."

Pearl nodded her head at Bass

He nodded back and grinned as he replied to Ben, "It wadn't me, I weren't there an' didn't do it."

Ben and Pearl both laughed.

"Nothin' like that Marshal. All good, I assure you, all good…Now how may we be of service to ya'll?"

"We had to arrest these ladies here an' we need to search their persons…Not proper fer us to do it, an' we was wonderin' if, uh, Pearl could git 'nother lady to help out?" Selden managed to stammer out.

"Certainly, Marshal, that widow lady, Miz Wilson has been stayin' here since her husband died…bless her heart…I'm sure she would be happy to help…I try to keep her busy, you know."

"I've sent over for Commissioner Garrett to stand guard outside the door and take custody of the ladies after ya'll have searched 'em."

"This is an outrage!" Jennie said as she stamped her foot. "I'll not submit to being searched like a common criminal."

"Don't see as you got 'ny choice, ma'am. Traffickin' in liquor does make you a common criminal an' as I mentioned, it's a Federal offense."

"If you ladies will come along with me, promise not to take too long. We'll go upstairs to Miz Wilson's room," Pearl said as she escorted the women to the stairway.

Commissioner Garrett entered the lobby from the street. "Got here quick as I could, Marshal," the twenty-eight year old up-and-coming local politician said.

"Appreciate it…Meet Bass Reeves…Marshal this is one of our County Commissioners, Buck Garrett."

Bass and Buck shook hands.

"Heard a lot about you, Mr. Reeves. It's indeed a pleasure to meet you."

"Pleasure is mine, Mr. Garrett."

"Miz Parker and Miz Wilson 'er searchin' the ladies we arrested over to May's with three gallons of whiskey. They passed a bank note from Longview, think they may have information on the whereabouts of the Dalton gang…"

"Dalton gang?"

BIG BUCK'S GUN SHOP

The big burly man walked quickly down the brick sidewalk, his long gait covering a full yard with every step. Tobe Bassett whispered to Jed Neal as the man stepped off the cut limestone curb and made a beeline for the entrance to the gun store across the street, "Looks like the man Selden described, all right. Give 'im a minute to git inside."

"Kinda wish ol' Bass was with us. Lindsey weren't kiddin' when he said the man was like a bear."

"Uh huh," Tobe agreed as he turned to face the display on the dry goods store. They could hear the slight ding of the door bell as the bearded man entered the gun shop. The older lawman watched in the storefront window reflection as the door closed behind Wallace.

Buck turned to greet the customer. "Good day to you, Mr. Houston. I got your order all boxed up for you in the back."

"That's good, 'cause I'm in a little bit of a hurry."

"Be right back," Buck said as he opened the door to the shop's back storeroom and retrieved an open-topped wooden ammunition box laden with the remainder of the original order.

Wallace watched him as he brought it to the front of the store and carefully laid it on the top of the counter next to the cash register. The front door opened and the two marshals stepped in—both of them had their morning coats pulled tight, covering the badges affixed to their vests.

"Be with you gents in just a minute," Buck said as he retrieved a small box with receipts from a shelf under the cash register. He flipped through the paperwork for a second and found the correct one. "Here we are, Mr. Houston...Your balance due is ten dollars and thirty-five cents."

Tobe and Jed had moved closer and were only five yards from their suspect as he stepped up the register and reached deep into his left front pocket.

"Houston Wallace! US Deputy Marshals...Yer under arrest!" Tobe announced in a loud voice.

The bearded man's eyes narrowed, his wild black eyebrows coming together like a single malevolent streak across his furrowed face. His dark eyes locked on Buck's for a moment. The savvy shopkeeper feigned shock and surprise. Wallace slowly turned and faced the two lawmen. "I think you done made a mistake, Marshal. The name's Benton Houston. Don't know nobody called Wallace," he said as his right hand snaked behind him and almost imperceptibly found the handle of his new .41 Colt.

"Git yer hands where we can see 'em, mister, and nobody gits hurt," Jed said in a calm voice.

In a flash, Wallace had the double action revolver out and pointed at the doorway leading to the storeroom. "One wrong move from either of you, and I'll put a bullet in that powder room and send us all to Kingdom Come!"

Jed and Tobe exchanged nervous glances, the speed of the bear of a man having caught both off their guard.

The sound of a single shot echoed off the walls of the small shop. Wallace's eyes rolled up to the top of his head as the .45

caliber slug exited above his left brow. He slumped forward, crashing to the wooden floor with a resounding thud.

Jed and Tobe looked across the counter as a wisp of smoke circled upwards from Buck's six shooter. The gray-haired gun dealer slowly stuck the Colt back in his pocket. "The hell you say! Whatever your name was...nobody, but nobody, comes in my shop and makes threats."

PARKER HOTEL

Pearl came back down the stairs with her sewing basket in her hand. "Marshal Lindsey, we found $300 in ten dollar bills and twenty dollar bank notes in Miz Brown's bodice and another $400 in Miz Pruitt's stockings." She held out the basket containing the money.

Lindsey took one wad and handed it to Bass while he looked at the other. "First National Bank of Longview...Thought as much."

"Same here," said Bass as he thumbed through the packet of money from Miz Pruitt.

"And something else...You know how a woman is more apt to talk to another woman? Well, it seems that Miz Pruitt is actually Miz Wallace and Miz Brown is...Miz Dalton," Pearl added.

"Well dog my cat...Hit the jackpot," Selden exclaimed. "Reckon we'd better go up stairs an' see if'n we kin make a deal. Know the Wallace place is near Elk...need to find out 'zactly where."

"All we got on 'em that'll stick is traffickin'. Don't imagine they's a jury nowhere in the world that will git wives an' mothers on accessory-after-the-fact...but they don't know that," observed Bass. "I 'spect they'll be happy to tell us how to git to the cabin, if'n we promise to let 'em go."

The marshals headed up the stairs.

"We kin have Garrett hold the ladies in the Commissioner's office 'til we check out the Wallace place," said Selden as they reached the landing.

"Shore hope Tobe an' Jed don't have no trouble with Houston Wallace," Bass said with concern in his eyes.

***

CHAPTER FOURTEEN

ARDMORE, I.T.

Loss Hart rode up with the four locals hastily recruited as additional possemen to capture the remainder of the Dalton gang. He had assigned them the duty to drive the Wallace wagon to Elk, and guard the prisoners on the way back to town. He reined up next to Bass. "How did the Houston's woman take to the news about her husband?

"As you would expect. Whole lotta screaming and hollarin'...She do have a mouth on her...Called Selden ev'rythin' in the book and then some...Cussed her old man out for gittin' hisself kilt. Glad I'm not married to a woman like that."

"I hear ya. Got four men to ride along with us."

"Howdy, gents," Bass said.

"Couldn't turn down a chance to ride with Bass Reeves. Now that's sumpthin' to tell our kids about," one of them said.

"Don't know if that be right, but glad to have the company," Bass said as he looked up and saw Selden, Jed and Tobe walk out of the Commissioner's office. "Looks like we 'bout to ride."

Selden untied his horse's lead rope from the hitching post and secured it to a nickel-plated ring on the saddle short skirt. He stepped up in the stirrup and swung easily into the seat, as did the other marshals. His horse shook its head from side to side, sending a small stream of stringy mucous flying from a nostril.

"Guess we're as ready as we're ever gonna be gentlemen."

Tobe nodded. "Time's a wastin'," he said as he reined his horse around and nudged it into a brisk walk. The five lawmen pulled out in front of the wagon and started the first leg of the trip to round up the last of the infamous bunch known as the Dalton Gang.

The sun was high as the four young deputies in the wagon approached the low water crossing at Caddo Creek between Ardmore and Healton. The man at the reins called out, "Whoa up thar, you slab-sided cayus." The horse responded, slowed to a stop, and then lowered her head and began drinking thirstily from the slow moving stream as he eased up on the reins and gave the Wallace mare some slack.

One of the others looked at him and remarked. "Dammit, Charlie, you didn't think to bring us a canteen, did ya?"

"Naw. They was so all fired in a hurry to get goin' that I plum forgot. If yer dyin' of thirst, there's a lot of water in the creek yonder."

Bobby Don looked down at the green algae on the surface of the mostly stagnant water with disdain. "Mind I'll just wait 'til Healton. Oughta be there in forty minutes er so. Don't think they's anythin' else 'fore we cut north towards Elk."

Another twenty-year old sat up in the wagon bed. "Startin' to git a bit hungry, too. Them marshals gonna feed us lunch?"

Charlie Dixon just shrugged his shoulders. "Hell I don't know. Never been on a posse 'fore...you?"

All the rest shook their heads.

"I'd ask 'em, but they's all gone up ahead. Must be a couple miles ahead of us by now. Just said for us to wait in Elk and they would meet up with us once the gang was caught...er kilt," Charlie said.

"Wonder if they would mind if we took a sip of this here whiskey? Loss says it be evidence agin them Dalton women," Ray Earl asked from the back of the wagon.

The four exchanged nervous glances, before Bobby Don made a suggestion, "Don't know 'bout ya'll, but this here ridin' for hours done give me a powerful thirst. May be that a little nip of who-hit-John is just what we need to make the time go by."

"Yeah," the others agreed readily.

"Hand it up here boys, on account I'm the oldest," Bobby Don said as he sat up a little straighter. "I better give it the taste test."

Tony and Ray Earl rolled the small keg out from under the wagon's bench seat and lifted it over the back. Bobby Don looked at the label, branded into the side of the keg.

"Hell's bells! This is the good stuff. Says from Kentuck...Not watered down ner nuthin'!" He struggled with the cork firmly planted in the bunghole. "'Nybody got a knife?" Charlie dug into his jeans for a well worn Barlow knife. "It was my daddy's...Don't bust the blade off or I'll thump yer ass."

"You and who's army?" Bobby Don countered as he fumbled with the blade and finally got it open. Taking the tip and inserting it into the side of the cork, he pried up on it and got the recalcitrant cork to yield slightly.

"Pries it from the other side!" Tony suggested.

"Shut yer trap...I know how to do this."

"Come on, ain't got all day!" Ray Earl urged.

Bobby Don shot him a sideways glance, and then pried up on the other side of the cork. It finally yielded to his repeated attempts and eased out far enough where he could grasp it, give it a twist and pull it out. "Got it!" He folded the knife and handed it back to Charlie.

Cradling the thirty pound keg in his arms, he opened his mouth wide and tried to seal the bunghole as he rocked the keg toward his face. A few ounces of the warm 100 proof bourbon filled his mouth. He struggled to swallow the throat searing hooch without spilling a copious amount. Tears filled his eyes as he gagged slightly and a small amount dribbled back out his nose.

He rolled the keg away from his mouth and gasped for air. "Damn, that's good," he mouthed, but no sound came out.

Charlie chuckled and stuck out his hands.

"Here! Let a man show you how it's done…panty waist."

Bobby Don struggled to get a breath as Charlie took control of the keg. Ray Earl and Tony awaited their turns anxiously.

"How was it? Tony asked impatiently.

Bobby Don wiped the excess off the tip of his nose and upper lip with the back of his hand. He blinked a couple times before he could actually form words. "Smooooth…really smooth."

All four took a couple turns each at the keg before Charlie popped the reins over the horse's rump. The wagon jolted ahead and Tony, the youngest fell backward in the wagon bed, howling from smacking his head on the rough unpainted planks. The other three broke into a fit of laughter at his misfortune.

"That there is the big town of Elk," Bass said as the five lawmen crested a hill. Not much more than a small hamlet of eight houses, it consisted of a small store/post office, a farrier's shop and a couple of barns—it was the closest thing to civilization near the Wallace house.

"We'll tie up in the farrier's corral and walk in from there. If'n we're lucky, we kin slip up through the woods an' git the drop on 'em," Selden said as they rode down the hill. "The wife said they's a trail past the blacksmith shop that leads northwest out to the house. Also the Russell Pretty Branch Creek runs north an' south a bit to the west of the cabin and a ravine with a wet weather stream runnin' east an' west…Ties into the creek at a right angle…House sits in the corner, 'bout forty yards south of the ravine…She said there was a newly planted corn field further to the south, so we'll have to go 'round it through the woods to git to the cabin without bein' seen."

"'Spect one er two of us kin work up the crick an' somebody else go completely 'round to the north to git to the ravine…Just gotta keep from spookin' 'em," Bass offered.

Jed dismounted and opened the gate to the corral. The others rode in silently and followed suit. Each loosened the girths on the saddles and drew out their long guns from their scabbards. Jed walked his horse inside and closed the wooden gate behind him. He removed his canteen from the saddle horn and looped the strap over his left shoulder and head—letting the bulky container drop to a resting spot just above his left hip.

There was an undeniable air of tension about the five lawmen. Not one said a word, and it appeared they were purposely avoiding even looking at each other, as if none wanted to truly consider that one or more of them might not survive the encounter that they were about to face. Tobe gave his horse a couple loving pats on the neck, and then took a long drink from his own canteen, but left it tied to the horn.

A curious eleven year old boy watched as Bass opened his saddle bags and removed a full box of .44-40 ammo and emptied it into the side pocket on his black broadcloth coat. He glanced around at the other strangers and noticed they all had a serious look on their faces. One of them, a tall white man with a large black mustache motioned for him to come closer. Reluctantly, he did.

"You work here, son?" Selden asked.

"Yes, sir. My Pa owns the blacksmith shop an' livery."

Selden reached into a vest pocket and drew out a shiny silver dollar. "See to it that our horses git watered and rubbed down good an' give 'em some hay. Will this cover it?"

The boy nodded.

"Give 'em a bait of grain, too. Be another dollar in it for you when we git back."

"Yes, sir!" the boy said with a definite hint of excitement.

Selden looked up at the other marshals. He took in a deep breath and let it out slowly. "It's time…Let's do it."

With that, he turned and led the group over to the gate. They soon disappeared up the trail.

WALLACE CABIN

"Gracie, 'bout time you go over to the meadow an' git the milk cow 'fore yer mama an' them git back. Reckon she'll need the fresh milk fer supper," Bill Dalton said.

"All right, daddy, in just a few minutes, need to finish this seam on my new dress," the twelve year old replied.

"If that's the right corn field, then the house should be just on the other side," Selden said. "Loss and I will circle round and cover the back side of the house. Tobe, take the front of the house from this side in the woods…you'll have a good field of fire if they try to get out toward the barn."

Tobe nodded.

"You want Jed and me to cover the west side?" Bass asked.

"Right…stay low in the creek to the south until you get in range. I'll be in the creek to the north. Wait for me to call to 'em in the house. We got a couple of their women in custody. Meby it'll make a difference."

Tobe shook his head. "Doubt it. Most of these jayhawkers don't show much tenderness for anyone 'cept themselves."

"Probably right. Give us five minutes to get in place…Ya'll check yer watches."

They all pulled out their pocket watches, looked at the time and nodded.

Loss and Selden were quickly out of sight. A couple of minutes passed before Tobe likewise moved out and was swallowed up in the dense woods. Bass and Jed slowly eased through the woods that showed a shallow drop off to their right toward the creek.

Gracie untied the Guernsey milk cow from grazing spot where she had been staked out for several hours. She was leading the cow back north along the creek past the corn field when she saw the silhouette of a man with a rifle in the woods crouching over and moving slowly toward the house. The twelve year old fought back the urge to run—her heart was pounding. She walked quickly as she could, leading Bessie to the barn and put her in a stall, and then headed back for the house.

Glancing side to side, she searched for other threats as she hid the panic inside and made out as if she hadn't spotted the gray-haired man with a gun. She took the front steps, two at a time, and burst into the main room of the one story house. She spied her father sitting at the kitchen table, reading a two-day-old newspaper.

"Daddy! Daddy! There's man on the other side of the creek! He's got a gun and he's sneaking up on the house!"

"You sure?" he replied as he sprang from the chair. "Did he see you?"

"I was out in the open with Bessie! 'Course he seen me, but I didn't let on that I seen him. Daddy, what'er we gonna do?"

"Calm down, honey," Bill said as he grabbed at a holstered Colt hanging on a peg. "Show me where he was." Bill moved to the front window overlooking the porch. He slipped the gunbelt around his waist as he peeked out the curtain-less window.

"Right up yonder there in the corner of them woods!" she said as she pointed.

Big Asa walked into the room. "What's all the excitement? What going on?"

"Comp'ny...and not the good kind. Get yer gun. Where's Jim and George?"

"Jim's taking a nap...don't know where George is...hell, ain't my day to watch him!"

Bill looked around the room in a panic. He ran to a shelf and pulled off a couple of hard covered books and shook them. A packet of bank notes and bills fluttered out.

"What we gonna do, Daddy?" Gracie asked again.

"*We* ain't doing nothin'. I'm the one with a bounty on me. Stay put! I'll be back when I can..."

Gracie started to cry. "I love you, Daddy," she blubbered as Dalton snatched up the money off the floor and shoved the notes in his overalls.

He kissed Gracie on the forehead and brushed the hair from her eyes. "Love you, too, baby girl...Gotta go!"

He turned and ran to the open back window, crawled out and sprinted toward the woods.

Selden, down in the creek bed, recognized him immediately and called out, "Dalton!" in a strong voice.

Bill heard the shout and saw the tall man stand up near the top of the embankment with a rifle in his hands. He threw up the revolver, pulled back the hammer and snapped a shot that flew just a bit wide, narrowly missing Lindsey, as he ran to his right.

Selden, instinctively ducked as the bullet hissed past his head, *Son-of-a-bitch. He's too good a shot to miss twice.* He quickly lined up his sights and dropped the hammer as Dalton was again cocking his Colt. The .38-56 bucked hard into his shoulder. Dalton stumbled at the impact and fell forward as a shot from Loss Hart's .44-40 rang out from the north. His body jerked again, went limp and slid to a stop in the bright green spring grass—Bill Dalton was dead before he hit the ground.

Bass rose up from cover and called out. "Hello the house! US Marshals! We got you surrounded...come out with yer hands up!"

The sound of glass breaking caused Bass to dive for protection. His reaction was well-timed. A rifle shot from inside a west facing window ripped a hole through the tail of his jacket. Bass fired a couple shots at the gunsmoke with his Winchester.

Inside the house, Big Asa stumbled back, a hole in his shirt just below the second button on his new shirt. He looked down in surprise at the spreading red circle that was just beginning to show bubbles, coughed twice, frothy blood filling his mouth and dribbling down his lower lip. Jim Knight ran into the room just in time to see his big brother's knees buckle. He lunged to catch him, but was a second too late. Asa crashed to the floor, his eyes no longer focusing—in a moment he was dead.

Jim picked up the rifle and ran out the front door. "You God damned bastard laws!" He started levering rounds into the Winchester carbine as fast as he could, shooting at the smoke from the marshal's rifles.

Jed rose up from the creek near the north end of the cornfield, aimed his newly acquired 1892 Winchester at Knight. "Drop it, mister!"

The outlaw swung his rifle in Jed's direction. "The hell you say!"

Jed fired just as Knight brought his rifle to his shoulder. His bullet struck Knight in the forehead, just below the hair line, as he squeezed off his last round. The poorly aimed shot plowed a furrow just to the right of Jed's foot and whined off as it ricocheted into the woods.

The multiple gun shots woke George Bennett from his afternoon nap with a start. He had sat up in the hay piled deep in barn loft and crawled to look out the loft door, just in time to see Dalton fall. Panicked, he scrambled down the homemade ladder, moved to the south door and cautiously peeked out. He watched Jim Knight make his last stand and go down. "Sons of bitches!...They ain't gittin' me." He reached in the back pocket of his new bib overalls and pulled out his .38 caliber Smith and Wesson. George glanced toward the house again and sprinted the opposite direction toward the woods.

The movement caught Tobe's eye—he raised his rifle, but hesitated pulling the trigger as he saw Loss directly in the line of fire beyond the running outlaw. Waiting until the man cleared Hart, Tobe squeezed off a single round, catching Bennett in the thigh and causing him to tumble. George quickly regained his feet, snapped a shot in Tobe's direction and limped into the deep woods. Loss and Tobe both fired again simultaneously, but it was too late—Bennett disappeared into the wilderness. The marshals wisely decided not to pursue the man into the dark woods.

The silence was deafening as the last traces of sulfurous gray gunsmoke drifted away in the soft breeze. From the back door of the cabin, a young brown-headed girl ran screaming toward the body of Bill Dalton. Two preteen boys came out on the back porch, both in tears, watching their sister as she knelt beside her father's body.

ROAD TO ELK

"Gwine to run all night...gwine to run all day...bet my money on the bobtail nag...Hey, guys, Looky! We're almost there!" Charlie sang out as the wagon topped the rise south of the town of Elk. The buckboard rocked back and forth in the springtime ruts.

Bobbie Don said nothing, as the Kentucky bourbon had worked its wonders on him a little too well. Tony was already passed out in the wagon bed.

Ray Earl stood up and hollered as he pointed a finger to the sky. "We made it...by God, we..." His sudden movement was a bit too much for the drunken teen—the young man's eyes rolled up as his lids fluttered. He toppled over the low sideboards of the unsteady conveyance, did a complete somersault and landed face down in the road.

Charlie didn't even notice, and the three young drunks continued their northerly path unaware. He also didn't notice the keg on its side, the plug out and the balance of the whiskey dribbling out onto the wagon bed and through the cracks between the wood planks to the ground.

LOG CABIN

Yellow Owl and One Dog had moved together and were hiding in a cluster of cedar trees on the south side of the cabin.

"Yellow Owl think other pindah-lickoyee no come back," he whispered.

One Dog nodded, and pointed to the privy some forty feet from the cabin on the opposite side from the barn. "Dalaa-Goshe wait by outhouse. White-eye odd, must have special place to leave scat, make big stink. Draw flies...Shis-Inday never understand."

"When pindah-lickoyee man come out again, he wounded...walk with shiny black stick. No hear Be-don-ko-he...Dalaa-Goshe take," said Múh-Jaune. "Me go in house get fire-hair white-eye woman."

One Dog slipped over behind the board-and-batt outhouse and waited with the patience known only to the Apache. The wait was not to be long, however. Jack stepped out on the front porch leaning heavily on the shillelagh, cautiously worked his way down the steps—one at a time—and hobbled toward the convenience. He opened the door with his off hand and went inside. In a few minutes, he pushed the door back open and finished pulling his suspenders up. With the help of the Irish cane, he stepped outside—where everything went black.

Yellow Owl, seeing Jack go down, moved to the front porch with the grace and quietness of a big cat. He opened the door and stepped inside.

Angie was at the kitchen counter, her back to the door when she heard it open. Without turning around, she spoke, "Sure and ye made it out and back in without falling. That's a good start." There was no response. She turned around and then screamed...

WALLACE CABIN

Bass, Selden and the other marshals cautiously left their places of concealment and congregated at Dalton's body with his daughter still collapsed on top, sobbing. They looked at each other, uncomfortable in their own way over the situation with the young girl—none knew exactly what to do.

"We git 'em all?" Selden asked.

"One slipped into the woods…had a hole in his leg though. He'll turn up somewheres next week, I 'spect," Tobe answered.

The sound of a horse trotting caused them to turn toward the road to the south.

A bearded man, somewhat resembling the late Houston Wallace, rode up on the group. "What's all this then?"

"US Deputy Marshals…Who would you be?" asked Selden.

"Bob Wallace, Houston's my brother…Got a place near two miles west. Thought I heard shootin'…Came to see." He looked around. "Where's Houston?"

"Got hisself kilt in Ardmore…Kin you identify this man?"

Wallace got down from his horse, moved over and gently raised Gracie to her feet and hugged her. "It's alright, Gracie, it's alright…" He released her, knelt down and rolled the body over face up. Gracie began to wail anew.

"Bill Dalton…this here is Bill Dalton…Dammit, tol' that hard-headed brother of mine when he quit marshalin' not to be consortin' with his kind, but no, he wouldn't listen…an' now looky here…Both of 'em are dead before their time." He got back to his feet and put an arm around Gracie again.

"Seems as though they's a couple more younguns at the house yonder...Trust you'll be a takin' care of 'em?" asked Bass. "Reckon we kin make loan of yer horse? Got a wagon an' our horses in Elk that we be a needin' to git here...Gonna have to load the bodies up an' take 'em to Ardmore."

Bob nodded. "Who kilt him?"

The marshals all glanced at one another before Selden spoke, "Cain't say...lots of bullets a flyin'." Bass and Loss nodded. "Jed, you mind ridin' back to Elk an' have the other possemen bring the wagon an' our horses?"

Jed nodded, picked up the reins to Bob Wallace's horse, mounted up and rode south.

ROAD TO ARDMORE

Jack woke up to a jolt as the wagon bounded over a rock in the road. It took a couple seconds before he figured out exactly where he was. He could see blue sky and recognized the familiar green painted sideboard of Angie's farm wagon. His head hurt anew, but this time, it was on the other side from where the bullet had creased him. *What the hell?*

He tried to sit up, and then realized his hands were bound behind his back and his feet were likewise tied together. His bandana had been stuffed in his mouth and knotted tight behind his head. He heard two men talking in a tongue he could not clearly understand. The words were some he had heard before—he wracked his brain and tried to remember where and from whom. Suddenly it came back to him—Apaches!

Jack gathered his strength and rolled onto his side. The sight of Angie, similarly trussed up with a bruise on the side of her left cheek sent his blood boiling as untamed rage built inside him. But, there was absolutely nothing he could do about it.

WALLACE CABIN

Bob Wallace walked a still grieving Gracie toward the house and her brothers, leaving the rest of the lawmen standing and looking down at the body.

"End of an era, boys...end of an era. The last of the old time outlaws...Reckon the press will have to quit makin' Bill Dalton into some kinda dang Robin Hood," Selden mused. "How they was thrilled when he shot his way out of scrape after scrape. Made fools out of posse after posse...Would drop in on a church social er send word back to lawmen a tailin' him which trail he would take...Press always makes it out different than it was...Wonder if'n it'll ever change?" He looked over at Bass who shook his head.

"Prob'ly not, Sel, prob'ly not. They'll always want to be a romanticizin' the outlaw. What with them dime novels an' magazines, play actin', an' even in them movin' pictures I heered about. They's gonna put play actin' on pictures an' show it up on a white wall fer people to watch...Train robbin', stage an' bank hold ups an' shoot outs...Know what's funny?"

"What's that?" asked Tobe.

"Folks 'er actually gonna believe it...like it was real er somethin'...Nosiree, you wait an' see...the world ain't never gonna give up the Old West...never."

"Bass, that sounds like some kinda fairy tale. Cain't swaller it, jest cain't...Next thin' I guess you'll be a sayin' is we'll all be a flyin around the sky like birds...er go to the moon like in that writer feller, Jules Verne's book. Haw!" said Loss.

"Wait, just you wait." Bass grinned.

***

CHAPTER FIFTEEN

WALLACE CABIN

"While we're a waitin' on Jed and the posse to come up, we best take the time to search the house…We know fer certain the gang got away with over two thousand dollars. Now, Dalton had $285 in his pockets. His wife had $300 an' Houston's wife had $400…My bet the rest is it hidden in the house," Selden said.

Tobe nodded. "No time like the present. We'll get Houston's brother to take the kids outside for a bit. Hate to have 'em watch it all play out, but…well, you know."

"Yeah, I do," said Bass. "Makes me sorry for the little ones. They likely had no choice in the business…You don't git to choose yer folks."

The four moved around to the front door and entered. All three of the Dalton kids were huddled around their *Uncle Bob*.

"Mr. Wallace, if'n you don't mind, we still have a little business to take care of here in the house. It might be better if the young 'uns didn't have to watch," Bass said.

"I'll take 'em outside for a walk...Where are the rest of Dalton's men, 'sides the big one in the house and Jennie and Maude?"

"We can talk 'bout that later, I 'spect the women'll be home by tomorra."

"I see," Wallace said glumly, as he herded the kids to the door.

ELK, I.T.

Jed rode up to the livery and spied the young stable boy holding onto the lead rope to the mare hooked to the Wallace wagon. Both Charlie and Bobby Don were passed out on the seat. "What 'n hell happened here?"

The young man couldn't help but laugh. "She walked in here all by herself. I seen it was the Wallace's rig right off, 'cause me and my Pa shoe all their stock...but these three strangers are drunker 'n Cooter Brown!"

"Oh, Jesus, Mary an' Joseph...Marshal Hart gonna have a big ol' piece of their white butts if'n they done gone and drank up all the evidence," Jed said as he rode up and looked down at the empty keg laying on the bed. "Son, you ever been in a posse a'for?"

"No, sir. Ain't but eleven."

"Old enough. Kin you drive that rig up to the Wallace place?

"Yessir."

"You swear to foller my orders?"

The freckle-faced child nodded.

"Fine...Yer deputized. Roll them two into the back an' hitch our saddle horses to the rear. We be needin' to head on back up there. They's a waiting fer us."

"Yes, sir!"

In thirty minutes, Jed and the wagon pulled into the yard in front of the cabin. Selden and the other marshals had brought Dalton and the two Knight brothers' bodies and laid them side-by-side on the porch. Loss Hart did a double take at the sight of the young boy driving the wagon.

"What in tarnation?" He jogged down the steps and ran up to the boy. "Where are my deputies?"

The tow-headed youngster grinned and pointed his thumb back over his shoulder. "You mean them three, Marshal? My Pa would say they done fell into the corn...Oh, I'm yer deputy now."

Loss' face flushed as he peered over the sideboards. "Consarn those inbred bunch o' cretins! By God, I got me half a mind to..."

"Easy there, son. I got a feelin' they're gonna feel bad enough in the mornin' to never touch another drop...leastwise 'til the next time," Selden said with a grin as he walked up beside the wagon. "Wait a minute...I thought they was four of when we left town."

"They wuz four, back in Ardmore. Two-bits on the chance we find one of 'em layin' in the road somewheres."

"No bet there, pard…Let's load up the stiffs. We'll be lucky to make it home before dark."

ROAD BACK TO ARDMORE

A half mile south of Elk, the procession came across a body lying face down in the road. Selden reined to a halt beside it and turned in the saddle to call back to Loss, who had taken over driving the wagon. "Look familiar?"

"Cain't see his face from here. Roll him over, Sel."

Lindsey swung down and ground-tied his horse. He slipped the square toe of his tall cavalry style boot under the young man's shoulder and rolled him over—his face was covered in dried blood from an apparent broken nose. The man moaned a couple times, but made no move to get up.

"Yep, that's Ray Earl Wilkinson, the dumb sumbitch. Serves him right." Loss set the brake on the wagon and tied off the reins before he stepped down.

Selden and Loss hoisted him upright, dragged him to the back of the wagon and dumped him on top of the other bodies.

"You know, when we get back, I might have to give you schoolin' of the finer points of posse selection…"

Loss shot a look back at the more senior marshal. "Go ahead, rub it in. I prob'ly deserve it."

Selden slapped him on the shoulder. "Well you gotta admit, it does add a little spice to the story of the final saga of the Dalton gang."

"That it does, Selden, that it does."

ARDMORE, I.T.
PERKINS COUNTY SHERIFF'S OFFICE

Yellow Owl and One Dog half drug Angie and a hobbling Jack into Sheriff Cobb's office.

"Here pindah-lickoyee woman Be-don-ko-he sent to fetch. Not know who ugly man is, bring anyway. You pay for him too," said Yellow Owl.

"Who are you, feller? An' what were you doin' at the widder's place?" Cobb asked.

He stood a little straighter and looked the sheriff in the eye. "I am Jack McGann...United States Deputy Marshal, Fort Smith, Arkansas."

The sheriff blanched for a moment then regained his composure. "Hell, man, anybody kin say they'er a law officer. Show me yer badge."

"I, uh, lost it...But you kin contact..."

"I ain't contactin' nobody. Far as I'm concerned, yer associatin' with a murderess the likes this country has never seen. Reckon that makes you a killer too...I'll jest add yer name to the warrant 'long with hers...How do you like them apples...Marshal?" Cobb laughed. "Yer gonna hang, right along with her..."

"What about a trial?" Jack asked.

"Oh, you'll git a trial alright...then we'll hang you."

"Barney, lock 'em up in cells one an' three."

The jailer nodded and escorted them toward the cells in the back room.

Cobb opened the top drawer of his desk and took out ten double eagles. "Here you are Yellow Owl, one hunderd dollars, the extra fifty fer the man," he said as he handed the Apache the stack of gold coins.

Yellow Owl took the top coin, bit down on it, looked at his teeth marks and nodded. "Shis-Inday go." Both men turned and left the office.

Damn glad they're gone. Apache bastards give me a cold chill, he thought as he got up and walked over to the stove for a fresh cup of coffee.

A cub reporter from the Daily Ardmoreite burst into the office causing the sheriff to spill the coffee he was trying to pour into his cup. He still was suffering from the broken right wrist.

"Dang it, boy!…Don't go bustin' in here like that!"

"Sheriff, Sheriff!…He's dead!…He's dead!"

"Who's dead? What in tarnation you babblin' about?"

"Bill Dalton, that's who. Marshals kilt him over to Elk this afternoon. They're bringin' the body to the undertakers."

"Well, well, well…That ought to keep them Federal boys busy fer a while."

The sun had set as the bone-weary lawmen turned down the street leading to Marston Appollas' funeral parlor. A large crowd of nearly a thousand strong had gathered to witness the sensational story of the killing of the great Bill Dalton. Tobe had ridden ahead to make certain the undertaker was prepared for three bodies, and one of his apprentices had run to alert the newspaper and the town sheriff. Several of the men held coal oil lamps in their hands to pierce the gathering darkness.

"Here they come!" one skinny older man called out when the two riders leading the procession turned the street.

"Appollas's gonna run plum outta caskets, them marshals stay around here much longer," said another.

The entire crowd began to murmur with excitement, children broke away from the throng and ran to tag alongside the wagon.

Loss pulled the wagon up to the sidewalk as Tobe tried to push the milling mass back to make room.

"Must be half a dozen of 'em kilt!" one man yelled as he leaned in for a closer look.

Men and women both pressed in for a better view.

Suddenly, Ray Earl sat up, his eyes snapped open wide and he turned to face a woman who was squashed up against the sideboard. She saw his bloody face and screamed just as he threw up on her embroidered bodice. She, along with two other women fainted from the sight. Ray Earl passed out again and fell back prone.

"All right people! Make a hole!" Selden yelled with authority. "Move back I say!"

Bass dismounted and pushed through the unruly crowd. "You heard the man…Give us some room!"

The throng slowly edged back as Bass and Jed reached the back of the wagon. Bass reached in and grabbed one body by the shirt collar and yanked it off the stack. Jed helped stand him upright. The crowd gasped in awe.

"Bobby Don is dead!" one of the onlookers shouted.

"Dead?...Dead drunk is more likely. You know this yahoo?" Bass asked.

"Sure, he's my nephew!"

"Good, he's all yers," Reeves said with no shortage of disgust.

The man put his arms around the limp former posseman and dragged him back away from the wagon. Loss Hart stepped over the six remaining water-soaked bodies.

"Anybody here claim to know Ray Earl Wilkinson?"

"That's my boy! He alive?" a man called out from the back of the crowd.

"Matter of opinion...Got 'im a good whiskey bump, you might say."

"But I don't allow no drinkin' in my home!"

"Figures...Well, he ain't drinkin' now...Come give us a hand. We got us two more drunk ex-deputies to move before we get to the Dalton gang."

Once the drunks and lifeless bodies were separated and the dead men laid out on the sidewalk, the crowd began to comment about the identities of the deceased.

"That ain't Bill Dalton! I seen him before and he ain't near that big...Look at the belly on that man!"

"Don't look like him a'tall," said another.

Selden and Tobe heard the comments.

"The man's bloated all ready, been a hot day is all. We poured water on 'em ever chanct we got...didn't help much."

297

"You shot the wrong man, Marshal. Don't look like the wanted poster no way," said another.

Tobe looked over at Selden. "I know one surefire way to find out, even if his neighbor did say it was him."

"And that would be what?"

"Bring 'em inside and go get his wife. I mind she'll break down when she sees him."

"Got a point there. Bass, you want to go over to the Commissioner's office an' git her?"

Bass nodded and pressed his way through the surging crowd.

Local newspapermen moved in to interview the lawmen.

"Who killed Dalton, Marshall? Who's the hero?"

"Ain't no heroes 'round here...No questions now. Cain't you see we got work to do? Give us chance to take care of the bodies first."

"Mighty fine shootin' though...right in the chest...or is that an exit wound?...How far away was he, Marshal Selden?"

"Dammit man! What part of *no* do you not understand?"

Jed and Loss lifted Dalton's body and carried it to the entrance to the undertakers.

"Give us some room, people!" Tobe shouted as he moved to open the door.

Once all the outlaws were laid out in the back room, Loss Hart stood guard by the front doors. Bass knocked loud to gain entrance.

"It's Bass...open up!" he said in his unmistakable deep voice.

Loss unlocked the double doors, allowing Bass and the two women to enter. Each took one by the elbow and led them back to the embalming room. Jennie Dalton was shaking with misapprehension, afraid of what she knew in her heart she would find. Three tables were lined up, preparatory to Doc Gibson coming over to do the autopsies—each with a body draped in a white cotton sheet. The room had a distinctive medicinal smell, plus an almost overpowering scent of pine oil to try to mask the scent of death and decomposition.

Selden stood beside a large corpse. "Can you help us identify these men for the record, Miz Dalton?"

She nodded almost imperceptibly as he pulled the sheet back to reveal Asa Knight.

"That's Big Asa, all right," she said softly as tears streamed down.

Selden pulled the sheet up and turned to the next body.

"Jim Knight, Asa's brother," she sobbed.

Selden nodded and moved around the table after replacing the sheet over Jim. He couldn't force himself to look the widow in the eyes, as he lifted the sheet revealing Dalton.

She stiffened and hesitated. "That's not Bill."

"What's that you say, ma'am?"

"I said that's not my husband, Bill Dalton!"

Bass and Selden looked at each other.

"Well guess we got 'nother fer Potter's Field, Selden," Bass said shaking his head. "Yep, jest another hooligan without a name er headstone."

It was then Jennie Dalton broke and let out with a long sobbing wail. "Oh, Bill!...Bill...God, what have they done to you?" she cried out as she slumped toward the floor.

Bass caught her as she fell and pulled her gently to him for support. Maude broke away from Loss and ran to her aid.

"You bastards! Is that enough proof for you!" she screamed.

Tears rimmed Bass' eyes. Identification of killed loved ones was never easy, even if the deceased were wanted criminals. "Sorry, Selden, I hated to do it thataway...but didn't see no choice."

Selden nodded and moved closer to Jennie. He placed a hand on her shoulder and spoke softly as her body racked with sobs. "I'm so sorry 'bout this, Miz Dalton...Sorry it turned out thisaway...You both 'er free to go...all charges against you 'er dropped."

She looked up and said nothing, the shock of the ordeal still too much to comprehend.

"Go on now, ma'am. Your children'll be needin' you...You wagon is right outside," Bass said with obvious caring in his voice.

"Let's go home," Maude Wallace said as she pulled Jennie away from Bass.

The morning's paper proclaimed the death of Bill Dalton in bold letters. The report gave credit to Loss Hart for the killing shot based on the initial observations of the mortician. The bullet had entered the back, just above the kidney and exited just below the left nipple—Marston Appollas said and he well knew a .44 caliber bullet wound. Selden Lindsey had carried a .38-56 Winchester. Dr. Gibson would make the final determination when the bodies were autopsied later.

At breakfast, well-wishers dropped by to congratulate the marshal for the accomplishment.

"Mighty fine shootin' there, Loss. Guess that kinda makes you a hero 'round these parts."

Loss just glared up at the man, then resumed eating.

"Like we agreed, Loss, jest gotta ignore 'em…Won't be made a spectacle of," whispered Selden.

Doctor Gibson washed his hands in the basin with lavender scented strong lye soap and then dried them on a towel. The white cotton surgical mask still hung around his neck. He turned to the marshals. "There were two bullets in Dalton's body. A .44 caliber ball that entered from the lower back and stopped, somewhat flattened, against the inside of the third rib on the left side…The other was a .38 caliber slug I found lodged in the heart…That was the kill shot. However, he would have eventually expired from the other round due to massive trauma and blood loss…but he was dead when he fell."

"Doc, we'd appreciate it if'n you'd keep the autopsy results to yerself. Folks don't need to know," said Selden.

"Why, for God's sake man? You killed the last of the Dalton gang. I'd think that you'd want…"

"Well, you'd be thinkin' wrong. The man who killed Bill Dalton would become a circus side show...won't have it. Best that they always wonder...Don't you see?"

"I suppose. Of course I have to file the report for court records, you understand."

"I understand, but it'll take 'em some time to go through all that stuff and by then this will have all blown over."

He was wrong...

Bass, Tobe and Jed were scattered about Selden and Loss's office, working on fresh cups of coffee. Lindsey was reading the article from the paper they brought over from Sally's after breakfast.

"Uh, huh, just like I said out to the Wallace place, damn newspaper reporters never git it right. They think they got to lay in their own opinion instead of just the facts. It's beyond me why they have to sensationalize ever little thang." He opened the four page daily paper to the second page and was perusing the obituaries and local arrest filings. "Great jumpin' horny toads!" He stood up from his chair.

"What is it, Sel?" Bass asked.

Selden walked over and handed him the paper. "Here, read fer yerself...Ain't gonna believe it."

"Uh, Sel, you'll have to read it out loud. I ain't very passable at readin' writin'. I kin recognize names an' such on warrants, but never learn't to read proper."

"Oh, right, sorry Bass...Uh, says here, bottom of page two:

'Local Couple Arrested on Multiple
Murder Charges, Trial Set For Monday.
Angela Maureen O'Reilly and M. Jack
McGann were arrested yesterday by the
Pickens County Sheriff's Department on
multiple counts of murder. Indictments
were handed down by the Grand Jury last
night. Trial is set for County Judge
Henry Graham's court Monday at 11:00am.'"

"Holy Mother…that bastard sheriff. Asshole did that whilst we were out scoutin' after the Dalton gang!" said Loss.

A deep furrow creased Bass' forehead. Tobe noticed his jaw muscles were working.

"Gonna bust a tooth, there Bass…Got somethin' on yer mind?"

"He's al'ays got somethin' on his mind, don't cha know?" Jed offered.

Bass jumped to his feet and headed to the door. "Be back in a bit."

"Don't do nothin' brash…Want one of us to go along with you?"

"No." He slammed the door behind him.

"Don't know where he's a goin', but I wouldn't want be where it is," said Tobe.

PICKENS COUNTY COURT HOUSE
CHICKASAW NATION

The small courtroom was packed—standing room only. Many of the observers were from the Chickasaw Nation. Angie

O'Reilly and Jack McGann, hands shackled in front of them, were led by a bailiff to chairs behind a long table in front and just to the left of the judge's bench.

A smirking barrister Jason Alexander Baldwin and his secretary, Hillary Kerry were seated behind an identical table to the right. Baldwin was acting as county prosecutor for the joint murder trial of Angie and Jack. They had been indicted for the murders of Percy "Cougar" and Bosco "Ox" Cole and Camillus "Bobo" Green.

Bass, Jed, Tobe, Selden, Loss, Winchester Ashalatubbi and Ben Sixkiller sat in the first row of church-style benches behind a railing. Each of the men looked as if they could chew nails.

"All rise for the honorable county judge Henry Bartholomew Graham," announced the middle age bailiff.

Everyone in the courtroom rose as a diminutive man—less than 5' 3" tall—in a black robe, strode into the room from his adjacent chambers. His movements and attitude were somewhat reminiscent of a Bantam rooster—commonly called a *banty*. He had what some might term a Napoleonic complex. The judge flared his robe and took his seat behind the large dark mahogany desk on a fourteen inch riser at the front of the room. What the attendees could not see behind his bench was an eight inch taller than standard custom chair and the small box set underneath for his feet.

"Be seated," ordered the bailiff. "The County of Pickens in the Chickasaw Nation versus Angela Maureen O'Reilly and Marmaduke Jackson McGann is now in session," he recited as the assemblage sat back down.

Bass glanced around the room and at the closed back doors.

"On your feet," the judge barked. "Angela O'Reilly and Jack McGann, you stand here in my court today accused of the heinous crime of cold-blooded murder of three of Pickens County's most stalwart and respected citiz…"

"Good God almighty! Those three no-accounts…"

"Quiet in the court!" the judge interrupted Selden, slamming his gavel twice. "Marshal Lindsey, you will refrain from any further outbursts in my court room or I'll have you ejected and fined. You are here only out of respect for the badge you wear, but I'll tolerate no disruption of these proceedings. Do you understand?"

Lindsey just glared at the little man.

"Do you understand?"

"Yes, sir," he said softly.

"I can't hear you!"

"I said yes, sir, *your honor*!…You little peacock," he added under his breath.

"What was that last part?"

"Nothin', nothin' at all…yer honor."

Judge Graham nodded his satisfaction. "Now where was I? Oh, yes. Do you have representation?" the judge addressed the pair.

"Reckon not, yer honor. We wasn't given enough time to find coun…"

"That won't be necessary," came a booming voice from the back of the room. A large man in a three piece black suit with a black cravat strode through the double doors

A low murmur ran through the court room as heads turned. Jason Baldwin and his secretary exchanged surprised glances. The entire row of US Deputy Marshals broke into wide grins and nudged one another. Sixkiller and Ashalatubbi exchanged curious glances.

The barrel-chested man stood almost 6' 4" with a full head of white hair, a white mustache and goatee and dark piercing eyes. "I will be their representation," he added as he took his place beside Angie and Jack.

"And just who are you, sir? I don't believe I recognize you...Have you ever practiced in my court?"

"I have not...I, sir, am Issac Charles Parker...from Fort Smith, Arkansas."

The color drained from Judge Graham's face. Jason Baldwin lurched as if he were gut shot.

Five full seconds of palpable silence ensued before Henry Graham was able to respond, "Judge Parker...uh, welcome to my court. It's an honor and privilege to have someone of your stature in jurisprudence to join these proceedings. I hope..."

"Interesting that you said *stature*, you little popinjay...I don't refer to you as *Judge* for you have disgraced the very robe you wear with this mockery of a trial. Not only are you subverting federal law and *my* jurisdiction, but you have tried to railroad these citizens by violating every legal precept of which I am aware...You, sir, had the temerity to begin a trial without affording the defendants proper representation and not even having a jury of their peers on hand...in direct violation of the Constitution of the United States of America, not to say anything of the small matter that this is Indian Territory and as such, is totally...I repeat, totally under federal jurisdiction."

Parker walked slowly and deliberately to the desk, placed both hands on the top, leaned in and looked down at Graham's cowering, ashen face. "Your *justice for hire* scheme, perfidy and malfeasance of office shall not go unpunished, sir. As of this moment, you are stripped of your position and I can readily assure you that you'll never practice law or again sit in judgment on *any* creature anywhere in this great land. I have ever had the single aim of justice in view...*Do equal and exact justice* is my motto, and I have often said to the grand jury, *Permit no innocent man to be punished...but let no guilty man escape.* The total absence of remorse and even common human decency typifies your pestiferous nature and I *will* see it eradicated.

"You and your partners in this nefarious and calumnious undertaking..." Judge Parker turned, pointed a finger at Jason Baldwin and then at Sheriff Cobb.

Baldwin sprang to his feet. "It was all Graham's doings, Judge. He ordered me and the Sheriff to obtain her property by any means. He's the one..."

He froze as Parker turned back to him and fixed his steely dark-eyed stare—known to actually make lesser men fall over in a state of apoplexy in his presence.

Parker continued, "The lot of you shall be transported *in shackles* to the 9th District Court of the United States in Fort Smith, Arkansas where you will stand before me in trial for your crimes…and may God have mercy on you…for I shall not."

He turned to Bass. "Marshal Reeves will you, Marshal Neal and Marshal Lindsey please take these two abominations in the eyes of the law into custody…along with that sorry excuse for a sheriff over there…pending transport."

"It will be a pleasure, your honor," Bass said as he, Jed and Selden got up from their seats and moved toward Graham, Baldwin and Cobb respectively—each removed a set of wrist cuffs from their coat pockets.

"I trust you have facilities for their temporary incarceration, Marshal Lindsey?"

"Yessir, do believe I have a vacancy."

"Marshal Bassett would you mind removing the cuffs from my deputy and the young lady?"

"Nothin' would make me happier, your Honor."

He approached Jack and Angie, removed a standard handcuff key from his vest pocket, unlocked both their shackles and dropped them on the table.

Angie and Jack embraced, then Jack turned and shook hands with Judge Parker. "You shore do know how to make an entrance, Judge."

Parker leaned over and whispered in Jack's ear. "I was waiting in the foyer for the right moment…I have been accused from time to time of being a trifle theatrical, but keep it under your hat, my friend."

"Well, we're both much obliged, Judge. Was shore surprised to see you come through the door when you did."

"Had to, Jack, your off time had completely run out...Marmaduke? Haw!" Parker grinned and slapped Jack on the back.

"Family name, Judge. Back to my grand daddy, Robert Marmaduke McGann. We just called him Granpa Duke." Jack grinned sheepishly and then glanced at Angie. "Uh...got me a big favor to ask of you, your honor, that is...uh, of course, Judge, uh...if you are of a mind."

"Jack McGann, just cut to the chase, man!"

He swallowed hard and took Angie's hand and squeezed it as she looked curiously at him.

"Well, sir, we would sure 'preciate it if'n you would do us the honor of marryin' us."

The question brought a huge smile to the usually taciturn Judge, but before he could speak, Angie interrupted him.

"Marryin'? By all that's holy!...Jack McGann...you would think it's proper to ask a woman such a question, before ye go and go making any cockamamie requests! Faith and are ye daft, man?" Her green eyes flashed and a touch of pink filled her cheeks.

"Didn't figure you'd say no in front of the Judge."

She crossed her arms defiantly. "Had it all planned out, did ye now?...All but a decent proposal! What kind of woman do ye..."

"Angie O'Reilly, would you do me the great honor of being my lawful wedded wife?" Jack blurted out in desperation.

"You leather-headed numbskull...I thought you'd never ask!"

"'Bout time, Pard," Bass said from across the room.

Jack swept her up in his arms and kissed her passionately as the still crowded courtroom erupted in applause.

***

EPILOGUE

LOG CABIN

The private reception, chivaree and fish fry after the wedding was in full swing. A number of the Chickasaw Council wives were in charge of the cast iron wash pots full of boiling lard—set over oak fires—for the frying of corn mealed catfish filets and bream. The pots cooking the fish, fry bread and sliced sweet potatoes were in the shade of a large red oak tree. Just a short distance away, were several yard tables covered with red and white checkered cloths laden with bowls of potato salad, creamed corn and pies. The tables were next to a small hand-carved headstone that just read:

BOOT - MY BEST FRIEND

Tobe stood for just a moment at the stone, his eyes beginning to fill with tears. Angie walked over to him with a thick-stemmed goblet—she put her hand on his shoulder.

"Thought you might like some cold cider, Tobe," she said softly.

He turned to her, quickly wiped his eyes and took the glass. "Thanks, Angie...you always seem to know when a man's in the dismals...You an' Jack 'er gonna make a great couple."

"It's I who'd be thankin' you and the other marshals, for bringing Judge Parker here and getting us out of that brobdingnagian fix we were in...Now, come along with ye and I'll be fixin' your plate."

The other men, including a number of council members and Chickasaw Lighthorse were all standing around in groups, sipping on the homemade apple cider and telling stories. Selden and Bass were deep in conversation with Judge Parker near the path to the falls.

"Really glad you decided to stay fer the fish-fry, Judge," said Selden.

"Ain't it the truth...don't think I've ever seen you in jest shirt sleeves, Judge. Makes you look almost..."

"Human, Bass?" He chuckled. "I'm no different than you men. I enforce the law...just do it from a different place, is all. Sometimes I wish I could ride the trail with you after outlaws on the scout, instead of dealing with them in my court."

"Yessir."

"You know, Selden, I'm glad I stayed too. It's almost like a vacation for me...I needed a break...and if you'd believe it, this was the first time I've ever performed a wedding ceremony for one of my own marshals...Haven't had this much fun since I can't remember when."

"I'll be danged. An' fer Marmaduke too." Bass roared with laughter.

Selden and Parker joined in the belly laughs.

"Now why is it, when a man gits married he becomes the butt of some jokester?" said Jack as he limped up with the shillelagh in one hand and his drink in the other.

"Oh, it ain't on account of you gittin' married, Mar...uh, Jack. You kin trust us on that," said Bass, still grinning as he slapped his partner on the back.

"Judge, 'peers as though I'm gonna need a little more off time...One, gotta finish healin' up an' two Angie an' I need to git in our plantin' 'fore it gits too dry...if it's alright."

"Certainly, Jack. Way ahead of you. I had already told Bass and Jed to stick around and give you a hand with getting your crops in and all...You need to spend a some time with your lovely wife and get to know one another...I can tell you from experience, that's very important...Your job will be waiting when you're ready."

"Really 'preciate it, Judge."

"Bass, how was it that you wuz able to git the Judge here so fast? No way you coulda give him all the information in a telegram," Selden asked.

"Used one of them new-fangled talkin' machines from Mr. Alexander Graham Bell an' jest called the Judge. Noticed Mr.

May had one in his store. He said it wuz a lot easier makin' orders on it than telegrams…Showed me how to use it."

"It was fortuitous that I recently had one installed in my chambers…It's the coming thing. Bass was able to fill me in with all the facts and I caught the first train out…You gentlemen know the rest."

"Say…Where'd Jack go?" Bass turned and looked around.

"There he goes, him and that white wolf of his," Selden said as he pointed at Jack and Boy slowly heading down the trail to the falls.

"Think I'll follow," said Bass as he motioned to Winchester Ashalatubbi.

The Chickasaw shaman moved over to Bass and the others. "What is it, Bass?"

"Jack's headin' toward the falls, followin' Boy. Somethin's up…Why don't you come along too, Judge?" He turned and started down the trail accompanied by the shaman, Selden and Parker.

Jack stood next to the shoreline, his gaze fixated on the water tumbling down the seventy-seven feet to the pool. The mist and spray boiled up obscuring the cave behind the falls. Boy sat beside him, staring up at his face. Anna walked from behind a clump of bushes, stopped beside the great white wolf and laid her arm across his massive shoulders.

"Thank you," she said softly.

Jack turned and looked down at the little girl. "For what?"

"For taking such good care of my mommy."

Bass and the others came around the corner and saw Jack and the wolf. Winchester put out his hands to stop everyone and then held a finger to his lips.

"What is it?" Judge Parker whispered.

"He speaks with the spirit of Anna," replied Anompoli Lawa. "We must stay back."

"Spirit?" questioned Parker. "I only see Jack and the animal."

"You're not allowed to see. The spirits select only a few. Even I cannot see her, but I sense she's there…We must wait."

"I kinda thought it was the other way 'round," Jack replied.

"You found each other. It was meant to be. I've been waiting for you…we've both been waiting for you to come…But now, you must help me. Come for me…daddy." Anna turned and slowly walked into the water until it was up to her waist. She looked back over her shoulder. "Come for me, please." She dissolved into a mist.

Jack looked up at the falls and then down to Boy. "Well, son, think I know what she wants." The wolf nudged his hand.

"Now we can approach, she is gone," the shaman said and began to walk toward Jack.

"You alright?" Bass asked as they got closer.

Jack did not turn around. "Fine, I'm fine." He then turned to the men. "Somethin' I gotta do tomorra…gonna need some help, Bass…Cain't do it by myself."

"What ever you need, Pard."

"Come on back up to the cabin an' I'll tell ya what I got in mind."

Bass, Jack, Selden and Boy started up the trail—Parker and Winchester stayed beside the pool.

"Tell me, what is this place, Shaman?" Parker asked. "It's beautiful."

"One of our holy of holies, Judge. Very sacred to the Chickasaw people...and to the people that were here long before us." He paused and looked at the big jurist. "Something you would find interesting, being a man of letters...Inside the cave...behind the falls where Angie found Jack almost dead, there are petroglyphs from thousands of years ago. Having been a student of divinity and studying Hebrew, I recognized several particular hieroglyphs as also being in the Masoretic Text. These hieroglyphs illustrate...*Jehovah - God of Isreal.*"

"Oh, my Lord!" Parker exclaimed.

"Exactly." Winchester nodded. "In the Muscogean language shared by the Cherokee, Chickasaw, Choctaw and Creek...one of our words for the Great Spirit, or God if you will, is...*Chihóa.*"

"Astonishing...So much for Columbus," the judge offered.

"I'm afraid he was a Johnny-come-lately to these shores...So you see why this is a holy place to us...We all worship the same God."

"So it would seem, so it would seem."

"Some think that when the Temple of Solomon was destroyed by Nebuchadnezzar II in 587 BCE, one of the tribes of Israel somehow made it across the Atlantic to America...and apparently some came all the way to the Arbuckles...Just supposition on my part, you understand."

"Who is to say it's not?...To quote from Shakespeare's Hamlet, 'There are more things in heaven and earth, Horatio, than are dreamt of in your philosophy'."

Winchester nodded and they made their way back to the cabin.

The morning dawned clear and bright with signs of it being a warm spring day. Angie sat a large platter of pancakes stacked five inches high on the table for the men. It had been decided the night before that it would be better for them to stay there in lieu of making two trips. Judge Parker was driven in by Ben Sixkiller and Winchester Ashalatubbi as he had a train to catch that morning back to Fort Smith. They would return in time for the planned event around noon.

"Whoa, but that looks good Miss Angie, er Miz McGann...but what 'er they gonna eat?" Loss said referencing the other marshals.

"Pay him no mind, ma'am. Selden tells me he's a bottomless pit...Ain't that so, Sel?" Bass said.

"Never seen him walk away from 'nythin' less than a clean plate yet."

"It's not worrying I'll be. Have more than enough batter, I do. Sure and be helping yourselves."

"See?...she don't mind, so there," Loss added. "Oh, say Jack, fergot to tell ya. We got yer saddle an' other tack at the office. Found it an' Montford's stuff at Baldwin's minin' camp. Reckon that locks in who bushwhacked ya'll...Bring it out on the next trip."

"Huh?...Oh, 'preciate it, Loss. Had that saddle a long time. Was hatin' the thought of breakin' in a new one." Jack returned to his reverie of staring off out the window.

"Yer bein' kindly quiet, Jack. Ain't like you," said Bass.

"Aw, jest been thinkin'."

"About what, me husband?"

He turned and looked at her with his limpid brown eyes. "That I want you to stay up here to the house, Angiedarlin'."

"And it's no such thing I'll be doing."

"I really think it would be best, ma'am," Selden offered sincerely.

The rest of the men all nodded and looked at her. Angie nervously brushed a lock of her red tresses away from her face. "It's outnumbered, I am. And it's a ninnyhammer I'd have to be to argue with the likes of this bunch."

Jack got to his feet and hugged his wife. "That's my girl...Everythin' will be fine, you'll see."

The sun was almost directly overhead as Jack and the group gathered on the north side of the falls pool. Included in the assemblage were Bass, Tobe, Selden, Loss, Jed, the just arrived Ben Sixkiller and the Chickasaw Shaman, Anompoli Lawa with his medicine pouch. Bass started linking three thirty-five foot hemp ropes together as Jack stripped down to his pants. He slipped the running noose over his head and down to his waist.

"You sure you don't want one of us to do this, Jack? Yer still a bit gimpy," offered Selden.

"Not likely. The good doctor here said my wounds have healed up enough that I should be fine."

"Long as you don't stay in there the rest of the day, Jack."

"Ain't plannin' on it, Doc...Now, since the best swimmer here, 'sides me, is Sixkiller...he says...He's agonna swim out with me an' carry these two eight pound Mother's Pure Lard buckets in this flour sack so's I'll have somethin' that floats to rest on. With the lids on tight, they hold air jest fine." He nodded at Bass. "An' seeing as how my partner here swims like a rock, he's gonna play out the rope and pull my butt outta there if'n I git in a world of hurt."

"Jest like pullin' in a big ol' turtle on a trot line," Bass said with a grin.

Jack nodded. "Wellsir, you ready?" he asked Ben.

"White-eyes wait on Sixkiller, he backin' up."

They started wading out into the large pool in the direction of the huge boulder that sat just in front of the falls. It was reasonable to assume that it was a chunk of the cliff that had fallen many years before.

The water was cold enough to take one's breath away. Both Ben and Jack gasped and their breathing became choppy and ragged as they ventured out farther. When the two men reached waist depth, they dipped under to the neck to further adjust to the cold water, put the lard can floater between them and side paddled toward the center.

Bass stood on the shore, close to the water's edge and played out coils of rope as they neared their destination—the boulder. Boy sat calmly beside him, never taking his eyes off his master.

Jack held on to the makeshift flotation device with Ben and began to take deep breaths. After five, he took one last big one, put his head down, lifted his legs above the water and kicked and pulled his way toward the bottom some thirty-five feet below. Normally, except for short periods after a heavy rain, the spring fed water was clear. Jack stroked toward the base of the rock as close to the bottom as he could get.

He rounded the north side and let out a muted scream as he came face-to-face with a blue cat that seemed to be almost as big as he was—in actuality, the catfish was only a little over sixty pounds, still big by any standards. Jack's startled scream had caused him to expel most of his air and he frantically began to kick toward the surface. "Jesus Christ almighty!"

"Jack scared…What you see?" Ben asked.

"Catfish…Big as you, you danged redskin!"

The normally stoic Lighthorse came as close to a grin as he could. "White man should have stuck arm in mouth. Big fish clamp down, hold on. You bring to shore. We have 'nother fish fry."

"Are you crazy? That damn fish was big enough to eat me."

"Meby that true too."

Jack just glared at Ben and began taking breaths again. Sufficiently re-oxygenated, he went back down—this time to the south of the boulder. As he neared the falls side, he could see a washout underneath the edge. It seemed to make a pocket. He pulled some of the small loose gravel from in front and saw the gleaming white crown of the skull of a child—whisps of blond hair waving softly in the current still clung to it. His air depleted, he returned to the surface.

"You find?"

Jack nodded. "Hand me the sack."

Ben handed him the empty flour sack. Jack repeated his deep breathing again and then dove back to the site. At the hollow under the boulder, he began to carefully recover the remains. Some of the limbs were still articulated, including her right hand. The bony little fingers were wrapped around something that appeared yellow. *What the Sam Hill?* He eased the phalanges away and discovered that in her hand she had held a gold nugget the size of a goose egg. *My God.*

Even underwater, the nugget picked up enough light from the surface to shine. Jack slipped the giant hunk of gold into his pants pocket, and carefully stowed the alabaster bones in the cloth bag. He returned to the surface one more time and refilled his lungs for a final trip. Arriving at the sandy bottom again, he added the last of the lower extremities and then felt around for any stray remains—there were none. He slowly kicked his way to the surface.

"Gettum all?" Ben asked.

Again Jack nodded and then waved to the shore. Ben grabbed on to the rope looped about Jack's waist as Bass started pulling them in hand-over-hand. Closer to shore, both men stood up and waded quickly out of the cold water.

"It's done," a shivering Jack said solemnly as Selden wrapped a blanket around him and then another around Ben. "She's all yours, Shaman." He held out the sack.

Winchester took the dripping flour sack from Jack's blue fingers. "Thank you...her spirit will find peace at last. You have done a good thing here today, my son." He took the small tin of red ocher from his medicine pouch, unfolded the beautifully beaded doeskin burial pouch he had brought and walked down the shore toward the base of the cliff to a more private area to sanctify Anna's earthly remains.

"Oh, Jack!" Angie exclaimed as she rushed up and wrapped her arms around him. Tears filled both their eyes.

"I thought I told you..." Jack began to say.

"It's sorry I am...I just couldn't stay..."

Suddenly the voice of a small child froze her.

"Mommy?"

Angie and Jack turned toward the pool. There, just mere feet away was a glowing translucent image of Anna just above the surface of the water, clothed now in a gown of the purest white. She smiled sweetly and softly said, "I love you mommy. Everything is going to be fine now. Thank you, daddy. We'll meet again one day."

She lifted her hand and waved, her image shimmered with a kind of light none there had ever seen before, then collapsed to a single point of brilliance that streaked skyward like a falling star returning to the heavens.

Angie gasped and looked at Jack with astonishment. "Blessed be the Virgin...Did ye see that?" She crossed herself.

"I did," he said as tears streamed down his face. "I did." He pulled her close to him and held her tight. Jack leaned back, reached in his pocket and pulled out the giant nugget. "She had this in her hand for you."

Angie took the heavy chunk of gold and held it to her chest. "The Saints preserve us...This is what she was reaching for when she fell in...Oh, Jack!"

At the cabin, Jack and Ben had put on dry clothes and each held a steaming mug of coffee with both hands as they sat on the porch with the others.

"'Preciate yer help, Ben...You kin go back down there and grab that catfish, now...if'n you want," Jack said with a grin.

"Sixkiller pass. Eat too much fish yesterday."

"How big did you say that monster was agin'?" Bass asked.

"Well, if'n he was to open his mouth all the way, I prob'ly coulda crawled inside to take a nap."

"An' next year he'll be a saying he could set up house keepin' in there," said Tobe. "What's this?" He looked down and Boy had taken his entire hand in his mouth softly.

"He wants you to go with him. I'd suggest you don't argue."

"Didn't plan on it." Tobe got to his feet and Boy led him out the gate by his hand toward the barn. "Slow down, if'n you don't mind."

Inside, the big wolf took Tobe to a nook behind the oat bin.

"Well, looky here." He knelt down close to a female white wolf and four fluffy white pups wiggling around next to her. "Don't reckon yer gonna bite me?"

Boy nudged first one, then another of the pups toward Tobe and looked up with his golden eyes.

"Guess not…You want me to pick them up, that it?"

He nudged them a little closer.

Tobe picked up the first. The male pup had freckle-like red spots on his ears. He licked the back of Tobe's hand and looked in his eyes. Tobe inhaled sharply. *Sweet Jesus.* Then he picked up the other and held them both close to his chest. The first one turned his head upside down against Tobe like Boot used to do. Tears began to form in his eyes. *Thank you, Lord.*

Boy and his mate each took one of the remaining pups in their mouths and headed out the rear of the barn. Tobe watched them leave, then he turned and headed back to the house.

"Boy left you a gift." Tobe handed the second pup to Jack when he got to the top of the porch steps. "Think he's done his job and took off with his mate. These 'er what he wanted me to see in the barn." He pressed the one in his hand to his cheek. The pup promptly licked him across the mouth and gazed at him with his golden eyes. "He done exactly what Boot did when I first got him."

"Whatcha gonna call him? I'm callin' this little feller, *Son*," said Jack as he held the white ball of fur in his lap. The pup looked up when Jack said the name.

The elder lawman looked down at the son of Boy in his hand. "Reckon I'll name him *Scout*. How's that?" He licked Tobe's hand again.

"He looks like a scout to me," offered Bass.

Tobe and Scout stared deep into each others eyes, then he looked up at the others. "Ya'll believe in reincarnation?"

"In the shamanic belief of the Chickasaw, there is no essential difference between men and animals. Death is thus but a temporary accident and the spirits will continue to come back as long as they are needed," said Anompoli Lawa. "You and Jack are blessed indeed."

From off in the distance they could all hear the long howl of a wolf, quickly joined by a second. Everyone looked south where the rocky outcrop of the jagged ridge above the falls was visible over the tree tops. On top of the peak two white wolves were silhouetted against the sky, their faces pointed upward, singing their song.

****

TIMBER CREEK PRESS

PREVIEW OF

THE NEXT EXCITING NOVEL FROM

TIMBER CREEK PRESS

by

KEN FARMER & BUCK STIENKE

LEGEND of AURORA

PROLOGUE

A fleet of twelve giant globular shaped, iridescent green space craft moved silently through the black void toward their destination, the third planet from the sun—a brilliant blue and white marble designated as Tellus, but known by the inhabitants as…Earth. As they passed the fourth planet—a red orb called Mars—an area of space far in front of them shimmered and a fleet of ten huge triangle shaped silver craft—five heavily armed Mauler cruisers and five gargantuan Superdreadnaught Carriers—emerged one at a time from the vortex. Each of the five larger carriers was over a mile wide and slightly over four miles long and carried two hundred fighters.

Ahead of the marauding green fleet, Earth and its moon were looming larger. The triangle craft quickly formed into an immense cornucopia-like cone formation that covered thousands of miles with the Maulers at the open end—like a giant maw—directly in front of the globular craft. The military grouping was able to encompass virtually the entire formation of globular craft.

Hundreds of smaller triangle shaped craft—tiny two-crew versions of their giant mother ships—began to spew from the Superdreadnaught carriers like angry wasps from a nest. They took positions inside the cone, between the Maulers and their carriers that completely encircled the globular craft formation.

The ball-shaped space vehicles—each over two miles in diameter—begin firing with pulse lasers of unimaginable power on the smaller craft. The multi-layered force fields of the small fighters began to flare with titanic intensity as they darted, looped, gyrated, dodged and spun to keep away from the ravening beams. Several of the smaller craft took direct hits, flared through the visual spectrum from violet to white hot incandescence and then vaporized into the cold inky vacuum of space, leaving only wisps of particles of metal where the craft formerly were like coruscant vapors.

The five huge Maulers were designed to lock on and hold an enemy with powerful tractor beams to prevent their escape or even movement. The great cruisers, Superdreadnaughts and the smaller fighters simultaneously would then begin a centrally coordinated pounding with massive annihilating purple beams of pure energy from their projectors and launch wave after wave of Tritium torpedoes at the green enemy. The cone of annihilation formation enabled the triangle ships to direct their concentrated force beams into the formation of the globes from multiple directions, overloading the layered shields surrounding the greenish craft of the aggressors. Nothing made of ordinary matter could survive in the center of this unbelievable display of pure power and energy.

The trapped globular craft fought back with savage ferocity and poured pulse upon pulse of powerful multiphased vibrating laser beams hundreds of yards in diameter in return. Protecting fields of force flared vividly on both sides with blinding regularity.

The smaller triangle craft flitted closer, encircling the giant ball ships like swarms of angry bees, constantly firing their force beams to add to the destructive power of their huge carriers and accompanying space cruisers. The overwhelming masses of silver fighters exceeded the number of defensive weapons on the larger green craft.

Inside one of the tiny fighters, small gray hands flashed over a touch screen, directing the craft toward one of the giant globes seen through the panoramic cockpit window. In the second seat, another set of tiny gray hands worked over a weapons console targeting a pair of ultra-deadly Tritium torpedoes toward the nearest globe—the fighter abruptly spun and darted away at maximum free velocity after releasing its missiles. The globe fired a pulse laser at the quickly retreating fighter and scored a grazing hit exactly where its force field was the weakest—along the aft quarterdeck. Due to the fact that the ship was in the *free* inertialess mode at the instant it was hit, the laser pulse knocked the craft out of the battle area like a bat striking a ball—but initially at near the speed of light.

LEGEND of AURORA

The globe's monstrous force field flared with sheets of whiteish-blue hot plasma as the first Tritium torpedo struck and partially collapsed it, creating a quarter of a mile circular area devoid of defense. The second torpedo followed on the tail of the first, penetrated the hull and detonated with a force well over a thousand kilotons. The two-mile diameter sphere shook with the power of the explosion deep within its bowels. Large chunks of debris flew out into the stygian darkness lit only by the repeated flashes of force fields repelling attacks or failing.

Three other fighters from the squadron darted in and targeted the weakened globe with force beams that sliced through its exposed aranak skin like a hot knife through butter. The globe's force field flared like a mini-sun to violet then through the entire spectrum of colors—then the globe vaporized into a billion points of brilliance and was gone into the absolute zero cold and vacuum of interstellar space.

The triangle ships and their fighters systematically began targeting the other globular craft and one by one, the force fields of the giant spherical ships flared into even more frenzied displays of pyrotechnic incandescence with rainbows of color and then failed as the ships were vaporized. Only clouds—merely silver mist—of tiny atom-sized metal droplets drifting through their own momentum in the ether were left in the center of the cone.

Many of the small fighters had taken near hits from the enemy vessels, but were able to return to their mother ship's docking bays—except for one. The damaged craft spun out of control in the direction of the blue and white planet some 57.4 million miles in the distance.

The two gray figures inside worked frantically to stabilize their fighter—to no avail. The tiny ship's inertialess drive was severely damaged at the moment of contact from the pulse laser, causing it to go inert and therefore Newton's First Law of Motion took effect: *Every object in a state of uniform motion tends to remain in that state of motion unless an external force is applied to it.*

The battle zone was positioned such that Tellus was at aphelion—its most distant point from the Sun—and Mars was at its perihelion—the closest point to the Sun. In other words, the two planets were orbitally on opposite sides of the sun. The gravitational force of the massive star began to slow the passing vehicle as it approached Earth.

The triangle mother ships continued the destruction of the remaining globular craft with a tremendous flare of expended energy until the last craft ceased to exist in this plane. The surviving viable fighters formed up and headed toward their giant space carriers and were taken back on board.

The fleet of triangle space Maulers and Superdreadnaughts reformed into a line with the carriers in the lead as a distortion in the very fabric of space appeared in front of the fleet. One at a time, the ships entered the wormhole with a bright flash and disappeared to reemerge from hyperspace thirty parsecs away on the other side of the galaxy just minutes later.

LEGEND of AURORA

APRIL 17, 1897
AURORA, TEXAS

The damaged fighter finally began to regain some degree of control as it entered the outer thermosphere portion of the Earth's atmosphere at a speed approaching Mach 5. The crew tried repeatedly to reactivate the inertialess drive, but it was too badly damaged and only functioned intermittently. As a result, the ship started to glow from the heat of the friction.

If the drive had been fully functioning, an elliptical bubble field in the shape of the craft would have been generated around the ship, not only making it invisible to any light spectrum, but also giving it full antigravity capability as well—known as being *free* and making it massless. The neutralization of inertia removed the limitation of any *free* craft to instantaneously reach the velocity which the force of her cosmic engines could generate—depending on size—in any direction. The larger the craft, the more ultimate velocity could be achieved—allowing the jump to hyper-space—per Newton's Second Law of Motion: *The relationship between an object's mass (m), its acceleration (a), and the applied force (F) is F=ma. Acceleration and force are vectors; in this law the direction of the force vector is the same as the direction of the acceleration vector.* The tiny fighters were not of sufficient size to permit hyper-jumps, but performed very well in dense atmospheres like Earth in their *free* inertialess state—but the little stricken vessel was subject to the normal atmospheric friction and gravitational forces exerted by the planet.

A full moon was setting on the western horizon and dawn was just starting to lighten the horizon to the east as the small silver craft—still glowing from the heat of its passage through the Earth's atmosphere—moved erratically north across the sky, losing altitude.

Small gray hands again flashed over a touch screen. Through the panoramic cockpit window the occupants could see a metal tower with a circle of numerous blades at the top in the distance, rapidly coming closer. The craft yawed sharply, shuddered, dipped, and then regained altitude and stability for a moment.

The three lights on the bottom of the craft flickered on and off. Then like a shot dove, it plummeted toward the surface, striking the tower and its adjacent water tank before hitting the ground, tumbling and exploding in a fireball, scattering wreckage for more than a hundred yards.

Some fifty yards away, in a large white frame house with a wraparound porch on three sides, a woman was startled awake by the resulting explosion and sat up in bed. Hazel Proctor nudged her husband, Judge Henry Proctor.

"Oh, my God!…Henry!…Henry, wake up! What was that?"

A small gray figure, silhouetted against the fire, stood shakily from a portion of the wreckage. The figure looked around, then knelt down for a moment in the wreckage next to another gray figure. The being stood erect again, picked up a metal looking case and disappeared into the darkness.

Judge Henry Proctor, a portly man in his fifties with full mutton-chop gray whiskers, stirred from a sound sleep and rolled over to face his wife. "What?…What are you babbling about, woman?"

"An explosion!…Over to the windmill!…Get up, Henry!" She looked out the open window. "There's a fire!"

He snapped awake. "A fire!…Where?"

"I told you…Over to the windmill!"

He jumped out of bed, threw a flannel robe over his long white night shirt, shoved his feet into his slippers and charged out of the door, followed by his wife, Hazel. She had grabbed a faded pink chenille robe and slipped it over her skinny frame.

Wreckage and flames were scattered everywhere. The windmill and water tank were destroyed as well as Judge Proctor's garden. Nearby neighbors, most still in night clothes, were rushing toward the wreckage. The top edge of the sun had just started peeking above the horizon.

"What the Sam Hill is it?" one of the neighbors asked.

"I seen it pass over downtown when I was gittin' up, a few minutes ago…It's some kind of flyin' machine," another answered.

"What on earth can fly?…'Cept a balloon."

"'Twern't no balloon…it was shaped like a triangle with three flickerin' lights on the bottom. I can tell you that…"

One of the ladies gathered at the wreckage gasped, "Look!…There in the wreckage…is that a body?"

The gathering crowd looked and pointed toward a large piece of the craft a short distance from the fire. Lying near the twisted silver metal—with strange hieroglyphics on it—was a small gray body.

"Everybody get back…get back," said Proctor as he and his wife Hazel arrived from their house.

She moved forward. "Oh, my goodness, Henry…It's a child!"

The judge moved forward himself for a closer inspection and knelt down by the body. "Meby…meby not, Hazle…but, whatever it is…" He looked up at the crowd. "…it's not of *this* world."

A small silhouetted figure watched from the darkness under a large bois d'arc tree at the edge of the cemetery, and then it shimmered very slightly and disappeared—metal case and all.

AURORA CEMETERY

Aurora, Texas, a small farming community located in Wise County, just northwest of Fort Worth boasted a population in 1897 of over three thousand residents. A somber group of the town's people gathered around a small grave that had been dug under a gnarled oak tree with a large L shaped crooked limb sticking out overhead.

A preacher opened a bible and began reading, "'The Spirit himself bears witness with our spirit that we are children of God, and if children, then heirs—heirs of God and fellow heirs with Christ, provided we suffer with him in order that we may also be glorified with him.'...Lord receive this creature to thy bosom that it may have everlasting life'. In Christ's Name we pray. Amen."

There was a scattering of 'Amens' as four townsmen lowered a small child-size wooden casket into the ground with ropes. At one end of the grave a stone marker of native rock had been placed. Carved into the sandstone was a *V,* lying on its side with three circles etched inside, and beneath was an inscription that read:

NOT OF THIS WORLD

April 17, 1897

A small figure watched the funeral in the shadow of a tree in the distance. It touched its left wrist and again shimmered and vanished...

***

TIMBER CREEK PRESS